Praise for

LIVER LET DIE

"Liz Lipperman delivers a sparkling new cozy star! Readers will cheer for Jordan, a Clueless Cook with charm and spunk in a mystery that really sizzles."
—Cleo Coyle, national bestselling author of the Coffeehouse Mysteries

"Jordan McAllister heads up an appealing cast of characters in the fun new Clueless Cook series from Liz Lipperman . . . Plot twists, action, and lots of scrumptious food make this a mystery not to be missed!"
—Misa Ramirez, author of the Lola Cruz Mysteries

"A culinary critic mystery with good taste, charming characters, and plenty of delicious twists. It's a recipe for a truly enjoyable story."
—Linda O. Johnston, author of the Pet Rescue Mysteries

Berkley Prime Crime titles by Liz Lipperman

LIVER LET DIE
BEEF STOLEN-OFF

BEEF STOLEN-OFF

Liz Lipperman

BERKLEY PRIME CRIME, NEW YORK

THE BERKLEY PUBLISHING GROUP
Published by the Penguin Group
Penguin Group (USA) Inc.
375 Hudson Street, New York, New York 10014, USA

Penguin Group (Canada), 90 Eglinton Avenue East, Suite 700, Toronto, Ontario M4P 2Y3, Canada
(a division of Pearson Penguin Canada Inc.) • Penguin Books Ltd., 80 Strand, London WC2R 0RL,
England • Penguin Group Ireland, 25 St. Stephen's Green, Dublin 2, Ireland (a division of Penguin
Books Ltd.) • Penguin Group (Australia), 250 Camberwell Road, Camberwell, Victoria 3124, Australia
(a division of Pearson Australia Group Pty. Ltd.) • Penguin Books India Pvt. Ltd., 11 Community
Centre, Panchsheel Park, New Delhi—110 017, India • Penguin Group (NZ), 67 Apollo Drive,
Rosedale, Auckland 0632, New Zealand (a division of Pearson New Zealand Ltd.) • Penguin Books
(South Africa) (Pty.) Ltd., 24 Sturdee Avenue, Rosebank, Johannesburg 2196, South Africa

Penguin Books Ltd., Registered Offices: 80 Strand, London WC2R 0RL, England

This is a work of fiction. Names, characters, places, and incidents either are the product of the author's
imagination or are used fictitiously, and any resemblance to actual persons, living or dead, business
establishments, events, or locales is entirely coincidental. The publisher does not have any control over
and does not assume any responsibility for author or third-party websites or their content.

PUBLISHER'S NOTE: The recipes contained in this book are to be followed
exactly as written. The publisher is not responsible for your specific health or allergy
needs that may require medical supervision. The publisher is not responsible for
any adverse reactions to the recipes contained in this book.

BEEF STOLEN-OFF

A Berkley Prime Crime Book / published by arrangement with the author

PUBLISHING HISTORY
Berkley Prime Crime mass-market edition / July 2012

Copyright © 2012 by Elizabeth R. Lipperman.
Cover illustration by Ben Perini.
Cover design by Sarah Oberrender.
Interior text design by Laura K. Corless.

ISBN: 978-0-425-25142-3

BERKLEY® PRIME CRIME
Berkley Prime Crime Books are published by The Berkley Publishing Group,
a division of Penguin Group (USA) Inc.,
375 Hudson Street, New York, New York 10014.
BERKLEY® PRIME CRIME and the PRIME CRIME logo are trademarks of
Penguin Group (USA) Inc.

PRINTED IN THE UNITED STATES OF AMERICA

10 9 8 7 6 5 4 3 2 1

ALWAYS LEARNING   **PEARSON**

This one goes out to my children,
Nicole and Brody,
for making my life so much fun.

ACKNOWLEDGMENTS

Penning a story is a solitary experience. However, the writing community is filled with many wonderful people who cheer when one of their own has a victory, offer help when it's needed, and soothe when there are tears. I've been very fortunate to have a lot of these awesome people in my life, and they need to know how much I appreciate them.

First and foremost is my agent, Christine Witthohn of Book Cents Literary Agency. I will forever be indebted to her for her loyalty and fighting spirit even in the face of adversity. I am proud to stand by her side as a friend as well as a business partner no matter what enemy we're facing. Then there's my editor, Faith Black. I can only say "wow!"—your faith in me and the gang at Empire Apartments never ceases to amaze me. Thanks for making my journey so easy.

And I can't forget all the hardworking people behind the scenes at Berkley Prime Crime, especially Sarah Oberrender, who designed my awesome cover; Ben Perini, who illustrated it; Laura K. Corless, who designed the interior; and Caroline Duffy, copyeditor extraordinaire, whose eye for detail astonished me.

A huge thank-you to:

The wonderful Cleo Coyle, whose generous spirit touched my

heart, and to Misa Ramirez and Linda O. Johnston. These three wonderful authors graciously agreed to take time from their own busy writing schedules to read my book and give wonderful blurbs.

The fantastic Book Cents Babes, who are always there for me—no matter what I need—and the ultra-talented Plotting Princesses (plottingprincesses.blogspot.com), who sat around the table one day and helped me plot this book.

My critique partner, Joni Sauer-Folger, who never lets anything slide and who should have WTF after her name. I'm a better writer because of her.

My talented beta readers, Chris Keniston, Sylvia Rochester, and Nora Friday Roth who helped me polish the manuscript.

Debbie Sheuchenko at Lazy S'S Farm, who helped me find the perfect murder weapon, and Leo Garcia, my expert for the Hispanic names.

The Bunko Babes, who keep me laughing, and my siblings, who shower me with support.

My children, Nicole and Dennis Bushland and Brody and Abby Lipperman, and my grandchildren, Grayson, Caden, Ellie, and Alice. Oh God! I love you.

And lastly to Dan, my real-life hero, who believed in me and made all my dreams come true. *Te Amo.*

CHAPTER 1

"You're looking at the new *permanent* culinary reporter for the *Ranchero Globe*." Jordan McAllister bent over in an exaggerated bow.

"What? That old bat kicked the bucket?" Victor Rodriguez threw his arms in the air. "Yea!"

"Victor," his partner and co-owner of the apartments, Michael Cafferty, scolded. "You didn't even know her. It's mean to call her an old bat."

Victor shrugged, turning back to Jordan, unfazed by the reprimand. "Give it up, girl. Does this mean you can say good-bye to your four-times-a-week fried-bologna habit?"

Jordan took a minute to observe the people who had become her second family since she'd arrived in Ranchero a few months ago with only a few suitcases, her goldfish Maggie, and a broken heart. The residents of Empire Apartments had taken her under their wing, offering her unconditional love in the process. There was no doubt in her mind all of them would risk their lives for her—and already had—as she would for them.

"Who's saying good-bye to bologna?" Ray Varga asked, walking into the dining room from the kitchen, carrying a clay pot.

"Jordan's about to," Michael answered. He leaned over to get a better look at the concoction in Ray's hands. "Good Lord, Ray, are those gummy bears in the middle of that—thing?" He poked the shovel jutting from the center of the chocolate dessert.

Ray beamed as if the Cowboys had just kicked the winning field goal at the Super Bowl. "Cool, huh?"

Lola Van Horn came up behind him and patted his bottom. "Yes, darling, you outdid yourself this time. How you ever talked Myrtle's niece into sneaking you a copy of her aunt's new recipe is beyond me."

Ray pulled the chair out for his lady and then plopped down beside her. "What can I say? I'm irresistible."

"Hogwash!" Rosie LaRue said, joining the group, her arms loaded with bowls and spoons. "Myrtle guards her recipes like a Rottweiler in a junkyard. She's going to cut off your sneaky little fingers and feed them to the pigs behind the diner if she ever finds out you snuck around her to get this." She pulled out one of the gummy bears and popped it into her mouth. "What's this called, anyway?"

"Dirt Cake, better known as La Suciedad Pastel for Jordan's column." Ray scowled, glancing down at his hands. "Now you've got me scared."

"Oh hush, dear. You should have thought of that before you stole her recipe." Lola's attempt to sound gruff couldn't disguise her amusement. She pouted with her Angelina Jolie lips, compliments of a plastic surgeon who couldn't go a week without one of her psychic readings.

"Enough chatter," Rosie chimed in. "Ray, you dish it up while Jordan tells us about her good news."

As the resident cook of the group, Rosie was the only reason Jordan ate at least one good meal a week, offsetting the effects of the fast food she consumed the other six days. Rosie, the femme fatale of the group, gave credit for her cooking skills to her third husband, who was really husband number four. She liked to forget about the night she and her first husband boozed it up in a little bar in Connor right after her divorce from hubby number two was finalized. She and "the love of her life," as she liked to call him, ended up catching a red-eye to Vegas and repeating their "I do's" at the Little Wedding Chapel. Once sober, they soon remembered why it hadn't worked out the first time; the marriage lasted two months and didn't count, according to her.

Rosie settled into the chair between Victor and Jordan and patted the table. "So did the old bat die?" Turning slightly out of Michael's view, she winked at Victor.

"Loretta Moseley ran off with her physical therapist and the big chunk of change she got in her settlement with the personal watercraft manufacturer. She's in Reno now, probably feeding it all to the one-armed bandits."

"What?" Victor rolled his eyes. "I never got any money when I flew off that Jet Ski I rented last year."

"You never broke your hip, either." Michael wiggled his eyebrows. "And if you ever run off with a hot physical therapist, sweetie, I'll hunt you down and break both your legs."

Victor's scowl quickly turned into a smile. "Point taken."

"Mmm!" Lola moaned, closing her eyes after the first bite. "I can see why Myrtle guarded this recipe with her life. A person could be tempted to do anything for a bowl of this stuff."

Ray leaned over and wiped the small droplet of chocolate escaping out of the corner of her mouth. "Anything, dear?"

"Oh, get a room, you two," Rosie said affectionately before turning her attention back to Jordan. "So your cheapskate editor finally gave you a raise?"

"Yes." Jordan lowered her eyes.

"Uh-oh. I know that look," Michael observed. "The penny-pincher did the old 'I'd give you more but the economy's in the toilet and fewer people are buying newspapers' song and dance, didn't he?"

Jordan looked up, breaking into a grin. "Yeah, how did you know?" She didn't wait for his response. "I did get a small raise, but I still have to write the personals. Mr. Egan did throw in a bonus, though. I'm going to sit with Jim Westerville in the press box for a couple of Cougars home games next season."

"If memory serves, sugar, that press box nearly got you killed not too long ago. Surely you wouldn't even consider going up there again, even if it is with the sports director at the *Globe*," Lola commented.

At the mention of her close call several months ago at Grayson County College's football field, Jordan shivered. She'd come so close to getting herself killed playing amateur sleuth, she'd vowed never to go near another press box again.

Until Dwayne Egan threw it in as a perk when he talked her into taking over Loretta Moseley's job permanently at the *Globe*.

Truth be told, she'd fallen in love with the job and the notoriety that came with it and would've taken it even without the hundred-bucks-a-week raise.

Six weeks ago, she'd jumped at the chance to write the culinary column temporarily, along with the personals, seeing it as a step up the ladder to her dream of becoming a sports reporter, but somewhere along the way her attitude changed. She still missed the good old college days when she and her ex-boyfriend had covered all the events at the University of Texas, and she still longed for the excitement of being right in the middle of anything athletic. But she'd have to bide her time if she wanted a shot at sportswriting at this small local newspaper.

The good news was, as of that very morning, the Kitchen Kupboard column was hers as long as she wanted it, even though her culinary skills and knowledge of fancy foods were nonexistent. When Egan first offered her the job after Loretta's accident, she'd nearly turned it down, thinking there was no way she could pull it off. But with Rosie and the gang coming up with casserole recipes every week, then slapping fancy foreign names on them, she had fooled the good people of Ranchero into thinking she was a fine food connoisseur instead of the clueless cook she really was.

She'd been ready to sign on the dotted line even before Egan dangled the press box carrot. At that point, her near fatal incident at the football field was conveniently forgotten. Growing up with four brothers, she'd loved anything athletic and still believed her sportswriting dream would come true one day. But while she waited for that to happen, having her own byline wasn't a bad gig, despite her feeling like a fraud every time she posted one of Rosie's or Ray's recipes from their weekly card game and potluck dinners.

"So, honey, have you told everyone where you're going tomorrow night?" Rosie reached for a second helping of the dessert.

Jordan shoved the plate toward her friend and licked her lips. "I will if you give me another spoonful."

"Ha!" Michael squealed. "Like one spoonful is going to satisfy you. We all know there's a chocoholic inside that skinny little body of yours."

Jordan shook her finger at him. "Look who's talking." He was at least six feet tall and couldn't weigh more than 160 pounds fully clothed. "I'm going to the Cattlemen's Ball," she announced, grabbing the bowl piled high with the chocolate dessert.

"What? Why would you go there?" Ray asked.

"Apparently Lucas Santana reads my column and called Egan last week to request that I be his guest at the party and then report on it. He thinks it could boost the sagging beef sales in the county if I write a good review."

"Sugar, you hate beef," Lola said, wrinkling her forehead. "I may be old but I remember reading about last year's event, and I'm pretty sure prime rib was mentioned."

"I know," Jordan replied. "But Egan says this year they're making it less fancy, both to save money and to put more focus on cheaper cuts of beef. Some big barbecue joint in Dallas is catering the event. Unfortunately, less fancy only applies to the food. I still have to go out and buy a prom-dress lookalike that I will probably never wear again." She paused before adding, "And for the record, I don't hate all beef, just the undercooked stuff that bleeds all over my plate. I love brisket."

"I'm so jealous," Victor said, jutting out his lower lip in a pout. "It doesn't seem fair that you get to be with all those big hunky cowboys . . . Ouch!" He grimaced as Michael kicked him under the table.

Ray shifted in his chair, his eyebrows hitched in a disapproving way. "You're going with Lucas Santana? His reputation as a womanizer goes way back."

"Oh, I'm not *going* with him. He set me up with his ranch foreman—a guy named Rusty Morales."

"Hot damn!" Lola cried out, nearly spilling her iced tea on the brand new caftan she'd bought that afternoon at Wal-Mart to go with the twenty others hanging in her closet. "He is one good-looking hombre."

Ray nailed Lola with one of his icy ex-cop glares, taking the heat off Jordan, at least momentarily. "And you would know this how, darlin'?"

Lola bit her lower lip in an attempt to wipe the smile from her face. "He came in with Santana not too long ago. Wanted to know if I could predict the future. Guess the old guy was upset because of the depressed beef market. Rusty wanted me to lie and tell him things were about to get a whole lot better. He even slipped me a twenty behind Santana's back."

"Did you do it?" Michael asked.

"Of course," the older woman said, flicking an imaginary piece of lint off her shoulder. "Twenty bucks is twenty bucks."

Rosie high-fived her before turning to Jordan. "I can't wait to get all the details. Maybe the night will end with a little romance."

Jordan nearly choked as she sipped from the coffee cup Ray had placed in front of her a few minutes earlier. "I'm not that kind of girl," she said defensively.

"Everyone's that kind of girl," Lola interjected. "Tell us that after you eyeball him." Her voice softened to a whisper. "When that man gets a look at those long legs and curly red hair of yours, I guarantee he'll make a pass, and it will be hard to resist. With that olive skin and those smoky black eyes . . ." She sighed and rolled her eyes, despite the fact Ray was still sending daggers in her direction.

Jordan smiled. Ray was a retired cop and the resident protector of the group, and he and Lola sometimes acted like teenagers in love. She couldn't help being envious of the relationship. Since her breakup with Brett after she'd followed him to Dallas several months earlier, she'd basically been "Single, party of one."

Not by choice. In the small town of Ranchero where over sixty percent of the twenty-two thousand or so residents were women, dating was not a happening thing.

"Speaking of getting lucky, what do you hear from Alex these days?" Ray asked, finally looking away from Lola.

Jordan took in a sharp breath at the mention of the undercover FBI agent who had saved her life on at least one occasion. "It's been a few weeks since he called. He warned me this might happen, so I'm trying not to worry." Had things gone as planned the night before he'd left for a new assignment in El Paso, things might have heated up. A candlelight lasagna dinner prepared by the amazing hunk would have had an intoxicating effect on her.

Instead, ending up in the hospital with a concussion put a damper on her plans. Now all she had were fantasies of what might have been. That and his twice-a-week phone calls when he could slip away from his undercover persona and sweet-talk her into imagining all kinds of romantic interactions.

She was jerked from her daydreaming when Rosie sprang from her chair and said, "Let's get this table cleaned up so I can start taking your money."

"Not in this lifetime, my dear." Michael scooped up the dessert bowls and made his way to the kitchen.

Jordan pushed away from the table, anxious to get

Screw Your Neighbor underway to take her mind off Alex. She pulled out fifty pennies and laid them on the table, thinking tomorrow night might not be too bad after all if this Rusty Morales guy was as hot as Lola claimed.

"I'll deal first," Jordan declared. While she doled out the cards, she mentally added a quick run to the mall to her morning to-do list; she needed to find something special to wear. "Get ready to part with your money, people. I've got a dress to buy."

Jordan's heart raced as she walked to the door and flung it open. Catching her breath, she stared into the darkest eyes she'd ever seen.

"Hi. I'm Rusty Morales." The beautiful creature extended his hand.

The minute her flesh made contact with his, a spark of electricity shot up her arm. "Jordan McAllister," she mumbled, aware he was sizing her up, just as she was doing to him.

"Lucas said you were easy on the eyes, but he never prepared me for this."

Jordan felt the heat crawl up her face. It wasn't the first time a man had complimented her, so why was she acting like a teenager on a first date?

"I could say the same about you," she blurted, mentally slapping her forehead for the lame response. Opening the door wider, she stepped aside to let him pass, rewarded immediately by the view from the back.

Dressed in a well-fitting black tuxedo with a starched white shirt that did nothing to hide the way his upper body narrowed at the waist, Rusty Morales could have stepped off the cover of *GQ* magazine, cowboy edition.

When he caught her staring, he grinned, and she felt her heart speed up. "Let me get my purse," she stammered before twirling around and walking toward the kitchen, hoping he enjoyed her back view as much as she'd enjoyed his. She added a wiggle just in case.

As soon as they walked out the front door of her apartment building, Jordan spied a sleek black Hummer limo at the curb. When the driver rushed out to open her door, she felt Rusty's hand on the small of her back, guiding her as she stepped in.

Chill, McAlister, she scolded herself. *This isn't a real date, so quit acting like it is.*

An inner devil's advocate chided that she wasn't fooling anyone. Who spends over a hundred bucks on an outfit for a job assignment? Only this morning, she'd splurged on the slinky black cocktail skirt and the emerald green and charcoal silky top that showed off her eyes. At least that's what the clerk said, but then she would have said anything to get the sale and her commission.

"Hello, Jordan. I'm so glad you were able to come with us tonight," an older male voice said. "Remind me to call Dwayne Egan and tell him he needs to have his eyes checked. There's nothing average about you."

Turning to face the speaker, she cursed the fact that it took very little to make her blush. "You must be Mr. Santana." She offered her hand, taking a few seconds to size him up.

Probably in his early sixties, Lucas Santana was exactly what she'd imagined a wealthy Texas rancher would look like—tall and husky with salt-and-pepper hair, dark brown eyes that peered at her from under a Stetson hat that had probably cost as much as her rent.

And those peepers were undressing her right now as

Ray's earlier warning of his womanizing skills popped into her head.

"Call me Lucas," he said, patting the seat beside him.

Hesitating only briefly before settling in beside him, Jordan attempted a smile. "I've heard a lot about you." *None of it good!*

Glancing up, she noticed a woman who looked to be in her midthirties seated across from them and caught a glimpse of her scowl before it quickly disappeared. Even from where Jordan sat, she could see that this woman, with her thick blond hair pulled back in a cascade of curls falling on her shoulders and the ankle-length hot pink and navy evening dress belted with a sequined blue sash that showed off her tiny waist, was what Ray would call a head-turner.

She leaned forward to shake hands. "Maribella Kensington." Her voice was sexy in that breathy kind of way with just a hint of a southern accent. "But everyone calls me Bella. I'm Lucas's personal assistant."

Jordan reached for her hand, aware of the strong grip. Judging by the way the woman was rubbing the fingers of her free hand up Santana's arm, she decided Bella's job probably went beyond paperwork and making appointments. "It's a pleasure to meet you."

Jordan's eyes connected with Rusty's, and she had to look away. She was nervous enough without discovering the sexiest guy in Grayson County still checking her out.

She directed her attention to Lucas. "I appreciate the invite, Mr. Sant . . . Lucas. I'm looking forward to getting to know all of you."

"Darling, that most definitely will be the highlight of this evening," Lucas said, his eyes trailing down to her chest, making her wish she hadn't spent the extra forty bucks on the Victoria's Secret push-up bra. "Tonight we're going to enjoy some great-tasting beef, throw back a Johnnie Walker or two, and dance to the sweet music of Lone Star, the best country band in the Southwest. I'm going to personally enjoy watching Rusty teach you how to do the Cotton-Eyed Joe. I only wish I could be out on the dance floor with you."

He patted his thigh, and for the first time Jordan noticed he was wearing a leg brace.

"Car accident ten years ago," he explained, apparently catching the curious look that crossed her face. "Broke my femur so badly the doctors thought I would never walk again. I surprised everyone except Bella." He shot her a sidelong look. "She was my nurse and insisted I could do it from day one. I couldn't have made it without her all these years."

"Jordan doesn't want to hear all about that, Lucas. She's probably wondering why she was invited to the ball." She turned her gaze toward Jordan. "Ever been to one of these shindigs?"

Jordan shook her head. "I do know it's the biggest fund-raising event in the Texas beef-producing community. People come from all over the state just for the party," she replied, reciting almost word for word from the article she'd found on the Internet.

Rusty laughed. "It draws a lot of interest from ranchers in Oklahoma and Nebraska, too. The Board of Texas Cattlemen goes all out to make it better every year. And that doesn't even take into consideration the standing-room-only crowd at the all-day cattle auction and rodeo the last night. You're in for a treat, Jordan." His eyes told her he'd like to be part of that treat.

She couldn't help herself and smiled back before remembering the handsome FBI hunk back in El Paso. "Mr. Egan said all the money goes to charity, right?" She forced herself to look away from Rusty's mesmerizing bedroom eyes.

"Yes—" Bella began before Santana cut her off.

"Like you said, it's the biggest money-making event in the area with the proceeds slated directly for cancer research. The board made sure most of the cash goes to Southwestern in downtown Dallas." He poured a Scotch on the rocks and handed it to Rusty. "What can I get for you pretty ladies?"

"A glass of Cristal, Lucas," Bella said, nodding at Santana before twisting toward Rusty. "Did you tell her we'd like her to write an article about the party and mention the great food?"

"Egan told me," Jordan answered for him, taking the glass of champagne from Santana.

Despite knowing she'd have a humongous headache in the morning, she took a sip. A few more sips convinced her this wasn't the kind of champagne you bought at the local liquor store. She could get used to it in a hurry, maybe even give up her preferred margaritas for the classy bubbly.

"Wonderful," Santana said, throwing back his head and draining his Scotch. "The people of Ranchero need to be reminded now more than ever that beef is the way to go, especially with the falling prices." He patted Jordan's knee. "I think you're just the gal to do it."

With his hand lingering on her knee and his eyes fixated on the little bit of cleavage peeking over the top of her blouse, he licked his lips.

Feeling his fingers creeping up her leg and his thumb and forefinger stroking her inner thigh, Jordan glanced toward Bella, surprised to see her chatting with Rusty as if she hadn't noticed. Gently, she removed Santana's hand, reinforcing the message with her eyes when his finally moved up to her face.

He winked, and she nearly threw up.

This is going to be one long ride to Fort Worth.

CHAPTER 2

Jordan bolted from the limo as soon as they pulled up to the Pavilion Hotel in downtown Fort Worth. After a few more glasses of Scotch, Santana had made another overt attempt to cop a feel, and she was more than ready to put space between her and the old codger. Thankfully, Rusty Morales had come to her rescue halfway there and suggested she change seats with him to get a better look at the Fort Worth skyline.

A hot-looking cowboy with good manners makes for a dangerous combination, she thought before quickly dismissing the notion.

Walking into the Pavilion, Jordan felt like she'd just stepped out of a pumpkin carriage into a marble castle. The only difference was she had on a black cocktail skirt instead of a flowing gown, Rosie's sequined black heels instead of glass slippers, and her almost-prince was back in El Paso.

She glanced up at Rusty, thinking she would be wise to remember that.

Turning her attention to the hotel lobby, she imagined that the price of a room in this swank hotel would gobble up her monthly paycheck.

"This way," Bella said, leading the group while holding on to Lucas's arm. For a guy with a brace, he managed fairly well on the slick marble floor.

If Jordan thought the hotel lobby was spectacular, the ballroom was even more impressive. A crystal chandelier the size of her kitchen hung in the center of the biggest room she'd ever seen, its prisms casting sparkles across the dimly lit dance floor. Linen-draped tables set with china and silver circled this area, each with a centerpiece of what looked like at least three dozen yellow roses.

On the stage next to the podium, a large ice sculpture in the shape of a longhorn steer glistened under a smaller chandelier. Jordan had never witnessed such beauty and extravagance in her life. She found herself wondering how much money would actually be left for charity when it was all said and done and that bovine was reduced to a couple hundred gallons of water.

She followed Bella and Lucas to one of the front tables, aware of Rusty's hand on her shoulder guiding her through the crowd. When he pulled the chair out for her, she realized she'd be sitting next to Bella instead of Santana and said a quick thank-you to the gods.

"Do you know anyone here?" Bella asked when they were finally settled around the table.

Jordan studied the two couples who had joined them and shook her head. "Only you and Lucas." She turned to her left. "And of course, Rusty." He rewarded her acknowledgment with a dreamy look that almost made her swoon.

"This is Blake Graham and Cooper Harrison," Bella said, pointing to the two men seated directly across from her. "I met Cooper about a year ago when he catered one of the charity events I sponsor," she explained. "Gentlemen, this is Jordan McAllister from the *Ranchero Globe*."

Both men stood and shook her hand. The shorter one, Blake Graham, who was decked out in a black tux, a light green shirt, and a tie that was dotted with rust-colored longhorns to match his cummerbund, spoke first. "Nice to meet you, Jordan," he said, and then, turning to the petite Asian woman seated next to him, added, "This is Amira Lee."

The tiny woman glanced up, then quickly lowered her eyes. Jordan couldn't help wondering if she was perched on a booster seat.

Cooper Harrison, the other guest at the table, was dressed similarly to Blake but without the livestock embellishments. He stared openly at her with a hint of mischief in his eyes, and although she immediately labeled him as a player, she smiled politely as he introduced the blond woman seated next to him. "Jordan, this is Carole Anne Summerville—"

"Her daddy owns North Texas Beef Distributors out by Lake Texoma," Bella blurted. "They supply most of the restaurants in the metroplex with the finest beef in the state."

Carole Anne flipped her hand dismissively toward Bella. "She doesn't care about all that. Tell me, are you the Jordan McAllister who writes the Kitchen Kupboard?"

Not waiting for Jordan's answer, she rambled on. "I love that column. I even had our cook make the chicken recipe. You know the Spanish one with potato chips?" She paused. "Anyway, it was divine," she added in a pronounced southern drawl that made the last word sound like a description of some young thing who had just lost her virginity—*de-vined*.

Rusty put his arm around Jordan's chair and leaned closer to whisper, "You'll have to make that for me someday."

Jordan lowered her eyes, hoping he hadn't seen the effect of his soft breath in her ear. What was up with her? She was acting like he'd just complimented her on her figure instead of suggesting she cook a casserole for him.

Yeah, like that's ever going to happen.

"I'm glad you liked it." She inched her body slightly to her right, toward Bella and away from the goose bumps she got with Rusty so close.

"So, Jordan," Cooper started, his eyes still sending out signals that must have been apparent to everyone at the table, including his date. "I didn't realize you and Rusty were an item. Last I heard, he and . . ." He caught himself before continuing. "Well, let's just say I didn't know you two had hooked up."

"We haven't," both Rusty and Jordan said in unison.

"Not that it doesn't sound appealing," Rusty continued, his riveting stare making the fine hairs on her arm stand at attention.

"We only met tonight," Jordan added, deliberately breaking eye contact with Rusty.

With that bit of news, Cooper's eyes widened, as if he had just gotten the green flag to go full throttle with his flirting. "Good to know. A girl who looks like you and can cook won't be on the market for long."

Jordan's mouth dropped, and she stole a glance toward Carole Anne in time to see her identical reaction. "I'm seeing someone right now," she blurted.

Are you freakin' kidding me?

Why had she felt the need to explain? Her almost candlelight dinner followed by an imaginary romantic evening did not constitute seeing someone.

"He's on an assignment right now," she added, deliberately leaving out El Paso and the undercover FBI part.

When will I learn to keep my big mouth shut?

Hearing Rusty take a deep breath, she realized she'd probably led him to believe she wasn't involved. Well, actually, she wasn't, so why imply otherwise? Was she afraid she couldn't handle this cowboy?

When Blake stood to reach for two cocktails from one of the many waiters circling the room with a tray full of every drink imaginable, Jordan could have sworn one of the longhorns on his cummerbund wiggled its tail.

"I don't see a ring on your left hand," Blake pointed out in a voice much deeper than Jordan would have expected given his short stature. He handed his date a drink and sat down.

"Like this one." Carole Anne held up her left hand to display a rock the size of a cherry. "Now if I could only get Coop to set a date." She squeezed his arm and shot Jordan a glare that clearly warned, Back off—he's mine.

Cooper's face registered his obvious discomfort, and he wiggled away from his fiancée as a waiter set a steaming plate of food in front of him. "Best barbecue in town," he said, clearly thankful for the distraction.

"Damn straight," Blake added.

Another waiter appeared with a tray of champagne glasses and set one at each place. Jordan waved him off, noticing that his misshapen nose suggested he'd been a boxer at some point in his life.

"It's for the toast," he explained, leaving the glass in front of her.

"Good evening, everyone," a voice boomed over the speaker system. "Welcome to the annual Cattlemen's Ball in the beautiful Pavilion Hotel."

Jordan focused on the stage, where a man resembling a chunky John Wayne, cowboy hat and all, was speaking. Her eyes diverted to the frozen cow next to him, which still looked pretty good for being dangerously close to stage lights.

"Before we dig in," the speaker continued, "I'd like to thank Cooper Harrison and all the great people down at Beef Daddy's for this wonderful food. It goes without saying they serve the finest barbecue in Texas, bar none, and it comes to us at a price that will allow us to write the biggest check in the history of this event to the dedicated people at Southwestern for their cancer research. Now if I can get you to raise your glasses, let's get this party started."

He lifted his champagne glass in the air. "Here, here. To a better economy, to putting all the thieving cattle rustlers behind bars, and to a prosperous year for cattle raisers across the entire state of Texas."

Jordan raised her glass for the toast, surprised by the overwhelming cheer of approval. These were serious cowboys who obviously loved what they did for a living.

"Now sit back and enjoy your evening."

Remembering how good the food was when she and her friends had splurged on takeout for their Friday night card game not too long ago, Jordan looked past Rusty to Cooper. "Do you own Beef Daddy's?"

The taller cowboy's eyes lit up like a grass fire in the middle of a Texas drought. "Yep. With the new restaurant in Abilene, I now have barbecue joints all over Texas."

Jordan heard Rusty huff. His dirty look quickly changed

back to indifference. *Is there bad blood between these two?* She filed that info on her mental laptop.

"It's so good because he pays top dollar for the finest cuts," Blake said. Despite his best attempt to sound southern, Jordan picked up on a northern accent.

"As the guy who programs my computers and deals with my financial records on a daily basis, Blake would know," Cooper said, giving a thumbs-up to the shorter man.

Jordan took a bite of the brisket, surprised it tasted even better than she remembered. "I'll have to make it a priority to come by your restaurant more often."

"You do that," Cooper said. "Matter of fact, why don't we just plan on you coming by in the next week or two—my treat. Afterward, I'll show you where we make all the food."

Jordan wasn't surprised to see Carole Anne glowering. Turning back to Rusty, now on his third Scotch and water, she smiled seductively, hoping Cooper's fiancée would think she was only interested in her own date.

Rusty raised his glass once again. "To good friends, both old and new," he toasted, never once looking Cooper's way, reaffirming Jordan's initial observations that there was history between them. By the way Carole Anne's eyes sparkled when her gaze met Rusty's, it seemed obvious what that history involved, although the blond woman looked more like Cooper's type than Rusty's.

Like I have a clue what either man prefers in a date.

And she wasn't the only one who had caught the look, judging by the way Cooper was glaring at Rusty with nostrils flared and eyed narrowed. For a minute Jordan thought he was about lose his cool before Rusty chugged the last of his drink, then began coughing violently.

"Are you okay?" Jordan asked, ready to pound on his back or do the Heimlich maneuver if necessary. She'd taken a mandatory first aid course in her early college days when she'd worked part-time in a day care center. As long as a choking person was still making sounds, the best treatment was to do nothing, which was what she did.

She leaned closer, handing him a glass of water. "Take a sip."

Wide-eyed, he grabbed the glass and did as instructed. A few seconds later, his face muscles relaxed, and he attempted a smile. "Thanks. Something must have gone down the wrong pipe." He set the glass on the table and reached for the replacement Scotch the crooked-nosed waiter had just brought over.

Despite Rusty's best effort to remain calm, Jordan noticed beads of sweat forming on his forehead. Without thinking, she reached up and wiped them with her napkin. His eyes questioned her.

She'd have to be careful not to lead him on. She had no idea where her relationship with Alex was going, but she wanted a chance to explore it. With him in El Paso, this was already proving to be a problem.

"So, Jordan, what do you think of the party so far?" Santana asked, breaking the intense moment.

She forced herself to look his way. "My readers will definitely hear about the excellent food."

My readers. How great that sounded, although she would have preferred the sort of followers who were more interested in the local high school football play-offs than how rich Texans schmoozed under the glare of a frozen-solid cow.

Sweating profusely now with his breathing rapid and shallow, Rusty grabbed the edge of the table with both hands. "I've gotta get some air." He sprang from his chair in a single motion.

"Do you want company?" Jordan asked, concerned.

Her first aid class never addressed this, but she could at least go outside with him in case he needed something.

Besides, she could use a breath of fresh air herself. The thought of sitting with Santana and Cooper without Rusty running interference didn't excite her.

He nodded gratefully, and for the first time Jordan detected a slight hint of fear in his eyes. Like the gentleman he was, he waited for her to go first.

Halfway across the room, a woman reached out and grabbed his hand. "Hey, stranger, you're not leaving already, are you?"

Petite, with jet-black hair that curled around her face in a stylish bob Jordan had seen only in magazines, the woman zeroed in on Rusty, her expression turning from playfulness to concern.

"Are you okay, honey?"

Rusty's breathing now came in short bursts. "Yeah, Brenda Sue. I just need a little air."

He broke free of her grip but not before Jordan noticed how the fingers on her left hand delicately caressed the inside of his wrist. One finger sported a huge wedding band with a diamond twice the size of Carole Anne's.

A little hanky-panky going on between these two? Jordan added another entry to her mental laptop.

She had to reach back to her high school track team days to keep up with Rusty as he bounded out the ballroom door, practically sprinting through the lobby and into the brisk Texas night. Once the cool October air hit him in the face, he sucked in a deep breath and made his way to a wrought iron bench. Plopping down beside him, Jordan waved off the valet attendant who inquired about calling a taxi.

"I can't feel my tongue," Rusty said, his voice unable to hide his panic. "What's happening to me? I can't feel the entire right side of my face."

She grabbed his hand and immediately felt his racing pulse. "Take a couple of deep breaths, Rusty. I'm sure this will pass in a moment." She hoped her voice hid her growing concern.

Suddenly, he slumped on the bench, his body falling into hers, convulsing. Jordan's scream for help was swallowed up by the raucous crowd arriving from some NASCAR event, all wearing DALE EARNHARDT shirts. Easing him to the ground with the help of one of the new arrivals, she ran back inside the lobby, shouting for a doctor. When no one responded, she raced into the ballroom, charging through the double doors and upending a waiter with a tray full of dirty dishes. The calamity drew everyone's attention.

"Help! I need a doctor."

Two men rushed toward her. Without a word, she turned and ran, praying they could help Rusty. As soon as they pushed through the revolving door, she pointed to the area beside the bench. Her heart dropped from her chest to her stomach.

Rusty lay still on the ground, a trickle of whitish spittle seeping from the left side of his mouth.

CHAPTER 3

The rest of the night was a blur of activity. The two gentlemen knelt beside Rusty and began administering CPR for what seemed like an eternity before Jordan heard the sirens approaching. She'd seen enough episodes of *Grey's Anatomy* to know the outcome wouldn't be good.

When the paramedics arrived and took over the emergency procedure, one of the doctors touched her shoulder and shook his head. "I'm sorry, miss. There's still no pulse, but maybe the paramedics will be able to revive him with a defibrillator."

Unable to hold back her tears, she allowed the older gentleman to take her in his arms while she cried silently. How could a man like Rusty be so vibrant one minute and dying the next?

By this time, it seemed as if the entire ballroom of people had packed the lobby, all trying to catch a glimpse of the drama in front of the hotel. Jordan stayed as close to

Rusty's side as she could without distracting the technicians, who now had him hooked up to an IV and were loading him onto a gurney.

"Who's with this man?" one of the attendants asked.

All eyes turned to Jordan, and she stepped forward "I am, but . . ."

"Jordan?"

She recognized the voice before she felt the hand on her shoulder. Twisting around, she faced Bella, who was waving her purse in the air, trying to get the attention of their limo driver among the mass of people scurrying around the hotel entrance.

"We all came to the party with Mr. Morales," Bella explained to the EMT. "We'll follow you to the hospital. You're going to Tarrant County General, right?"

The technician nodded, then climbed into the driver's seat and sped off.

Bella turned toward the hotel entrance and spotted Lucas making his way through the crowd, and she waved. "Lucas is as distraught over this as I am and will want to go straight to the hospital. Rusty's been with Santana Ranch since he was a young boy, and Lucas has a special place in his heart for him. You can either go with us, or we can call a cab for you."

A deep sadness washed over Jordan, thinking about Rusty. "I'd like to stay with you, if that's all right." She glanced over at the taxi line that snaked all the way back into the hotel. It would be well into the wee hours of the morning before she got home, anyway. Although there was nothing more she could do for Rusty, not that she'd been any help to him earlier, she felt she owed it to him to be there in case a miracle happened and he regained consciousness.

Bella patted her shoulder just as Lucas came up behind them, his eyes red and swollen. For a second, Jordan contemplated putting her arm around him to comfort him before remembering his previous behavior toward her. She'd have to empathize with him from a safe distance.

He fell into Bella's arms, sobbing.

"I know how much you love him," she said, stroking his back. "We have to hope for the best."

Jordan's concentration was diverted when the woman Rusty had called Brenda Sue rushed out of the lobby, screaming hysterically.

"Ohmygod! It can't be Rusty. Oh God, not Rusty."

The doctor who had been so comforting to Jordan minutes before rushed to Brenda Sue's side and kept her from running after the ambulance. Seconds later, he handed her over to another man, who cradled her in his arms and whispered something in her ear.

Jordan was unaware she was studying the couple until the man looked up and met her gaze.

Is that a hint of a smile tipping his lips?

Quickly, he looked away and whispered something to Brenda Sue.

The crowd closed in around Jordan, bombarding her with questions. "What happened? Will he make it?" Over and over, they drilled her until the police arrived.

The officer in charge addressed the crowd. "Let's back up, folks, so the drivers can pull up in an orderly fashion and get you all home." He jerked around when a commotion broke out in the taxi line. One partygoer who'd had one too many was causing a scene trying to cut in front of everyone.

Just then, the Hummer pulled up, and Jordan followed Bella and a still-sobbing Lucas to the car, where the driver waited with the door opened. Before getting in, Jordan took one final look at Brenda Sue and the man she figured was her husband huddled on the same bench where Rusty had slumped only minutes before. Brenda Sue was still crying, and from the look on the man's face, he was not too happy about her public display. She'd bet money Brenda Sue and Rusty had been more than friends.

Rusty with Brenda Sue and *Carole Anne?* If her gut feeling was right, the man got around.

Lucas finally stopped crying halfway to Tarrant County General and stared silently out the window. As soon as they arrived at the ER, they were rushed into a waiting room and told the doctor would be with them shortly. Jordan didn't have a good feeling about any of this but was afraid she'd only upset Lucas even more if she voiced her concerns. If ever there was a time to be quiet, it was now.

An hour later, two young doctors in scrubs walked into the waiting room.

"I'm sorry. Despite our best efforts, we weren't able to save Mr. Morales," one of them said, his expression full of sympathy.

The sound that escaped from Lucas's lips was heart-breaking, and he crumbled into Bella's arms once again.

"What happened to him?" He finally asked when the sobs quieted and he could speak.

"We don't know. It could have been a heart attack or stroke. We'll have to wait for an autopsy." The doctor turned to Jordan. "I was told you were with him when he collapsed. Is that correct?"

"Yes."

He sat down beside her and flipped open a notebook. "Did you notice Mr. Morales acting strangely prior to his death?"

"A few minutes before he had the seizure, he said his

entire face was numb," she answered, wishing she didn't have to relive it.

"Whose idea was it to leave the ballroom?"

"His. He said he needed a little air."

"Do you know of any underlying medical problems Mr. Morales had that might have brought on his death?"

"I only met the guy less than four hours ago," she explained. "I'm no medical expert. He could have had *anything* wrong with him, and I wouldn't have known it. Why don't you ask the two real doctors who tried to save him?"

"We've got the EMT report," he replied gently. "I just wondered if there was something you might have seen since you were there when he seized."

She shook her head.

He stood up. "We'll try to get answers for you as soon as we can."

When the doctors left, Jordan sat quietly with Lucas while Bella made arrangements with the hospital staff for the body to be transported to a Connor funeral home following the autopsy. Hearing her worst fear verbalized had left Jordan in shock. The sweet thoughtful man who had been so alive one minute was now dead. And she had been powerless to prevent it from happening.

Finally, Bella returned. "There's no need to stay here any longer, so we're going to start back to Ranchero now, Jordan."

Jordan nodded, then stood up and followed them out to the car. Once settled, Lucas immediately reached for the Blue Label Johnnie Walker and poured two fingers into the glass. He downed the liquor in one swift motion. Visibly upset, he refilled the glass, his hands shaking. He took a sip before asking if either of them wanted a drink. Both Bella and Jordan nodded.

"Could I have more of the champagne?" Jordan asked, knowing the Scotch would set her insides on fire.

When he handed her a nearly full glass, she took a couple of big gulps, then leaned back against the seat to let the expensive Cristal do its thing by warming her insides and calming her emotions.

Her mind raced back over the last few hours, searching her brain for any sign she might have missed before Rusty's seizure. Other than the shortness of breath, he really hadn't complained of anything inside the ballroom. Not until he sat on the bench did he mention his numb face and tongue. She'd watched her grandmother live through angina attacks before a major heart attack killed her. Nana always had chest pain but never complained of numbness around the face and mouth.

And she'd never had a seizure.

Jordan remembered how she'd panicked when Rusty went into convulsions. Could he have had epilepsy? She'd never been around anyone with the disorder, so she had no idea if the symptoms that precede an actual seizure matched Rusty's.

She caught Santana staring at her.

"It would be nice if you'd come out to the ranch for the memorial service and the luncheon afterward," he said, more as a statement than a question.

"Of course," she replied, wishing she could say no without feeling guilty.

All she wanted to do was forget about tonight. Although she barely knew Rusty, her first impression was that he was a nice guy. She wondered if that would've changed if she'd had more time with him, remembering how sitting near him had given her goose bumps.

By the time the limo pulled to the curb in front of

Empire Apartments, Jordan had finished her second glass of champagne. Thankfully, there had been little conversation during the hour's drive back to Ranchero.

Before getting out of the car, she reached for Santana's hand. "I'm so sorry, Lucas. If there's anything I can do, please let me know."

He held her hand a little too long before releasing it. "I'll call you in a few days to tell you when my driver will pick you up for the memorial service."

She nodded and got out of the car. She would attend the services. She owed Rusty that much.

Jordan showered under a spray of the hottest water she could stand, then quickly dried off and slipped on a Cowboys T-shirt and a pair of running shorts, her usual sleep attire. It was much too late to tell any of her friends about Rusty. With the exception of Ray and Lola, none of her apartment pals made it past the ten o'clock news.

Funny that the two oldest residents were Empire's night owls, but even their lights had been out when the limo pulled up to the curb.

Climbing into bed, she wondered whether Brenda Sue had calmed down or was now suffering through a totally sleepless night. And what about Cooper and Blake? She'd only caught a quick glimpse of them after the police arrived, but unlike Brenda Sue, they hadn't looked too grief stricken. When Cooper whispered something in Blake's ear, they had both laughed. That was just after the ambulance arrived.

An odd reaction to Rusty's death, she thought, certain she wouldn't see either of them at the memorial service.

The memorial service. No way could she even think

about going without a friendly face beside her. Ever since her grandmother's funeral, she had developed a genuine hatred for the ritual. Even the cloying scent of gladiolas now made her nauseous.

She'd bribe Victor into accompanying her. Maybe if she had a guy with her, Lucas would keep his hands to himself. As if anyone would believe Victor was her boyfriend. The man dressed better than she did and flirted outrageously with every male in the room.

After tossing and turning for over an hour, Jordan finally fell asleep, although it wasn't a restful one. She awoke the following morning still thinking about Rusty and wondering what had caused his death.

As soon as her feet hit the floor, the little man with the hammer began pounding in her head, and she cursed the two glasses of champagne she'd had in the limo on the way home. Padding to the kitchen, she made a cup of coffee with her new little one-cup coffeemaker, compliments of Loretta Moseley.

Well sort of. She'd actually bought the machine on sale, justifying the purchase with the extra money she would make as the new Kitchen Kupboard columnist.

Okay, so she had yet to see any extra money, but Egan promised it was coming, and coffee tasted so fresh made one cup at time. She blew out a slow breath and stretched over the sink to get the bottle of ibuprofen on the shelf above. Maybe between the drugs and the caffeine, she could squash the little pest in her forehead.

She opened the cabinet looking for something to fill her stomach. No Pop-Tarts or English muffins. Another Mother Hubbard moment. She moaned, remembering today was grocery day. Snagging the last Hostess Ho Ho, she threw the empty box in the trash and plopped into a chair at the kitchen table.

Rusty continued to weigh heavily on her mind. Turning on the TV, she was disappointed when after fifteen minutes she didn't hear one word about the freakish death at the society event the night before. She guessed a thirty-something, otherwise healthy man having a heart attack after eating a high-fat meal didn't warrant the Sunday morning Dallas news. She switched to the Texoma station, thinking a local rancher's death for any reason would get at least a few minutes of airtime.

Nothing. Apparently, even the local news didn't think Rusty's demise was important enough to interrupt the Sunday morning cartoons.

Wishing she had a paper, she decided to run to the 7-Eleven, maybe even grab a breakfast burrito and a bag of powdered doughnuts while she was there. She slipped on a bra under her T-shirt, grabbed her purse, and headed for the door.

Halfway there, the doorbell rang.

It's Sunday, people. Even God didn't have to answer the door on the Sabbath.

Thinking about that, she scolded herself for missing church yet another week. After nearly dying twice in the past few months, it would be wise to stay in His good graces.

Annoyed, she flung the door open, fully expecting to go off on some kid about how she had neither the time nor the money for overpriced magazines. One look at the person standing there, his eyes and hair color almost identical to hers and wearing a sheepish grin on his face, made her gasp with pleasure.

"Hey, sis, where you going?"

"Danny, what are you doing here? Does Mom know you're here?" She pulled him into her apartment and shut the door. "Are you in some kind of trouble?"

Danny McAllister laughed. "You wish," he said, crushing her in a bear hug. "You'd love nothing better than to call Mom and rat me out."

"What are you—like twelve?" she asked between giggles.

Two years older than her, Danny was her favorite of all four brothers and still lived close to their parents. He'd gone straight from college into the Texas Department of Agriculture where he was basically a gofer.

"I'm starving. I've been driving since four this morning looking for this godforsaken place. Why in the hell did you move here, Jordan?" He dragged his five-eleven frame to the kitchen and stared at the empty cupboards. "Okay, give it up. I know you have Ho Hos stashed somewhere. You'd be shaking like an addict if you didn't."

She grinned. He knew her so well. "Sorry. Just ate the last one less than five minutes ago. I was on my way out the door for doughnuts."

His eyes scanned the countertop. "You must be coming up in the world, little sis. This is some fancy coffeepot. Didn't Dad teach you the best cup of java comes from a percolator?"

"Talk to me after you've tasted a cup from this jewel," she fired back. While she fixed him a cup, she took a few minutes to study her brother.

She hadn't seen him since last summer, right after Brett dumped her in Dallas, and she'd had nowhere else to go but back home. Of course, she hadn't told her family about that, or they would never have let her leave Amarillo and return to the big city all alone.

She loved all her brothers, but Danny really was special, probably because he didn't tease her mercilessly like the other three. In fact, he caught a lot of their teasing himself, so the two of them had bonded.

"What brings you here at ten in the morning?"

He took a sip of coffee, and from his expression, Jordan could tell he was impressed. Not that he would ever fess up.

"I'm on a case."

"A case? Since when did you get cases? Last I heard, you were working a desk in downtown Amarillo."

"Yeah, well, you heard wrong. I left that job in September. Didn't Mom tell you?"

Jordan bit her lower lip to hide her amusement. He looked like a kid who had just been told he hadn't made the team. "She may have, but your job isn't a high priority with me right now," she teased. "Congrats, bro, I knew you'd either piss someone off and get fired, or knock the socks off your employer and have your boss's job by now. You never could do anything halfway."

"Oh, like you can?" He flashed an impish grin. "Mom told me what happened to you a few months ago. Freaked her out that you almost got yourself killed. It's a wonder she didn't send the McAllister Swat Team down here to hog-tie you and drag your sorry butt home. Sean and Patrick wanted to drop everything, and even Mr. 'I'm so important' Tommy told his boss he needed a few days' personal leave."

Jordan found herself at a loss for words. Her mother had gone psycho when Jordan's friends had called from the hospital to assure her that Jordan was all right. This was the first time she'd heard how close her mom had come to sending the band of brothers to drag her out of Ranchero, kicking and screaming.

Lord only knew what might have happened if her parents had known the whole story.

"It was nothing," she lied, thankful she'd been given nine lives and still had seven good ones remaining. If she'd learned anything from that adventure, it was that she was a reporter and not an amateur sleuth. The bad guys were best left for the police.

"So what's this new job?" she asked.

"You're looking at a field officer for TSCRA," he said, beaming.

"TSCRA?"

"Texas and Southwestern Cattle Raisers Association—"

"You don't raise cattle."

"I know. For once in your life, will you listen without interrupting?"

When she nodded, he continued. "Like I said, I was sent here on my first big case. I have no idea how long this investigation will take, but I need a place to crash." He grinned sheepishly. "That's why they handed me this case. We don't have a huge budget, and when I said I wouldn't need a hotel room—voilà! They couldn't get the case files in my hand fast enough."

"You still haven't told me what this big case is."

His eyes lit up like they had when he told her about the fish he caught the first time he was allowed to go out on the boat with their dad and older brothers.

"You can't tell anyone," he said, moving closer. "Did you know some of the biggest ranches in Texas and Oklahoma are being hit really hard by cattle rustlers?"

"What? Have you gone loony on me? We're not talking

about the old *Bonanza* episodes Gramps used to make us watch when he babysat us. This is the twenty-first century, Danny boy."

"Some things never change. You're still a smart-ass. For your information, not only have the ranchers already lost millions in revenue this year alone, but they're also finding themselves in danger. Three weeks ago, one owner caught the thieves in the act and fired at them. They jumped in their pickup and nearly ran him down to get away."

A sound bite from the toastmaster at last night's Cattlemen's Ball replayed in Jordan's head. The man had raised his glass to "putting all the thieving cattle rustlers behind bars." She'd had no clue what he meant. Now she did.

"Why you? That doesn't sound like something for a newbie to undertake."

Danny frowned. "I may be a newbie, but you're forgetting how I got all that extra money in college to wine and dine the ladies." His stern expression turned to amusement. "When they discovered I'd worked at that Lubbock ranch and had a criminal justice degree, they foamed at the mouth to get me."

Jordan couldn't stop the grin from spreading across her face. Danny always did have an inflated view of himself, despite the other three brothers' nearly constant attempts to bring him down a notch. He might not have been the biggest guy in the huddle at the Amarillo High football games, but no one on the other team wanted to get hit by him. His reputation earned him a free ride at Texas Tech, where he still held the record for most quarterback sacks in a single season.

"So they sent you to investigate. Why Ranchero?"

"They sent about six of us all over the state, and one guy even went to Oklahoma. I was supposed to go to Abilene to help out the agent there, but last night something big happened and my plans changed. I was packed and on my way here in less than two hours."

"Something big in Ranchero? What?" He had her full attention now.

"Not in Ranchero, per se," Danny explained. "In Fort Worth, but it involved a guy from here."

Jordan cocked one eyebrow. "You don't mean Rusty Morales, do you?"

Danny shook his head as if he didn't hear her right. "You know him?"

"I was the last one to see him alive."

"Shit, Jordan! Why didn't you tell me that ten minutes ago? I could've been on the phone telling my boss about it and not wasting time jawing with you."

Jordan took a deep breath, not sure she should ask the next question but too curious to stop. "Why are you interested in a man who died of a heart attack after dinner?"

"Because Rusty Morales has been on our radar for over a month. We think he was the brains behind the biggest cattle-rustling ring in the state, operating right here in North Texas."

CHAPTER 4

"How are we going to play this, Danny? Since I know these people, I think I should ask the questions," Jordan said, groaning when the pickup hit a bump on the back road to Santana Circle Ranch and her head connected with the roof. "You think you could slow down a bit? I'm pretty sure Rusty's not going anywhere anytime soon." She added an extra touch of sarcasm as she rubbed her head.

"I thought you'd lose that smart mouth when you became a big-time reporter." He chuckled. "Oh wait—I forgot. You write personals."

She slapped his shoulder playfully. Too much time had passed since her brother had teased her, and she'd missed it. "I have my own column, loser."

"Yeah, writing recipes you've never heard of and have no clue how to cook."

"Shut up! At least I didn't get my job because I came cheap." She paused and then laughed out loud. "Okay, maybe that is how I got the job, but I still think you should let me do all the talking."

"No way! I'm the one investigating this cattle-rustling ring. My job, remember?"

"Yeah, but I'm the one who held my date in my arms while he was dying." She huffed. "And *I'm* the one who got the invite to come to the memorial service and the luncheon. My original plan was to bring Victor until you whined like you did when you were eight and Mom wouldn't let you go hunting with Dad and the 'three musketeers.'" She tsked. "Don't make me regret my decision."

Danny pressed his lips together in a move Jordan recognized as his retreat-and-reload tactic. She prepared herself for his zing back.

"You might have a point," he said, disappointing her a little. She loved the back-and-forth one-upmanship they usually shared. "But for the record, Patrick was only eight when Dad took him on his first hunting trip."

"Mom always called you the sensitive one. When she thought she'd never get her little girl, she decided to keep you away from all that macho stuff." Jordan paused, remembering how her mom had shifted all that focus onto her, dressing her in frilly clothes like a baby doll. But she lost that battle when the testosterone in the McAllister house overpowered the estrogen, and her brothers discovered Mama's little girl could throw a precision touchdown pass in traffic better than any of them.

"Okay, I get it. If any of Rusty's partners in crime are there today, I'm sure the last thing they want is to get chatty with me."

"My point exactly," she agreed. "That's why we shouldn't tell them you're here for an investigation. Let's just say you're hanging out with me while you job hunt."

He made a sharp right turn off the road and stopped in front of an ornate gate with a huge, wrought iron banner swinging above that read SANTANA CIRCLE RANCH.

"Whoa! You said this guy was rich, but you didn't say how freakin' big this ranch was." He pointed to the clumps of black cows grazing to the left of them in a pasture that seemed to extend as far as the skyline.

"You obviously weren't listening when I said he was one of the biggest cattle raisers in the state," she said, but even she was impressed.

"And Rusty was his right-hand man?"

"Yes, and from what I gathered at the ball the other night, the two were tight."

"Hmm. Wonder if Santana was in on the rustling."

"You don't even know for sure if Rusty was involved." Jordan turned to face her brother. "Why would he risk ending up in jail when he had the perfect setup here? It was crystal clear Santana thought of him as more than an employee. And don't forget the male ego. Most guys would flash that kind of money around to impress a date. He didn't." She shook her head. "I'd bet good money he wasn't involved."

"Because he didn't pull out his wallet to impress your skinny bones? Ha! Maybe he wasn't interested. Did you ever think of that?" He snickered and then got serious again. "Our sources tell us his name showed up on several questionable bills of sale for Wagyu bulls that were probably stolen."

"Wagyu bulls?"

Danny turned down the gravel road, and a ranch house came into view several miles away. "Wagyu cattle are like the Rolls Royce of cows. Think Kobe beef and go one step better."

"I thought Kobe beef was imported from Japan."

"It is, but plenty of ranch owners raise their own around here."

Danny slowed down near a mass of cars lining the side of the road. After parking the truck in the first available slot, about a mile from the house, he got out. Jordan followed suit, pulling at the hem of the black jersey number she'd worn on her first assignment at the newspaper, swearing it had shrunk. Since it was the only black dress she owned other than the slinky black skirt she'd bought for the Cattlemen's Ball, she hoped it wasn't too short for a memorial service.

Nothing says white trash like slutty funeral clothes.

No sooner had they started the trek to the house than an elderly man wearing jeans and a SANTANA RANCH golf shirt pulled beside them in a three-rowed golf cart.

"Hop in," he said, flashing a smile that covered almost the entire width of his face. "I'm Farley Williams."

Danny allowed Jordan to step up first, then quickly followed. Once they were settled, the driver sped away with a jolt, causing Jordan to grab the seat in front of her to keep from falling out the side.

"Sorry about that," he apologized. "Sometimes the gas pedal sticks."

He rounded a curve in the road without slowing down, but this time Jordan had a grip on the seat in front of her.

"Shame about Rusty," he said. "I always did like the kid."

Jordan leaned forward to hear. "I only met him a few nights ago. How well did you know him?"

The old-timer shook his head. "All his life, it seems. I remember when his mother first brought him to the ranch. He couldn't have been more than a few weeks old. Mr.

Santana made an exception to his rule about his employees bringing kids to work because nobody cooked like Maria. That woman made the best damn tamales around, no doubt about it." He smacked his lips before a long sigh escaped. "I watched Rusty grow into a fine young man."

"So, does his mother still cook for Santana, Mr. Williams?" When the cart hit yet another bump, sending her momentarily airborne, Jordan decided this man must have a built-in radar system for finding every single pothole in the road.

"Mr. Williams is my grandpappy. Call me Farley." The old cowboy lowered his eyes, shaking his head. "Maria Morales had a stroke about six months ago. Last I heard she was in a wheelchair and required round-the-clock care."

"What about Rusty's father? Does he work for Santana, too?"

"Oh, hell no," the driver said, drawing out "hell" like it had three syllables. "He and Mr. Santana had a falling out years ago."

Jordan's body slammed into the back of the driver's seat when the golf cart stopped abruptly in front of the big house.

"Well, here you are," Farley said. "The service is around back in the entertainment room. Mostly everyone is there already."

Danny stepped down and helped Jordan out.

"Thank you for the lift and the interesting conversation," Jordan said.

"No thanks necessary." The old cowboy jerked the cart forward and then drove off, hollering over his shoulder, "I'll pick you up when the service is over." He disappeared down the road, heading back to the area where several new cars had pulled over behind Danny's pickup.

"Okay, so what's our plan again?" Jordan asked, linking arms with her brother. "I'm dying to find out what kind of beef Rusty's dad had with Santana." She laughed at her own play on words. "Good cop, bad cop?"

Danny halted. "You watch way too many TV shows, Jordan. Let's just concentrate on the service and keep our eyes and ears open. If our sources are correct, the cattle-rustling ring is too big for a solo thief. I guarantee someone in the crowd—probably a slew of someones—knows something about Rusty's extracurricular activities. We don't want to scare anybody off."

Jordan was about to argue they still hadn't confirmed Rusty was even involved when Bella opened the door and immediately hugged Jordan as though they'd been friends for significantly longer than one evening. She was decked out in a black skirt and a frilly, charcoal silk blouse that definitely had not come off the racks at Macy's. The mid-calf black leather boots that showed off perfectly shaped legs were probably custom-made, too.

"Hello, Jordan. Lucas will be glad to see you again. He thought when you turned down his offer to send the limo, you weren't coming." She turned to Danny, licking her lips as she took her time checking him out. When her eyes finally settled on his face, she asked, "And who do we have here?"

"Danny McAllister," he said, offering his hand.

She linked one arm with Danny's, casually brushing up against him as she did so, and the other arm in Jordan's and then led the way down the long hallway. As soon as they entered the entertainment room, Jordan's mouth dropped. It was bigger than the local theater in Ranchero.

Painted a deep maroon, its walls covered with the mounted heads of what looked like the entire animal kingdom, the room had at least twenty-five rows of theater seats, each with a retractable tray like those in the front rows of airplanes. The only light in the room besides that from the two skylights on the twenty-foot ceiling came from the sconces lining each side wall.

The massive screen spanning the entire front wall told Jordan that Santana watched a lot of movies in here, and she was pretty sure most of them weren't PG.

"It's nice to see you again, Jordan," a sexy southern voice drawled.

Jordan pivoted to greet Carole Anne Summerville, but the woman had already turned her attention to Danny.

Sheesh! This was a funeral and already two women had practically devoured him with their eyes. What was this— trolling for mourners?

"Carole Anne, this is my brother, Danny. He's staying with me while he's in town on an—for a few weeks."

Crap! She'd come this close to telling Carole Anne the real reason Danny was in town. She glanced toward her brother, wondering if he'd caught her mistake. The look he sent her way said he had.

"Jordan never mentioned she had a brother and cer- tainly not one that looked like you," Carole Anne said, inching closer to Danny, giving Jordan an up-close-and- personal look at her ensemble.

Wearing a dress cut low in front to show off her impres- sive cleavage, Carole Anne looked like she might have just stepped out of *Sports Illustrated, Swimsuit Edition* and thrown the dress on over a G-string bikini.

She was with a man in his late fifties with flecks of gray dotting his jet-black hair around his ears and at the base of his temples. "This is my father, Jerald Summerville. Daddy, this is Jordan McAllister and her brother, Danny."

At well over six feet tall, he towered over them as he extended his hand first to her and then to Danny. "I haven't seen you around, Jordan. How did you know Rusty?"

Jordan noticed the catch in his voice when he said the dead man's name. "I was with him at the Cattlemen's Ball on Saturday . . ." She stopped herself from adding "the night he died."

Jerald Summerville lowered his eyes, but not before Jordan was sure she'd seen tears welling. When he glanced back up, they were gone. "I loved that boy like he was my own flesh and blood, and he should have been . . ."

"I'm sorry for your loss, Mr. Summerville. In the short time I spent with Rusty, I could tell he was a gentleman and—"

"Call me Jerry," he interrupted. "Rusty was the son I never had."

Jordan stole a look Carole Anne's way in time to see the hurt flash in her eyes before she recovered and attempted a smile.

"He would have been family if Carole Anne hadn't gone and screwed things up with him."

"Daddy," Carole Anne said, her voice unable to hide the hurt this time. "I did no such thing. If you remember correctly, it was Rusty who decided he wasn't ready to settle down." She grabbed her father's arm and pushed him toward the front row. "Come on. Go sit down over there, and I'll get you a drink."

"Make it a double," he said, allowing her to nudge him to the front.

When they were too far away to overhear, Bella shook her head. "That girl practically runs his company, and he still makes her feel like she's not good enough."

Before Jordan could respond, she felt a hand on her

shoulder. Turning, she came face-to-face with Cooper Harrison, decked out in his cowboy finest.

"Where have you been?" Bella asked with a touch of irritation in her voice. "Lucas is already upset enough today without worrying about you."

"He didn't need to worry. I said I'd have the food here on time, and I did. Traffic on I-35 was a killer, though. A tractor trailer hauling produce jackknifed near McKinley and spilled the entire cargo across the interstate. There were vegetables everywhere."

"Cooper, I'd like you to meet my brother, Danny," Jordan said, trying to defuse the tension between him and Bella.

Cooper accepted Danny's outstretched hand. "Nice meeting you. I'm sure I'll see you again." He scanned the room, spotting Carole Anne up front now, waving furiously to get his attention. "I'll talk to you later. Carole Anne is going to kill me for being late." He started in the direction of his fiancée and future father-in-law.

Just then, an older man pushing a wheelchair entered the room, and all eyes turned toward the back. Jordan took a step out of the aisle when the man started her way.

Tall with a full head of gray hair and enough wrinkles on his tanned face to suggest he worked outdoors in the Texas heat, the man maneuvered past the people standing in the back. As he got closer, Jordan got her first look at the woman in the wheelchair.

Olive-skinned with eyes nearly as dark as Rusty's, she was dressed in a black suit with a matching pillbox hat, Jackie O style.

When they reached Jordan, the man stopped. "Is she the one?" he asked, pointing to Jordan.

Bella nodded. "Yes, Diego, she is."

The man leaned toward Jordan, sadness blanketing his swollen eyes. "My son would have liked you, I'm sure," he said before fixing his gaze back on Bella.

For an instant, Jordan saw the grief in his eyes disappear, momentarily replaced by something else. Was it anger? Hatred?

"You were with him when he died?" Rusty's father asked Jordan, finally breaking eye contact with Bella.

"Yes, sir. I am so sorry for your loss."

"Thank you for that." He leaned down to the woman in the wheelchair. "Maria, this is the reporter who was with Rusty Saturday night."

The woman attempted to speak, but nothing came out except a garbled sound.

"She had a stroke a while back and hasn't been able to speak since. Doc called it aphasia. Said her voice may or may not come back." He patted the woman lovingly on the hand. "Come on, dear. The priest's ready to begin."

As Jordan moved back a few steps, Diego pushed his wife toward the front of the room. Halfway past her, Maria Morales reached out and grabbed Jordan's wrist in a death grip.

Jordan flinched when the pain shot up her arm. Before Diego could unclench his wife's fingers, the woman's squinting eyes drilled into Jordan.

What was it behind that stare? Pain? Sadness?

No, it was fear. Jordan was sure of it.

Help me, Maria mouthed before her husband wheeled her to the front row for her son's memorial service.

CHAPTER 5

The eulogy was short and sweet despite several pauses while Lucas Santana swiped at his eyes. Although Rusty had been raised Catholic, he'd stopped going to church many years before. Nevertheless, the priest led the rest of the service and at one point, even stopped to walk over and comfort Maria Morales.

Jordan couldn't stop thinking about the way Maria had clung to her. Did her mouthing "Help me" mean anything, or was it merely something said out of grief? Jordan's only experience with stroke victims had been her ex's grandmother, who'd had no noticeable physical effects except right-sided paralysis. Emotionally, however, she'd been a time bomb, one minute laughing, the next crying.

Was Maria having that same kind of poststroke mood swing?

Jordan couldn't shake the feeling there was more to it, and her imagination ran wild with the possibilities. Was

Diego Morales abusing her behind closed doors? He'd seemed so loving toward his wife that Jordan quickly dispelled the notion. What then? Was the woman asking for help to speak again?

Maybe Danny was right when he said she was watching way too many TV shows and imagining something more sinister. Perhaps "Help me" was all Maria could say.

"It was a nice service, wasn't it?"

Jordan turned as Lucas walked over. Dressed in jeans and a starched white shirt, he still looked good for a guy her father's age, even with swollen eyes.

"It was, Lucas. I'm glad I'm here and could give my personal condolences to Rusty's family."

He harrumphed before catching himself, and the words of the old cowboy who'd given them a lift to the door that day sprung into Jordan's head. Lucas Santana and Diego Morales were not on the best of terms.

"Since you were there the other night, I feel like you're part of the family now, Jordan. I hope you won't be a stranger to Santana Ranch."

Jordan absently crossed her arms over her chest, aware of his interest in that area.

Yeah! Like I'd ever visit the ranch without a bodyguard.

"Come on," Lucas said, reaching for her arm. "The food's ready in the bunkhouse."

On her feet now, Jordan suddenly remembered she hadn't come alone. "Lucas, I want you to meet my brother. He's—"

"The special agent sent to our neck of the woods by TSCRA. I know." He reached over and shook Danny's hand. "'Bout time you guys showed up. Some of my friends have already lost thousands in cattle revenue just this month alone."

Both Jordan and Danny were speechless. *So much for anonymity.*

"So Danny—that is your name, right?" When Danny nodded, Santana continued. "I figured they'd send someone with a little more experience. Guess we'll have to take what we can get. Anyway, how are you going to go about finding these good-for-nothing thieves?"

"I'm working on that, sir," Danny replied. "Right now we don't have much to go on. But if it helps you sleep easier tonight, I was in the Department of Agriculture for a lot of years before I got this assignment, and I have a criminal justice degree. I can assure you, I know what I'm doing."

Jordan watched Santana's reaction, looking for any hint that Danny might be right about the rancher being in on the crime. Other than a grunt, there was nothing.

"That's good to know. Fortunately, I haven't been hit as hard as some of my friends, but that's only because I now have men patrolling the west pastures at night. Told them to shoot first, ask questions later. Word must have gotten out."

Jordan shrugged. "I can see where that would be a deterrent."

"Damn straight." Lucas leaned closer. "If you ask me, putting a bullet in a few chests would make them think twice, seeing as the organization taking our good money to protect us can't seem to find their own behinds with both hands." He glared at Danny. "No offense, but how hard can it be to find a stolen cow at an auction when they're branded?"

Danny inhaled sharply. "That's the problem, Mr. Santana. Not everyone is branding their livestock. Without a brand, it's difficult to find your stolen Elsie when she's standing next to someone else's Sophie. You know what they say—they all look alike after a few beers." He stopped then added, "No offense taken, by the way."

Santana puffed out his chest. "No need to get snippy, young man."

"I'm sorry if I came across that way. I'm just saying if every ranch owner would take the time to brand their herd and register that brand with the department, it would make my job a whole lot easier."

"Easier, maybe, but you still don't always get it done. Joe Rosco over at the Starboard Ranch in Ellis County lost ten head last month alone, and every single one of them wore his brand and was registered with TSCRA."

Danny cleared his throat. "That's a problem we're working on. There's a possibility the stolen animals are being transported across the border. Our agency now has inspection points for every trailer hauling cattle to Mexico." He held up his hands. "If you have any better suggestions, I'd love to hear them."

"Just catch the yeller-bellied slime." Santana looked away when Cooper Harrison tapped his shoulder.

"My crew's ready to serve lunch, Lucas. They're waiting on you."

Santana turned back to Danny. "Maybe you and I will have more time to talk about this now that Jordan will be coming out this way more often."

Before Jordan could respond, he added, "You're part of the family now, remember? We have a sit-down dinner every Sunday afternoon, and I expect you here even if it means I have to put a bug in your editor's ear." He turned and followed Cooper to the bunkhouse.

"Now that man's a piece of work. Why he's attracted to your skinny butt is beyond me."

Jordan ignored him, still thinking about what Santana had said earlier. "Danny, if it's as simple as branding the cows, why doesn't everyone do it?"

"Cattle rustling wasn't a big problem until the last ten years or so. Many of the smaller ranches are slow to implement branding. In today's economic downturn, stealing cattle has become the new carjacking."

"Get out! How much can a cow be worth?"

"You think you know everything. For your information, one cow can bring in as much as a grand or two at auction. Wagyu, a whopping ten to twenty thousand."

She gasped. "Twenty grand?"

"Some more than that. Ever eaten Kobe beef?"

She tsked. "You know darn well I don't do steak."

"Well, if you ever decide to give a big juicy steak a try, Kobe is the way to go."

"I still don't get it. What's so special about Wagyu?"

Danny lifted a cocky eyebrow, apparently loving that he knew something she didn't. "They're treated like royalty, pampered more than most humans, with massages, first-class food, and even beer."

She laughed. "You gotta be kidding me."

"Nope. All that coddling makes their flesh highly marbleized with interspersed flecks of fat. Marbling so subtle it bastes a steak in its own juices. Shoot! I've been told a Wagyu burger in Manhattan will set you back over forty bucks."

Before Jordan could react, Bella appeared and gently pushed them toward the door.

"Come on, you two. Cooper brought his special chopped beef that melts in your mouth. For the life of me, I don't know how he gets it so tender." She accompanied them out the back door and across the lawn to the bunkhouse.

As soon as they entered the building where Jordan assumed Rusty had spent much of his time, she made eye contact with Maria Morales.

Tears streamed down the older woman's cheeks while she held Jordan's stare, and then her husband pushed her across the room to a table of Rusty's coworkers. Bella led Jordan and Danny to the back, where Cooper Harrison and his fiancée, along with Carole Anne's father, had a table to themselves.

Throughout the luncheon, Jordan caught herself watching Rusty's mother, feeling a surge of guilt for not being able to help her son when he was dying. She realized it was stupid to feel that way, but seeing Maria so heartbroken made her wish she'd been able to do more. The woman's grief tugged at Jordan's heartstrings.

Even though she'd just met Maria, and her son only a few days before, she felt a special bond with the grieving woman. She could only imagine how hard it would be for a mother to sit through the funeral of one of her children. Her own mother came to mind. No wonder she'd been so upset when Jordan's friends called her from the hospital several weeks before.

Jordan straightened in her chair when she saw a woman approach Rusty's mother and bend down to kiss her forehead. It was the same woman Rusty had spoken with on his way out of the ballroom that night, the one who was so upset when the ambulance took Rusty away.

"Brenda Sue Taylor," Carole Anne said, obviously noticing Jordan's interest. "She and Rusty used to be an item before he dumped her and then introduced her to her husband, who by the way is twenty years her senior and rolling in money." She shook her head. "He did the same thing with me. Introduced me to Cooper one night on a date and then quit calling a week later. Guess he thought it was the perfect way to let us down gently."

Jordan was positive she detected a hint of anger in Carole Anne's voice, but before she could find out more, Danny blurted out why he was in Ranchero, and the conversation at the table turned to cattle rustling. Both Cooper and Carole Ann bombarded him with questions, making Jordan believe it was a bigger problem than she had assumed.

"Fortunately, we're not affected by it," Carole Anne said, nodding toward her father. "We only process the meat and ship it to buyers for the ranchers."

Danny put down his coffee cup and leaned forward slightly. "And you make sure every cattleman who brings the animals has legitimate proof of ownership?"

"Of course," Mr. Summerville answered, his speech slurred from the three double Scotches he'd had with lunch. "We've been doing business with most of the ranchers for over thirty years. Everyone has to show a bill of sale or proof the brand is theirs, or they go someplace else."

"Did y'all get enough to eat?"

Everyone turned when Bella approached and stood behind Carole Anne. Not waiting for their response, she continued. "Lucas asked me to tell you that he'll call your editor this week, Jordan."

"Why?"

Bella shook her head. "He didn't say, but I think he wants to work out some kind of arrangement with Egan." She turned to walk back to the front but not before Jordan noticed how her fingers had absently massaged the back of Carole Anne's neck. They hadn't seemed that friendly at the ball.

"What was that all about?" Cooper asked, narrowing his eyes. "Why would Lucas need to work out an arrangement?"

Jordan stood up. "I have no idea. Now, if you'll excuse me, I want to give my condolences to Rusty's mom one last time." She turned to her brother. "I'll only be a few minutes, and then we can head out."

"Take your time. I'll get another cup of coffee and finish your cake." He grinned, sliding over the plate with her half-eaten dessert. "What's up with you leaving chocolate?"

Jordan shrugged, then headed toward Maria Morales, thinking it might be advantageous to talk to Brenda Sue as well. The way the woman had caressed the inside of Rusty's arm that night didn't jive with a woman scorned. Still, she might reveal something that could be helpful in figuring out why Maria felt threatened.

Today Brenda Sue was dressed in an elegant black suit that showed off her tiny waist and slender legs. Jordan wondered if the woman's husband had come with her. Glancing around the room, she quickly spied the man watching his wife's every move with an annoyed look on his face.

Standing in front of Maria, Jordan cleared her throat, and Brenda Sue straightened up. Again, the woman in the wheelchair tried to say something but failed. Jordan reached for her left hand and squeezed.

"Pardon the interruption," she said to Brenda Sue. "I just really wanted to tell Maria again how sorry I am about Rusty. A mother should never have to bury her child."

Tears welled in the young woman's eyes. "I remember you from the other night . . ." She looked away monetarily before meeting Jordan's eyes again. "Rusty was in such a hurry to . . ." Her voice trailed off before she took a deep breath and continued. "We were never formally introduced."

"Jordan McAllister."

"Brenda Sue Taylor. I've been told you only met Rusty that night. Is it true?"

"Yes, I was on an assignment with my newspaper, and he was kind enough to be my escort."

Brenda Sue sighed, and Jordan could have sworn it was out of relief.

"I can see how much his death has affected you," Jordan began. "You must have known him well."

This time Brenda Sue couldn't stop the tears and dabbed at her eyes. "We lived next door to each other. Rusty and I have . . ." She swallowed. "Had been best friends since we were in preschool."

And a whole lot more.

"My mother died when I was in junior high. Maria and Diego were unbelievably kind to me during that terrible time in my life." She patted Maria's shoulder and smiled down at her, through her tears. "I love this woman and owe her and Diego so much."

Suddenly an idea formed in Jordan's mind. Who better to ask about Maria than someone who knew her intimately like Brenda Sue? As Maria gripped her hand even harder, Jordan made the decision to find out why this terrified woman in the wheelchair was asking her, a perfect stranger, for help.

"I'm fairly new to the area and haven't made many friends yet. I was wondering if you'd have lunch with me one day next week to talk about Rusty. I have a lot of unanswered questions."

"Okay," Brenda Sue said hesitantly. "Nothing that will end up in the newspaper, right?"

"Absolutely nothing. It will simply be me, hoping to make a new friend. Maybe if I learn more about Rusty, I won't feel so guilty that I wasn't able to help him."

"From what they're saying, no one could have helped him." Brenda Sue turned as her husband called her name and impatiently gestured for her to return to the table. "I have to go, Jordan. Tuesdays are always good for me as Marcus goes into Fort Worth on business, and it will be quieter at my house than in a restaurant. I make a mean chicken salad, so come hungry. Say around noon?"

Jordan attempted to pull her hand out of Maria's grip to shake Brenda Sue's, but the older woman wouldn't let go. Jordan reached with her other hand for the business card the dark-haired woman held out to her.

Alone with Maria, she leaned closer and whispered, "Are you afraid of someone?"

Maria nodded.

"Is it your husband?"

This time Maria shook her head adamantly.

"Well, honey, it's time for your medicine and your nap. Say good-bye to this pretty young lady." Diego Morales pried his wife's fingers from around Jordan's hand a second time. "It was nice meeting you," he said over his shoulder, wheeling his wife toward the door.

Once they were gone, Jordan glanced down at the business card Brenda Sue had given her.

TAYLOR'S WAGYU RANCH—GET READY TO TASTE THE BEST BEEF IN THE COUNTRY.

Jordan tucked the card in her pocket and headed back to her table, grateful Brenda Sue had agreed to talk to her.

Hopefully, she could put the guilt behind her once and for all and get on with her normal boring life.

And then there was the free chicken salad, one of her favorites. Maybe she and Brenda Sue could become friends.

CHAPTER 6

As Jordan stepped into Dwayne Egan's office, she had a flashback to the first time she'd been summoned there by the boss. Two months ago she'd been so sure she'd get her walking papers, she'd barely noticed the décor of his office. The entire left wall was now lined with pictures of the Texas Rangers baseball team, one even signed by Cliff Lee, the amazing pitcher who'd helped them win the pennant two years before. Apparently, her editor was as big a sports junkie as she was.

"Thank you." She reached for the cup of coffee Jackie Frazier offered.

With a tilt of her dark curly hair, the Gilda Radner look-alike directed her to the chair across from Egan's desk. After nodding to her boss, the secretary exited, leaving Jordan alone with him and wondering what he had up his sleeve now. The few times she'd been in this office, he'd always wanted something from her.

"Heard you made quite a hit with Lucas Santana at the funeral last week," Egan began.

By now, Jordan had gotten used to seeing the man who resembled Joe Pesci behind the desk and hardly even noticed his ears, which connected to each side of his head at the oddest angle.

"I suppose," she replied, wondering if Santana had followed up on his intentions to call Egan when she hadn't shown up for dinner at the ranch on Sunday.

"I just got off the phone with him, and I can assure you that wasn't me making small talk."

Question answered.

"Whatever went down between the two of you left an impression." He leaned back in the chair with his hands behind his head, studying her. "I assume Jackie told you we no longer need the article on the Cattlemen's Ball."

Jordan nodded.

"Lucas decided, given the circumstances, the less said about it the better. Do you agree?"

Again she nodded, bracing herself for what she was sure would come next. Even though she'd only dealt with her editor a few times since she'd been at the *Ranchero Globe*, she recognized he was going somewhere with this conversation.

Somewhere she probably didn't want to go.

"Instead, I'll need you to spend some time at Santana Circle Ranch documenting the daily operation of a successful cattle ranch."

"No," she blurted.

"No?"

Jordan turned away from his intense stare. "The man makes me uncomfortable."

"Uncomfortable like you're afraid of him or like he gives you the willies when he's in the same—"

"Oh, I'm not afraid of him." Her strong denial brought back memories of facing off with her four brothers, and she nailed Egan with a defiant gaze. "I'm not some fragile female, you know. I can't explain why. I just don't like being around him."

The editor leaned forward and rested his chin on his hands. "Are you aware Santana Circle Ranch makes up about a third of the advertising budget at the *Globe*?"

Here we go again. She'd already heard this spiel when he talked her into going to the Cattlemen's Ball in the first place.

"You made that perfectly clear the last time you summoned me to your office." She tilted her head back as she glared, ready to give as good as she got.

Egan didn't even flinch. "Then let me put it another way. If Santana pulls his ads, some of the *Globe*'s employees suddenly become expendable. I don't really want to see that happen. Do you?"

Egan was playing hardball, and they both knew it. Although the young woman occupying the cubicle behind hers was the only employee who'd made an effort to talk to her in the five months she'd been there, Jordan wasn't prepared to jeopardize anyone's livelihood just because some old guy liked staring at her boobs.

And that's exactly what Egan counted on.

She took a deep breath. "What do you want me to do?" she asked, annoyed he'd played the perfect trump card.

A satisfied smile spread across his face. "That's my girl. You're tough enough to handle anything Santana dishes out and—"

"Just tell me what I'm doing."

He took a sip of his coffee before continuing. "He wants you to join him and Bella at the ranch for Sunday dinners for a few weeks. Says he'll have his cook prepare casseroles using his own beef. Not only can you write about them, but you can also use the recipes in your column. He thinks that might get people excited about beef again."

Jordan felt her resolve slipping and knew she was fighting a battle she wouldn't win. She took a relaxing breath, wishing she had a Ho Ho. Shoving one of those chocolate treats into her mouth always produced an instant endorphin high and gave her a different view of the world.

Okay, that was a load of crap, but she really wanted one right now.

"All right, I'll do it," she said after making her editor sweat it out for a few more minutes. "But this is it with Santana. No more pimping me out to him."

Egan threw back his head and laughed so hard he nearly fell over backward, chair and all. "Jesus, McAllister, where'd that come from?"

"It's true," she said, unable to hide her disgust. "First, you send me to a party where my date up and dies in my arms. Now, you want me to play nice to Daddy Warbucks on my day off."

Egan was still grinning. "It's my job to do whatever it takes to keep the newspaper solvent," he said, attempting to sound serious, without success. "Come on, McAllister, how bad can it be to enjoy a home-cooked meal on a Sunday afternoon? And don't forget, you won't have to come up with a recipe for the Kitchen Kupboard for the next three or four weeks. If you think about it, I'm actually doing you a favor."

Jordan huffed, but there was some truth to what he said. Lately it was getting harder to come up with a different casserole every week and slap a fancy name on it. This might be a nice reprieve.

"Did I tell you I have two seats on the fifty yard line for the Cowboys game tonight?"

Her head jerked up. She loved the Cowboys, and this week they were playing their division rival, the New York Giants, on *Monday Night Football*. Danny had checked online, but the cheapest available tickets were two hundred bucks a pop, way out of their price range. And that was for end-zone seating.

"And you're giving them to me?" She tried not to let her excitement show and began tapping nervously on her pants leg, out of Egan's view. Danny would freak out if she came home with fifty-yard-line tickets.

"One of my friends has season tickets, but he's out of town tonight for the big game. I thought you might be able to use them." He paused. "That's if you agree to play nice on Sundays and talk up the local beef industry."

"Done," she said, holding out her hand and feeling much like a dolphin who did tricks for a fish.

Never breaking eye contact, he reached in the top drawer and pulled out an envelope. Handing it to her, he said, "There's a parking pass in there, too."

She grabbed it, noticing her name clearly written on the front. "You knew I'd cave, didn't you?"

He nodded. "Who could resist the Cowboys from the fifty yard line?"

Sensing that agreeing to pacify Santana was a big deal to Egan, she decided to press her luck. "Since I'm giving up the next few Sundays for the newspaper, I want Friday afternoons off."

"You got it."

She couldn't believe how easy that had been and decided to go for broke. "And I want that empty office downstairs."

"Get out of here, McAllister, before I change my mind about Friday afternoons."

She popped out of her chair and bolted for the door, surprised when Jackie Frazier looked up and gave her a nod. There was no doubt the woman had been eavesdropping.

After sprinting back to her desk, she called her brother. "Guess who has tickets for the game tonight?"

"Yeah, right. What'd you have to do to get them—rob a bank?"

"You really don't want to know."

Jordan fought to keep her eyes open as she drove down the country road. Last night's game had gone into overtime, which ended with the Cowboys finally kicking the winning field goal. By the time she and Danny had pulled up to Empire Apartments, it'd been well after midnight.

She had huge bags under her eyes and was hoarse from screaming, but being in the awesome new stadium and pigging out on nachos and hot dogs had made it all worthwhile. Unfortunately, with the lack of sleep, she'd nearly forgotten today's lunch date with Brenda Sue Taylor.

When she'd called for directions that morning she'd detected a hint of hesitancy in Brenda Sue's voice. From the way she whispered on the phone, Jordan got the feeling the woman hadn't told her husband they were meeting that day. Or maybe she was having second thoughts about it and didn't know how to back out. Either way, Jordan had ended the conversation before she'd had a chance to cancel.

Pulling up to the gate, she scanned the miles and miles of land on both sides of the road, and she whistled. She had no idea Taylor's Wagyu Ranch was as big as Santana's. After rolling down her window and punching in the code

Brenda Sue had provided, she waited while the massive wrought iron gate swung open. Heading down the paved road, she drove for over five minutes before a three-storied brick house came into view. Several smaller structures dotted the landscape off to the right of the building.

After parking the car, she got out and saw Brenda Sue waving from the wraparound porch.

"I'm so glad you came," the dark-haired woman said, her tone a direct contrast to their earlier conversation. "It's been a long time since I enjoyed lunch with a friend."

Jordan did the compulsory girl-hug thing and then followed the petite woman through the huge front door laden with stained glass and heavy wrought iron. The entire wall of the long hallway was filled with pictures of Brenda Sue and her husband and a lot of cows. It didn't take a rocket scientist to conclude the Taylors probably didn't have children.

"Let's visit here for a while, Jordan," Brenda Sue instructed when they reached the living room, pointing to the caramel-colored leather sofa. "Can I get you a glass of wine?"

"I'll have to pass on the wine. I'm heading back to the office after lunch," Jordan replied, leaving out the part about how wine and hiccups were synonymous as far as Jordan was concerned.

"Then let me get us both a glass of tea." Brenda Sue turned and walked to the kitchen, giving Jordan a chance to study the room.

Her dad always said you could tell a lot about people by the way they lived. If that was true, Brenda Sue was sophisticated and smart, without being snooty.

Decorated in warm earth tones, the couch and matching love seat along with an antique rocking chair were the only pieces of furniture in the room. A massive stone fireplace that went all the way to the ceiling served as an incredible focal point. With the temperature still in the low seventies during the day, a roaring fire would have been ill advised to say the least; instead, rows and rows of lit candles decorated the inside of the fireplace.

Jordan breathed deeply, taking in the sweet fragrance that reminded her of the herbal shampoo she used. She felt her shoulders relax. The entire room gave off a warm and friendly vibe, as if she were in the living room of a good friend instead of a wealthy stranger she barely knew. Her first instinct when she'd seen the size of the ranch was that Brenda Sue would be all about how much money she had. If the house was any indication, so far, Jordan was pleasantly surprised.

She looked up as her hostess came back into the room and handed her a glass of tea, noting that Brenda Sue didn't have kitchen help. Taking a sip, she was bowled over by the sweet delicious flavor. "This is fantastic. What's in it?"

"Orange pekoe with fresh mint added. The wife of our ranch foreman has a greenhouse out back where she grows herbs for homeopathic medicine, among other things. Her mint is the sweetest I've ever tasted."

"I have to agree," Jordan responded, taking another sip before settling back in the soft leather cushion of the sofa. "So what did you want to talk to me about?"

Jordan set her glass on a coaster on the end table and glanced at her watch. "I'll jump right to the point, if you don't mind, since I have to be back at work by two."

She'd made a deal with Egan to have this afternoon off instead of Friday this week but wanted an excuse to cut and run if things got uncomfortable. Besides, she had her heart set on a nap when she got home. "I'm worried about Maria Morales."

Brenda Sue's face displayed her confusion. "Because of her health?"

"No. Because she seems terrified and even admitted she was afraid of someone. I was hoping you might be able to shed some light on who might be giving her trouble."

Brenda Sue thought for a moment before shaking her head. "Everyone loves Maria, especially Diego. He wouldn't hurt a hair on her head, and he'd kill anyone else who tried." She shook her head again. "Honestly, I can't think of anyone who would deliberately hurt that woman." She met Jordan's stare. "Did she actually say she was afraid of someone, or did you suggest it?"

Jordan pondered the question before answering. "I may have led her there, but twice she grabbed my arm and wouldn't let go. Then she mouthed the words 'Help me.'"

Brenda Sue laughed. "Since her stroke several months ago, Maria hasn't always seemed rational. The doctors keep telling Diego that the aphasia may go away in time, but the longer she goes without speaking, the less chance there is of that happening."

Jordan straightened on the sofa as a thought suddenly came to her. "Can she write on a notepad?"

Brenda Sue shook her head. "She was right-handed and that's the side that was paralyzed. They've tried to teach her how to use the left one, but she's never mastered it. She gets frustrated and throws the pad across the room every time."

"It must be hard not being able to communicate."

"I'm sure. She had her stroke just a few months after having her left hip replaced, which made it that much more devastating. She was just getting used to walking without a cane when she had the massive bleed into her brain. As I understand it, she mistakenly took too many of the blood thinners she'd been on since the surgery. The doctor said it was a miracle she survived."

"Did she get confused about the pills or what?"

"That's the funny thing. When Diego counted the remaining tablets to see just how many she had ingested, none were missing. Yet her blood tests showed her clotting ability was five times slower than normal."

"Wow, that is weird," Jordan responded.

Brenda Sue pushed away from the table and stood up. "Enough about Maria. Ready to eat yet? I'm starving."

"Me too." Jordan got up and followed her through the French doors onto a veranda overlooking miles of green pasture dotted with grazing cows. "Are those Wagyu?"

The hostess looked surprised. "You know Wagyu?"

Jordan hurriedly looked away, thinking she had screwed up again before remembering she no longer needed to keep Danny's reason for being in Ranchero a secret. "My brother's staying with me for a few weeks. He's a TSCRA agent sent here to investigate the increase in cattle rustling. He gave me a ten-minute 'all you ever wanted to know about cows but were afraid to ask' lecture."

"Yeah, I'd heard an investigator was in town. Marcus and I lose about three or four head every few months despite our best efforts to prevent it. We move them to a new pasture nearly every night to confuse the thieves, but they always seem to know where to find the cows."

They sat down at a small table covered in crisp white linen and adorned with rust-colored stoneware plates and the most beautiful yellow carnations Jordan had ever seen. "These are gorgeous."

"Another of Karen's greenhouse miracles. She makes

pretty good money selling her flowers to the shops all over the metroplex."

"I thought you said she grows herbs for homeopathic medicine."

"That, too. She has customers all over the world."

"Amazing," Jordan exclaimed. "I'd love to see the flowers."

"Karen adores showing off her beauties. If you want, we can check them out after we eat." She reached for Jordan's empty tea glass. "Do you want a refill, or would you prefer water or a soft drink with your lunch?"

"I can get those anywhere. I absolutely want more tea. I still can't believe a little mint can change the taste so much."

Brenda Sue picked up the plates from the table. "Sit tight. I'll be back in a flash with our lunch and more tea."

Jordan used the time alone to contemplate their earlier conversation about Maria. The journalist in her moved straight to a more sinister explanation for the woman's accidental blood-thinner overdose. Was it possible Diego had slipped her an extra pill or two and then lied about how many were missing?

A vision of Maria mouthing "Help me" popped into her head. Although she barely knew the woman, she vowed to at least check it out. She added a visit to the Morales house to her list of things to do in the next week or so. First, she'd have to research the kind of medicine Maria would have been prescribed after a hip replacement.

Waiting for Brenda Sue to return, she formed a plan.

CHAPTER 7

"Here you go," said Brenda Sue, carrying a tray with the tea and stoneware plates filled with the chicken salad, a small spinach salad, and a greenish concoction.

After her first bite of the chicken salad, Jordan was glad she'd come. Next she tried the greenish stuff, licking her lips to get every last drop. "This is yummy. What is it?"

"Watergate Salad." Brenda Sue beamed. "My mother made this every time we had company. The pistachio pudding makes it so good."

"I'd love the recipe for my column," Jordan said, taking the last bite. "The chicken salad, too. It's the best I've ever eaten." She was already seeing both recipes as next week's entry in the Kitchen Kupboard, hoping Victor and the gang could come up with some exotic name to go with them.

When they'd finished eating, Jordan glanced at her watch. "I'll help you clean up, then I have to get going. It's about a half-hour drive back to the office."

Brenda Sue waved her off. "Don't be silly. Marcus won't be back until dinner time, so I have all day to tidy up. Let's go out to the greenhouse, and I'll introduce you to Karen and her garden. Bring your phone. You'll want pictures."

"Terrific. Lead the way."

Grabbing her cell phone, Jordan followed Brenda Sue out the door to the small building sitting back about three hundred yards from the house.

"Come on around back. Karen's always there pampering her plants." She led Jordan through the gate and behind the greenhouse where a yellow Lab rushed to greet them, nearly knocking Brenda Sue off her feet.

"Hey, Lucky. Look what Aunt Brenda has for you." She reached into her pocket and pulled out a dog biscuit. The dog snatched it and ran, his tail wagging his thanks. "Karen and David never had kids, so her plants and animals are her babies. Marcus and I have our cows, and of course, all of Karen's critters."

They were greeted at the entrance by a fortyish woman with dark hair tinged with gray at the temples and pulled back into a tight bun. Jordan watched the two women embrace before Brenda Sue introduced her to Karen Whitley.

After making a fuss over the beautiful flowers near the front, Jordan headed down the aisle, scanning the rest of the huge structure. It was like walking through a professional nursery filled on both sides by flowers of every size and color.

She bent down to smell a huge yellow rose with pink-tipped petals. "I'm totally dazzled, Karen. How did you get them to grow so large?" Pulling out her cell phone, she asked, "Do you mind if I snap a few pictures? My friends won't believe me when I tell them how beautiful these are."

"Take as many pictures as you like. I figure it's good advertising. Flowers To Go in Connor is one of my biggest customers." She paused. "I'll send you home with a bouquet to entice your friends to visit the shop."

"I'd love that," Jordan said, already checking out which flowers she wanted.

Near the back of the greenhouse, she spotted a large area cordoned off with rope. Inside were rows of shrubs, a few she recognized as oleanders by their pretty white flowers. Beyond those were large pots of unfamiliar vines. Some were covered with yellow-green blooms that resembled little helmets, while others were adorned with a mixture of purples and blues. The sweet fragrance coming from these flowers tickled her nose, and she pulled out her camera. After snapping several pictures, she leaned over the rope to pull one closer.

"No!"

She jerked back as Karen ran up.

"Those are all poisonous," the older woman said. "You have to wear gloves to touch them."

"I thought only ingesting oleander was unsafe," Jordan said, leaning away from the rope.

"That's true, but what you were reaching for is monkshood." Karen pointed to the purple and yellow flowers. "We're extra careful with those, even wear gloves when we get them ready to ship to the drug companies."

"Monkshood?" Jordan stared at the beautiful plants, finding it hard to believe something that lovely was so dangerous. "They're used in medicine?"

"Homeopathic remedies," Karen explained. "We ship them to health food stores all over the country. They make what they call aconite with the dried leaves and roots."

"Aconite? What's it used for?" Jordan asked.

"A variety of things, mostly to treat inflammatory ailments like arthritis and rheumatism. Some people even use it for colds and the flu."

"I thought you said it was poisonous."

"It is, in high doses," Karen said. "That's why we have to be very careful when we handle it."

"Wolfsbane is another name it goes by," Brenda Sue added. "In older times, they coated the tips of arrows with the juice and used it to kill wolves."

"It's also been used to commit crimes," Karen continued. "One dentist even filled his father-in-law's teeth with it and almost got away with the perfect murder." She laughed. "Know anyone you'd like to see dead?"

Jordan grinned, remembering the man who'd left her tied to a tree surrounded by feral hogs several months before. Thank the Lord he was behind bars, because if she'd known about the poisonous flower then, he might not be protected by the criminal justice system now.

"Don't you worry about working with it?"

"We've never had a problem, although I have gotten nauseous once or twice after processing it for several hours at a time. I'm sorry I scared you, but there's no sense taking chances."

"I agree," Jordan said, nodding. "So I guess I won't be choosing this one for my bouquet. What's the yellow stuff behind the oleander?"

"Saint-John's-wort," Karen said. "That's my money-maker."

"They're pretty enough to lift someone's spirits just by looking at them," Jordan commented before glancing once again at her watch. "I could spend the entire day here with all these colorful flowers, but I'd better wrap this up and get on my way."

"Did you decide which flowers you want for your bouquet?" Karen asked, pulling a pair of snippers from her apron.

"I love the yellow roses at the front."

Karen headed that way. "Then that's what you'll take home."

Jordan started to follow, but both she and Karen stopped when Brenda Sue's phone rang.

"It's Marcus. I'll just be a minute." Brenda Sue turned her back to them and spoke so low, Jordan couldn't make out what she was saying—not that she was eavesdropping.

A few minutes later, Brenda Sue faced Jordan, nervously biting her lower lip. "Marcus finished up his business in Fort Worth earlier than expected, and he's on his way home." She grabbed Jordan's arm and gently pushed her to the door. "The next time you visit, we'll spend more time with all these wonderful flowers, Jordan."

After thanking both Karen and Brenda Sue, Jordan walked to her car, confused by the hostess's abrupt dismissal. On the ride back to town, Jordan glanced down at the beautiful bouquet, hoping the flowers wouldn't wilt before she found a vase for them. The day had been surprisingly pleasant, and she could see Brenda Sue becoming a good friend. The subject of Rusty's death hadn't come up, which was just as well. Jordan had already decided the relationship between them had been more than just friendship.

From what Carole Anne Summerville had said at the memorial service, Rusty had introduced her to Cooper and Brenda Sue to Marcus Taylor right before he ended his relationships with them. Jordan got the feeling that Rusty might have had a wee bit of a commitment problem. Setting up the women in his life with other men was one sure way to get out from under the pressure if he'd been unwilling to give either of them what they'd obviously wanted.

But Jordan suspected things were not all rosy in the Taylor household, and she wondered if Rusty's death had anything to do with it. She'd picked up on subtle signs, like Brenda Sue being so distant on the phone that morning and then acting like Jordan was her long-lost friend later when she'd arrived.

And she'd been the perfect hostess until that last phone call from her husband.

Talk about a one-eighty demeanor change!

What was up with that? Was she so jealous that she didn't want any of her female friends around him? Or did she not want him to know Jordan had come to the ranch for a visit?

No matter the reason, after the call, Brenda Sue couldn't get Jordan out the door and on her way back to town fast enough.

CHAPTER 8

Jordan spotted the only available table at Mi Quesadilla the next day at lunch and quickly set her tray down to claim it. She hadn't been back here since she'd first met Alex, and the memory made her insides tingle. It was probably the only time in her life she'd ever left chips and queso on the plate.

What was it that made a girl pretend to eat like a bird when there was a good-looking man nearby? Growing up with four brothers had taught her if you didn't eat everything on your plate—and eat it quickly—there was a good chance someone would swipe it and shove it into their mouth before you could open yours to protest.

She and her siblings had inherited their mother's metabolism. Unfortunately, Patrick, the oldest, was beginning to sprout a spare tire since he'd broken his ankle and had been unable to play pickup basketball for a few months. Thoughts of her childhood in West Texas always made her homesick, although having Danny stay with her for a few weeks was probably more than enough of a brother fix for a while.

Jordan glanced at her watch to make sure she had enough time to sit and eat her lunch. She'd have to inhale it if she wanted to get back to the office in time. She'd stopped by Tomorrow's Treasures to chitchat with Victor and had gotten caught up in his excitement over a shipment of antiques he'd purchased from across the Texas border in Durant, Oklahoma. Ever since he'd bought the store from his former boss, he'd gradually added inventory as his wallet allowed. This latest purchase came from an estate sale and, according to him, was a steal.

As she slid into a chair and reached for one of the tacos on her plate, Jordan spied a young woman she recognized from the *Ranchero Globe*. She remembered her name was Sandy because once when Brett, her ex, had called, the woman had rescued her by buzzing in and giving Jordan the perfect excuse to hang up.

In her early thirties, Sandy wore her short dark hair in an old-fashioned style. With her nondescript black slacks and a white blouse, she was the stereotypical girl next door.

When she caught Jordan staring, she made a vague effort to smile, but Jordan noticed tears streaming down her face before she closed her cell phone and glanced away.

Jordan picked up her tray and carried it over, feeling like she owed her a return gesture of some kind. "Mind if I join you?"

Sandy swiped at the tears. "I'm not much company today." She pulled out a tissue and blew her nose.

Jordan flopped down across from her and took a long sip of her Diet Pepsi. "I'm Jordan McAllister."

"I know who you are."

"It looks like you could use some company. I'd like to return the favor."

Sandy glanced up. "Favor?"

"Remember when you rescued me from a phone conversation I didn't want to have?"

First confusion, then remembrance reflected on her face. "Oh, yes, I do remember." She sniffed. "I'm usually more social, but I'm not having a great day." Reaching across the table, she shook Jordan's outstretched hand. "I'm Sandy Johnson, by the way."

"You're way more social than anyone else at the newspaper, Sandy," Jordan said before she could stop herself. Her mom always said she needed a filter before she spoke.

But Sandy didn't look annoyed at the obvious rip on her coworkers. "They'll come around. Big-city girl with all your smarts coming to their neck of the woods scares them, I guess."

"Big-city girl?" Jordan laughed. "I grew up in Amarillo in a house with two acres. We never even locked our doors at night. Does that sound like 'big city' to you?"

Sandy grinned, reaching for her lunch. "Guess not, but we all heard about how you were the sports reporter at UT. Most of us at the newspaper graduated from Grayson County College and will probably never work anywhere but the *Globe*." She sipped her drink. "Guess everyone thinks you're going to act high and mighty."

"That's interesting," Jordan said. "Here I thought everyone avoided me like the plague just because I wasn't a local."

Sandy laughed out loud. "There is that. Ranchero is very cliquish."

"Tell me about it. I—" Jordan stopped midsentence when Sandy's phone rang.

After glancing at caller ID, Sandy put the phone in her purse. "No way I'm talking to that man again. He's already ruined enough of my day."

"Men have a way of doing that," Jordan offered. She shoved one of her sopapillas across the table. "A little pastry with a lot of honey goes a long way in making you forget an annoying boyfriend, if only for a while."

Sandy reached for the dessert. "It's not a boyfriend." She snorted. "I've just about given up on finding anyone in Ranchero who doesn't still live with his mother."

Jordan grinned. "You know what they say about men—that all the good ones are taken."

"Or gay," Sandy added. The smile faded when her phone rang again. "Dammit. I wish he'd leave me alone."

Jordan leaned closer. "Anything I can help with? I grew up with four brothers, and I know how they think."

"I appreciate the offer, but unless you have an extra three thousand bucks lying around, you can't help."

"Why do you need that kind of money?" Jordan asked before slapping her hand over her mouth. Where was that filter when she needed it? "I'm sorry. I didn't mean to get so personal."

"It's all right," Sandy said, blowing out a breath and glancing up to stop the lone tear from spilling down her cheek. "I have to pay the back taxes on my grandfather's house."

"Oh," Jordan said. "Can't your grandfather go to the bank and see about getting a loan or maybe even a second mortgage?" She thought of Alex and his cover as bank manager when he'd been in Ranchero. "There's a possibility someone I know might be able to help." The next time Alex called, she would ask him to contact the bank to plead Sandy's case.

This time Sandy made no attempt to hide her tears. "My grandfather died about six months ago."

Jordan reached across the table and grabbed Sandy's hand. "I'm so sorry. I remember when my grandfather died. He was my hero."

"Gramps was mine, too. Since my parents are missionaries and always traveling to who-knows-where, I spent a lot of time out at the lake with him. When he died he left the house to me, knowing how much I loved it out there in the woods so close to the water." She sighed. "He named every single duck on the lake, and they still hang out on his dock even though he's not there to feed them anymore."

"Sounds wonderful. What a great place to go after a mad day at the newspaper."

"I don't live there," Sandy said, a hint of sadness still in her voice. "I wish I did. Then I wouldn't have an apartment in town, and I could start saving to pay off the county tax assessor before the city steals the lake house right out from under me."

Jordan shrugged to hide her confusion. "So why don't you just move out there?"

"I can't." Sandy bit her lip. "You'll think I'm nuts if I tell you why."

"Hey, I grew up with brothers, remember? I can handle anything after that." Jordan scooted her chair closer to Sandy's. "What on earth is keeping you from moving to a house you love, especially when that's the only way you can save it?"

"It's haunted."

"Haunted? Like spooks and bumps in the night?"

"Exactly."

Never having been one to believe in such things, Jordan had to resist the urge to make light of this. The last thing she wanted was to give Sandy the impression she thought she really might be crazy. She'd finally found someone her own age who could actually turn out to be a friend—two, counting Brenda Sue. She didn't want to blow it by coming across as judgmental.

"Why do you think it's haunted?" she asked, thinking that going along with the idea might be the safest way to play this.

"I hear the ghosts at night."

"Do they talk to you?" Jordan was beginning to worry about her new friend. What if she was like Sybil and heard people conversing in her head?

"They don't talk, but they're there. I hear them pounding."

"Pounding what?"

Sandy shrugged. "I don't know. It doesn't happen every night. The last time I spent the weekend out there, it only happened twice. I tried to brave it out, telling myself it was nothing, but I got spooked and went home immediately when I heard it the second time."

"Could it be a neighbor working on a project or something? You know, maybe someone fixing a barn or a fence?"

"At three in the morning? No way. It's ghosts. I'm sure."

There was no doubt in Jordan's mind that her new friend genuinely believed what she was saying. An idea formed in her head. "Do you play cards, Sandy?"

"I love cards. I used to play Texas Hold 'Em in college nearly every day. Why?"

Jordan thought about Lola and how she had convinced Lucas Santana, just by reading his tarot cards, that the beef market would rebound. Although Lola wasn't a psychic, Jordan was sure she could help Sandy somehow.

"Can you come to my apartment on Friday night?" she asked, thinking ahead to the next Screw Your Neighbor potluck night. "There's someone I want you to meet."

"Cooper, why are you calling me?" Jordan leaned back, knocking a stack of papers from her desk. Scrambling to retrieve them, she nearly fell out of the chair.

"The newspaper seemed like the easiest way to reach you." He paused. "Personals? I thought you wrote the food column."

"I do both," she responded, anxious to find out why he was really calling and end this conversation. It was already Thursday, and she still hadn't finished her post for this week's Kitchen Kupboard.

"Two jobs, huh? I hope they pay you well."

"What do you want, Cooper?" she asked, unable to hide the annoyance in her voice.

"Right to the point? Okay, then. I'm following up on that conversation we had at the Pavilion and calling to invite you to Beef Daddy's for dinner tomorrow night. Afterward, you can swing by the warehouse on Greenville Avenue, and I'll give you a tour of the facility."

Spending time with Cooper was at the bottom of her list of fun ways to spend a Friday night. The man had flirted openly with her in front of his fiancée when she'd first met him. No way she'd chance one-on-one time with him, even though she loved Beef Daddy's food.

"Thanks, but I spend Friday nights with my friends. Maybe some other time."

"Bring them along," he fired back. "The more the merrier." He laughed. "There's something I'd like to talk to you about."

The sound of his laughter ground on her last nerve. She didn't like this man, and free food wouldn't change that.

"I don't—"

"Think about it and give me a call back. I'd really like to show you my Greenville Avenue facility." Before she had a chance to decline his invitation again, he hung up.

For a few seconds Jordan stared at the receiver, unable to come up with a single reason why Cooper might want to talk to her. Did he know something about Rusty's death? Or about Maria?

She pushed the conversation to the back of her mind, positive she wasn't about to find out.

Unfortunately, that night she made the mistake of mentioning his call to Rosie and Victor, who'd popped in to watch *Grey's Anatomy* with her and Danny. The idea of taking their Friday night get-together on the road plus the lure of free food was too tempting, and they ganged up on her. Finally, she'd agreed to call Cooper back and set it up, if only to be able to watch the end of one of her favorite shows in peace. When Victor sprang from the couch and ran out the door to tell the others, she bit her lip to hide her smile. The man loved anything free.

The next day, Jordan put the finishing touches on the typed recipes for Sunday's edition of the Kitchen Kupboard, certain the Ranchero citizens were going to love both the Chicken Salad and the Watergate Salad. When she'd called Brenda Sue for the recipes on Wednesday, Jordan was surprised that her new friend had reverted back to her jovial hostess persona. Apparently *Mister* Taylor wasn't around.

Good grief! Why were some women so intimidated by the men in their lives?

First there was Bella, who looked the other way while

the man she'd given the last ten years of her life to flirted outrageously with other women. Then there was Carole Anne, who spent way too much time trying to please her father when it was painfully obvious he would never see her as anything other than a mindless female. Even though, according to Bella, the woman was the reason North Texas Beef Distributors was the overwhelming leader in beef sales in the metroplex.

And Jordan still hadn't figured out the relationship between Brenda Sue and Marcus Taylor. It was obvious the woman still had feelings for Rusty Morales, and even more obvious that Marcus knew about them. Is that how he controlled her, by using that guilt to keep her at home like a Stepford wife?

Jordan shook her head, vowing to never give a man that much power over her for any reason, before she remembered how easily she'd caved when Egan had dangled the Cowboys tickets in her face.

"Are we still on for tonight?"

She looked up just as Sandy Johnson approached her desk. She'd already forgotten she'd invited her coworker to join the gang for cards that night.

"Oh geez, Sandy. I meant to call you, but things got really hairy around here." She tapped Send, praying the recipes were the big hit she predicted.

"If you've changed your mind, it's okay," Sandy said, disappointment flashing in her eyes. "One more take-out pizza won't kill me."

Jordan sighed, remembering Sandy's story about her grandfather's haunted house on Lake Texoma. "My friends aren't playing cards tonight. I—"

"Just my luck," Sandy said, lowering her eyes.

Jordan wondered how many times the shy girl's hopes

had been dashed in the past. "We've been invited to have dinner over at Beef Daddy's Barbecue Joint in Dallas and afterward to tour the warehouse where the food for all the metroplex franchises is made."

Sandy's eyes lit up. "I love their sliced brisket, although I don't make it into Dallas very often to get it."

"Then why don't you come with us?"

"Really?"

Jordan couldn't help herself and smiled, wondering if Sandy had any other friends. "Sure, why not? You can meet the woman I think will be able to help you get rid of the ghosts."

Visibly excited, Sandy hugged Jordan. "What time should I be at your apartment?"

Jordan glanced at the clock above the main entrance. It was already after five, and she'd have to hustle to get home and squeeze in a shower. "How about six thirty? We'll all pile into my friend's Suburban and head down to Beef Daddy's."

"I'll be there." Sandy raced back to her desk, reminding Jordan of an excited ten-year-old.

She made a mental memo to try harder to get to know the people at the newspaper. Maybe she had misjudged them. What if she'd misread their behavior as cliquishness when in fact they were all as shy as Sandy?

She glanced up just as the middle-aged woman in the cubicle next to her stood to leave. Even though she made eye contact with Jordan, the frumpy woman in a black pantsuit and matching shoes turned quickly and left without ever changing expressions.

Nothing shy about that rebuff!

Jordan opened the desk drawer and grabbed her last Ho Ho and threw it into her purse, adding a trip to the grocery store to her list of things to do that weekend. God forbid she had to go through the coming week without them.

She shut down her computer and headed for the door, thinking Lola would have her work cut out for her if she was to succeed in convincing Sandy she could actually scare the ghosts out of the secluded lake house.

Her last thought as she slid in behind the wheel of her Camry was, *What if there really were ghosts?*

CHAPTER 9

Sitting between Michael and Rosie in the middle seats, Jordan was so bloated she was tempted to unsnap her jeans. She and the rest of the gang had eaten way too much at Beef Daddy's and were now on their way to the company warehouse to thank Cooper Harrison for the great meal. She'd especially enjoyed watching her brother put the moves on Sandy. From the moment she'd introduced them, Danny had taken an obvious interest in getting to know her better, which surprised Jordan. Danny usually went for the extroverts who loved to party.

He'd been a ladies' man as far back as junior high, when he'd stolen the most popular girl out from under the richest kid's nose. Jordan never could figure out why the girls gravitated to him, but she was pretty sure he didn't burp or ask them to pull his finger like he did with her.

The guy's smooth. Halfway through the meal, he'd reached up and pushed a stray lock of Sandy's hair behind her ear. For the first time she could sort of understand the intoxicating effect he had on the West Texas girls.

Eew! Even thinking now about it sent shivers up her spine, and she quickly forced herself to look out the front window. She had no intention of turning around again to see him flirting with Sandy in the last row of seats in the Suburban.

"How far down Greenville Avenue did Cooper say we had to go, Jordan?" Ray asked, interrupting her thoughts.

Grateful for the diversion, Jordan reached into her purse for the directions scrawled on the back of a napkin. "He said the warehouse was about ten miles or so, almost into downtown Dallas."

"And we're finally going to meet the guy who comped that fantastic meal back there?" Lola asked, letting her finger stroke the back of Ray's head as he drove.

"Yes. Cooper apologized for not being able to meet us at the restaurant, but some business-related thing came up," Jordan answered.

"That was really sweet of him to feed us all," Rosie said before arching her eyebrows in a Groucho Marx kind of way. "Is this guy married?"

"Engaged," Jordan replied. "Matter of fact, his fiancée runs a company that supplies all the beef for his restaurants." She failed to mention Cooper was a big flirt, but unless he suddenly developed laryngitis and couldn't speak, they'd see it firsthand. And knowing her hip fiftyish friend who made no secret of her battery-operated social life and her penchant for marrying a guy every time she sneezed, Jordan was positive Rosie would love every minute of it.

"And how did you meet him, sugar?" Ray asked.

"Cooper and his fiancée sat with us at the Cattlemen's

Ball. He and Rusty knew each other through Lucas Santana." She stopped short of saying they were friends, remembering the interaction between the two of them that night.

"That reminds me," Danny said. "I forgot to tell you—"

"There it is," Victor hollered, pointing to the huge warehouse on the right. "Maybe he'll give us some freebies to take home."

"You already have half a cow in your doggie bag, love," Michael chided.

"The waiter said we could order as much as we wanted—all gratis, Michael," Victor said, trying unsuccessfully to look pouty before breaking into a cat-that-ate-the-canary grin. "Nobody gave me a time limit, and I can't help it there was so much left on my plate. They would have had to throw it away." He flipped his hand in the air. "Remember those starving kids your mom always told you about when you left food on your plate?"

"Yeah, my boy here was just looking out for the less fortunate, right, Vic?" Rosie twisted around and gave him a fist bump.

"Tell that to the young man who waited on us. Did you see the look on his face when Victor asked for his fourth helping?"

"Oh Lord, I hope he doesn't tell Cooper," Jordan said, joining in the laughter. It was a known fact that Victor liked to eat. Michael was always reminding him to watch his weight, and Victor was always ignoring him.

Ray turned off the main road and drove around to the parking lot at the back of the building. "The place looks deserted."

"Cooper said the night shift doesn't come in until midnight to start smoking the beef and preparing the side dishes. That's why he invited us to tour the facility now."

Rosie playfully punched Jordan's shoulder. "Obviously, there are some perks with this new job of yours, sweetie. I'll bet the tab would have been a few hundred bucks tonight."

"Easily," Michael said, pointing to the bag on Victor's lap.

"Some of us know how to take advantage of a free meal." Victor patted the food and made a big production of taking a whiff. "While I'm enjoying barbecue sausage tomorrow, you guys will be eating bologna."

Lola laughed. "You're confusing us with Jordan. Ray and I are grilling steaks."

"Yes, but you had to pay for those steaks, my dear," Victor said.

"Okay, guys, let's not let this man hear us talking about how we took advantage of his generous offer," Ray said when they'd piled out of the car and were headed for the door.

"Cooper said to pick up the phone and dial this number." Jordan handed the napkin to Ray and watched while he punched the keypad next to the door.

Before long, a buzzer sounded and the door opened. Cooper walked toward them as they filed in. He moved right to Jordan's side and hugged her as if they'd known each other all their lives.

"Cooper Harrison, meet my friends," Jordan said introducing each one.

"We sure did appreciate the meal tonight, Mr. Harrison," Rosie said, inching closer to the attractive host.

Ohmygod! She did not just bat her eyelashes.

"It was my pleasure," Cooper said, either ignoring Rosie's outlandish display or missing it entirely. "Let me show you around the place."

He grabbed Jordan's hand and nudged her down the long hallway where boxes were piled high on metal racks. "These are the supplies that don't need refrigeration—condiments, napkins, paper plates, et cetera."

Next Cooper led them to a room full of smokers where the smell of barbecued meat overwhelmed them before he'd even completely opened the door.

"This is where all the cooking is done."

"Wow! Your barbecue is the best I've ever tasted, Mr. Harrison. And believe me, I've tasted a lot of it. Do you ever give out your recipe?" Rosie gave him another eyelash flutter, followed by a hair flip that could only be interpreted as a possible play for husband number five, or four by her count.

"Call me Cooper," he said, flashing a grin that probably melted Rosie's thick mascara. "And no, the recipe is a secret that only a few people in the company are privy to. You can't be too careful nowadays."

Jordan coughed to cover her laugh as Rosie flashed him an adoring smile that Jordan recognized as the one she used whenever there was a good-looking man on her radar. Despite the fact Cooper was twenty years her junior, Rosie looked ready to show him exactly how much she appreciated the free meal.

Cooper led them farther down the hall, stopping in front of a double stainless steel door. "This is the refrigerator. It's frickin' freezing in there, so we won't stay long. Then I have a surprise for you."

Jordan shivered as they walked down one aisle and up another. Rows and rows of boxes filled the shelves, all marked with the logo of North Texas Beef Distributors, Carole Anne's company.

No surprise there.

"Come on." Cooper beckoned from the door. "I had my cooks whip up their signature banana pudding for you. It's all set up in the break room around the corner."

He led them to the tables already set with bowls of the delicious pudding. No one mentioned they'd already pigged out on desserts back at the Greenville Avenue restaurant, all compliments of him.

"There are soft drinks and bottled water in the refrigerator, and coffee and hot chocolate over there." He directed them to the corner where a huge beverage center lined the wall, the kind Jordan had seen at the car dealership when she took her car in for maintenance.

She headed that way while the others sat around the table. Even though she had on a sweater, she was still a little cold from the meat locker, and she hoped a cup of steaming hot chocolate might warm her back up.

As she reached for a cup, Cooper touched her shoulder, making her jump.

"Jordan, can you come with me for a sec?" he asked. "There's something I want you to see. I promise it will only take a minute."

She hesitated momentarily, wondering what he had to show her that the others couldn't see. "Sure, Cooper." She decided if he wanted to show off a little more, a little indulgence was a small price to pay, considering how he had just fed her friends. She followed him toward the door. "I'll be back in a flash," she said to Ray, who glanced up as they passed.

Cooper led her back down the hallway toward the meat locker.

"Please tell me what you have to show me isn't in there." She pointed to the big refrigerator they'd just left. "I'm just now feeling my fingers again." She tried to sound playful, but the truth was, she was getting a little nervous and wished she had insisted the gang come with her.

Cooper stopped abruptly in front of an unmarked door. "It will only be cold for a minute." He punched a code into the keypad, and the door clicked open. "This is where we store the really good cuts of beef that we use for special occasions. No one comes in here but Blake and me, so it's the perfect place to keep my office."

Jordan wrapped her arms across her chest and stepped around him into the room. Following him down the aisle, she glanced at the boxes lining the shelves, noticing they weren't labeled with the same North Texas Beef Distributors logo as the cartons in the big refrigerator. She was still trying to process why that might be when Cooper opened a door at the back wall. The warm air hit her before she even walked through it.

"Much better." Glancing around, she couldn't help but think this hardly looked like the office of the man who ran a million-dollar barbecue empire.

Except for one picture that hung behind the massive filing cabinets, the walls were bare. A computer screen and stacks of manila folders covered the medium-size oak desk.

She walked toward the cabinets to view the lone photo. "Who's that with you and Blake?" She pointed toward the picture taken in front of Buddy's Barbecue Pit.

"Buddy Wilson, the owner."

Jordan eyed him suspiciously. "Isn't he your biggest competitor around the metroplex?"

"Not anymore. This year we kicked his butt in overall sales, and that doesn't even take into consideration all the charity events we did." Cooper snorted. "He thought we were just a couple of Yankee hicks without a clue when we mentioned we were thinking about opening a restaurant."

"You and Blake are Yankees?" Jordan wasn't as surprised as she tried to pretend, since she'd picked up on that fake southern drawl the minute Blake had opened his mouth.

"Yep." Cooper leaned back against the desk. "Blake and I were executives at CLM for a lot of years."

"CLM?"

"Computerized Logistics Management. We were based in Washington, and Blake was my boss."

"So how did two computer geeks from DC end up in Texas running a successful barbecue franchise?"

"Blake only does the programming for me. He owns a very successful computer software franchise."

"Why did you leave DC?"

Cooper grabbed her hand and pulled her to him. "Shit happens—and then you move on. When the military budget was sliced in half, we lost a lot of accounts." He tightened his grip on her wrist. "Best thing that ever happened to us."

"What are you doing, Cooper?" Jordan tried to twist away but couldn't.

He leaned in until his head was so close she could smell the Listerine on his breath. He must've gargled right before they'd arrived.

"I never really got a chance to tell you how sorry I was about Rusty." He leaned closer and closed his eyes.

"Cooper!" she yelled. "What the hell do you think you're doing? You're engaged and I'm seeing someone."

He opened his eyes, never letting up on his grip. "I think you and I could have some fun together, that's all. I dig you and think you feel the same. Carole Ann doesn't have to know. Hell, I'm sure she has"—he waved one hand in the air—"little indiscretions of her own."

In that second when he held her with only one hand, Jordan managed to catch him off guard and wiggle out of his grasp.

"Cooper, I apologize if I gave you the wrong impression." She stepped backward. "Right now, I'm in a committed relationship." She crossed her fingers behind her back before continuing. "But you're right. I do like you, and if my status with the other guy ever changes, you'll be the first one I call."

She wondered if this was what he'd wanted to talk to her about and chided herself for not seeing it coming, especially when he'd maneuvered her away from her friends.

He eyed her suspiciously before a slight grin turned up the corners of his lips. "I could be your rich benefactor—open a lot of doors for you. Ever think of that?"

She pursed her lips, trying not to gag. "It's tempting, but right now we need to get back before the others wonder what we're up to."

"How about one little kiss to make you forget that other guy?"

She took a deep breath hoping he wouldn't realize she was lying or that standing this close to him disgusted her. The niggling thought that even if the gang came looking for her they'd never find Cooper's office forced her to rethink her strategy. She had to get out of there.

Trying a different tactic, she batted her eyelashes as she'd seen Rosie do earlier and tried to look seductive. "Oh, no, big boy, I want you to think about how good that first kiss will be."

She licked her lips, nearly cracking up at his reaction. She must be better at this than she thought. "Come on, sugar, you know anything this good is worth waiting on."

The victory smile spread across his face faster than a water stain on a paper towel. "I'll be waiting," he said, stepping in front of her to open the door, making sure to brush against her chest on the way.

As she walked past him, he patted her behind. When she turned to confront him, he held up his hands. "Just a little taste of what's to come."

"Of course," she said before nearly sprinting down the aisle past the rows of boxed meat.

Almost to the door, her arm caught on one of the boxes sticking out, and she nearly got clobbered when it fell to the floor.

Cooper rushed over and grabbed it. "That would've hurt."

She was glad he needed both hands to put the box back on the shelf because she was sure he would've used the opportunity to cop another feel.

When he lifted the box up, Jordan noticed the handwritten word on the top. "This is Wagyu?"

Cooper stopped midway and turned, his eyes questioning. "How do you know about Wagyu?"

She decided the faster she got out of the room and away from him, the better, and a conversation about what she had learned from Danny might mean more time alone with Casanova.

"Only from the business card Brenda Sue Taylor gave me."

He slid the box into the slot and gave it another push toward the back. "How do you know Brenda Sue?"

"I met her at Rusty's memorial service when I went to give his mother my condolences." She shivered. "Come on, Cooper, I'm freezing."

He opened the door slightly, then turned to her and undressed her with his eyes. "I can warm you up in a hurry."

"I'll bet you can, but now's not the time." She pushed into him so the door opened, allowing her just enough room to squeeze under his arm and take off for the break room.

"Where were you?" Danny asked, glancing up at her with a sheepish grin. "You're too late, Jordan. I ate your pudding."

Ignoring her brother, she tapped Ray's shoulder. "Let's go. I have a lot of things to do tomorrow, and I want to get an early start."

"Hey! I thought you said we were sleeping in tomorrow?" Danny blurted.

Jordan shot him a look that screamed, Don't argue or you'll be sleeping on the sidewalk.

"Okay, then," Ray said, obviously picking up on what she wasn't saying. He turned to Cooper. "My friends and I want to thank you for your hospitality. Anytime we can repay the favor, let us know. Rosie here cooks a mean beef—ouch!" He flinched, then turned to Jordan and shrugged.

"I just may take you up on that," Cooper said, focusing on Jordan. "I'd like to get to know you all a lot better."

Jordan rolled her eyes, then turned back and pasted a phony half smile on her face. "Take me home, Ray. I'm tired."

Somehow they managed to make it out the door without Cooper getting close enough to say anything else to Jordan. Climbing into the backseat of the Suburban, she wondered what it was about her that sent totally different vibes than she intended. Why had Cooper acted like she was some love-starved girl desperate enough to fool around with him?

Maybe he'd gotten the desperate part right, but he'd sure missed the mark about her agreeing to play hanky-panky with someone she hardly knew. Even if she were that kind of girl, she hadn't met anyone yet who even tempted her to go down that road.

Leaning back into the Suburban's plush seat, she closed her eyes. Okay, that was a lie, she admitted to herself, thinking about Rusty Morales's smoky black eyes. As his face popped into her head, she opened her mouth to tell Danny about seeing the Wagyu in Cooper's secret meat locker, then decided to wait until they were home alone. She had no idea what it meant or if it was even important.

"So, Jordan, why were you in such a hellfire hurry to get out of there?" Victor asked. "I saw another bowl of pudding in the refrigerator."

"Yeah, she kicked my ankle so hard, I'll probably need ice tonight," Ray added.

"Oh, honey," Lola said, patting his shoulder. "What you need is heat, not ice." She leaned over and kissed his cheek.

"Geez, you two are going to steam up the windows," Michael said, turning around to face Jordan. "Why the mad dash to get out of there?"

Jordan blew out a loud breath. "Cooper made a pass at me," she said, deciding not to tell them the whole story

No way she wanted to think about that again. Besides, Danny would tease her and say she misread the guy. He still saw her as his little sister with braces and a flat chest and couldn't imagine anyone else viewing her any differently.

"Thought you said he was engaged?" Lola said.

"He is. I met his fiancée at the Cattlemen's Ball that night with Rusty and—"

"Speaking of Rusty," Danny said, slapping his thigh. "I knew there was something I wanted to tell you earlier. They found out what killed him."

"What?" Jordan asked, hoping it wasn't something she should've picked up on.

"Poison."

CHAPTER 10

"Poison?" Jordan shrieked before lowering her voice an octave. "How could he have been poisoned? I sat right next to him the whole night." She gripped her throat. "I may have been poisoned, too, since I ate exactly the same thing he did."

"You and the other fifteen hundred people at the party," Danny interjected. "Don't be so dramatic, sis. If I were you, I'd be more worried about the cops looking at you as a suspect."

Jordan twisted 180 degrees in the seat, straining the shoulder belt until it dug painfully into her skin. "You're kidding, right?"

A slow grin crossed Danny's face—the same kind of grin she recognized from the past when he knew something and wouldn't tell her. She half expected to hear, "It will cost you," as she had so many times back in Amarillo.

"The cops are taking a look at everyone who was at the table with Rusty."

Jordan let out a deep breath, trying to remember who all was there that night. Lucas and Bella, Carole Anne and Cooper, Blake and his teensy-tiny date, and she and Rusty.

She shook her head. "Everyone at the table was a friend of Rusty's."

"Apparently not everyone," Danny said, pointing at Jordan. "You said you'd only met him that night. Maybe *everyone* else did, too."

"That's absurd. You were with me at the memorial service, Danny. You heard Farley say Rusty and Lucas were really tight when he drove us from our car to Santana's house that day. Blake and Cooper also had some kind of relationship with him. I could tell. And I got the impression Carole Anne and Rusty had been an item at one time."

"Is Carole Anne the blonde I met at Santana's with a figure that could stop a train and boobs that . . ." He paused and turned to Sandy. "Sorry."

"That was her," Jordan said. "Remember how upset her dad was? Said Rusty was like a son to him."

Danny leaned forward. "Yeah, I remember, but didn't he say Carole Anne screwed up the relationship?"

"Holy crap! What kind of father says that to his daughter?" Rosie asked.

"A bad one," Jordan said before turning back to Danny. "It was obvious she still had feelings for Rusty." She slapped her forehead.

"What?"

"While Cooper was trying to talk me into a 'you squeeze mine and I'll squeeze yours' thing, he implied that Carole Anne played around, too."

"Sounds to me like she's the perfect candidate for

dropping a little arsenic into Rusty's water glass," Ray commented from the front seat. "A scorned lover can be deadly."

"Oh, baby, that sounds like it came right out of a romance novel," Lola said, snuggling closer to him.

"My kind of romance novel," Victor said, forming a gun with his finger and thumb. "Pow! Love 'em, then kill 'em. That's kinda like a praying mantis, right?"

"Girlie praying mantises don't just kill their mate after sex. They eat the dude's head off," Rosie said. "I could rattle off the names of a few men who should be counting their lucky stars that I'm not an insect."

Deep in her own thoughts, Jordan ignored the joking that followed. "Do they know what kind of poison killed Rusty?"

The laughter stopped abruptly as everyone turned to the only person there who could answer that question.

"I shouldn't be telling you this, but it will be in the paper in a couple of days, anyway. Initially, the autopsy suggested asphyxia, as if he'd been strangled—which, obviously, he couldn't have been. After rechecking the stomach contents, they didn't find any evidence of anything that could have killed him."

"So why do they think he was poisoned?" Jordan asked impatiently.

"From your description of his symptoms moments before he died and the fact that the autopsy showed no definitive cause of death, the ME concluded that's the only thing it could be. They're bringing in a forensic toxicologist from Dallas next week. He's supposed to be an expert on poisons."

"And I'm really a suspect?" Jordan realized for the first time that she'd been the closest one to Rusty all night and had a better opportunity than anyone else to throw a little poison on his sliced beef.

She covered her mouth in time to stop the audible gasp as she remembered that wasn't entirely true. There was someone else sitting on the other side of Rusty. Her mind raced back to less than an hour ago when she'd been locked in a hidden back office with that someone.

She shivered as the realization hit. There was a distinct possibility that very same *someone* just might have had a jealous streak.

Watching the gate slide open at the entrance to Santana Circle Ranch, Jordan glanced down at the clock on her dashboard. Twelve thirty. Bella had called earlier that morning to tell her how excited she and Lucas were that Jordan had agreed to do a piece on Santana Circle.

Yeah. She'd agreed all right—more like she'd had her arm twisted.

Okay, so she sold her soul for fifty-yard-line Cowboys tickets, and now she was paying the devil with an afternoon she wasn't looking forward to. She figured they'd eat around two, and she could be on her way home by three thirty. In essence, she'd be giving up only three hours of her Sunday afternoon in exchange for getting four hours off on a busy Friday. When she looked at it that way, it didn't seem so bad.

Plus, she would be collecting recipes that would take care of the next few weeks' entries for the Kitchen Kupboard. She hoped her boss had explained to Lucas that she wasn't a big fan of steaks, thanks to all those years of watching her dad and four brothers eating theirs bloody.

Pulling into the circular driveway, she waved at Bella by

the front door. Telling herself she could make it through the next few hours, she got out of the car and walked up the steps.

"Hey you, I'm so glad you've agreed to do this. I think I'm more excited about seeing my recipes in the newspaper than knowing they'll boost beef sales in the county." Bella hugged her, then grabbed her hand and headed for the den.

Jordan stopped at the doorway, feeling as though she were about to step into a jungle instead of a living room. Like the entertainment room, the den was teeming with big game trophies; every wild animal known to man seemed to be glaring at her from all four walls of the massive room.

"Pretty impressive?"

The voice drew her attention from the mounted animals, and she turned to face Lucas Santana. "Obviously, you're a big hunter."

"Used to be," he said. "Since I messed up my knee, the only hunting I'm able to do now is sitting in here looking at these guys and trying to remember what it felt like." He pointed to the walls. "Bagged every one of these myself, most of them right here on my own land. Not that polar bear over there, of course." He pointed to the center of the room, where a beautiful white rug covered the floor in front of the fireplace. "That one came from Alaska. Got it from a buddy of mine."

"To each his own," Jordan said. "I prefer to see these beautiful creatures running wild in their natural habitat, not on a wall."

"Lucas didn't tell me you were an animal rights activist."

For the first time Jordan noticed the man sitting in one of the two chairs by a fire burning so briskly she felt the heat across the room.

He eased out of the chair and walked over to where she stood. "Bobby Carvella. I've heard a lot about you," he said, offering his hand.

"Bobby was Rusty's right-hand man," Lucas said. "Now he's mine. I thought it would be a good idea for you to meet the people responsible for bringing Santana beef to the public since you'll be writing about it." His eyes turned mischievous. "And did I mention he's single?"

Smiling, she reached for Bobby's hand, thinking everyone and their mother must be in on the plot to hook her up.

"Nice to meet you, Bobby."

Making sure she sat as far away from Lucas as possible, Jordan settled next to Bella on the couch. She looked up just as a petite Hispanic woman entered the room with a tray of drinks. "Looks yummy. Thanks."

"I did a little research and found out you liked margaritas," Bella said, breaking into a grin. "Thought I'd introduce you to a wonderful drink Rusty's mother, Maria, used to make for us whenever we had company. Margarita Swirls. The homemade sangria is what makes them so good. That's also Maria's recipe." She reached up and took a glass from the tray. "Thank you, Lily."

At the mention of Rusty's mother, Jordan straightened in the chair. "How long did Maria work here?"

"Nearly forty years," Lucas said, unable to hide the sadness in his voice. "She was like family to me. Hell, except for the year or so when she went back to Mexico, I saw her everyday."

"And what about Diego? Did he work here, too?" Jordan remembered what Farley Williams had told her about Lucas and Diego having a falling out.

Lucas narrowed his eyes. "At one time. Why do you ask?"

"No reason," she lied. "I thought I heard someone mention that at Rusty's memorial."

The old man sighed. "One day Diego strolled into my office, threw his keys to the barn on the table, and told me literally to go screw myself. I never could figure out what made him so angry that he would leave a well-paying job for one that paid only a third as much as a night watchman—"

"So how do you like the drink, Jordan?" Bella interrupted, clearly bored with the conversation.

Jordan took a sip and licked her lips. Bella was right. From now on, Margarita Swirls would be her drink of choice. She wondered if her favorite karaoke bar in Connor knew how to make them. "These are delicious. I'll have to tell Maria how much I enjoyed them."

"You talk to Maria?" Bella asked, wrinkling her forehead.

Jordan debated whether to share her suspicions about Maria and her husband with these people, then decided it was best to keep that to herself. She had no proof Diego Morales was hurting his wife—or worse, trying to kill her, and she'd sound foolish if she mentioned it. It was probably crazy even thinking that, especially after Brenda Sue had been so emphatic about how devoted Diego was to his wife.

"Jordan, I asked if you talk with Maria often," Bella repeated.

"Not really. I just feel so sorry for her, losing her son and all. I thought I would visit her and take some flowers."

"Good idea," Lucas said. "She was a wonderful mother to that boy from the day she brought him back from Guadalajara."

"Rusty was born in Mexico?"

"Yeah," Lucas said, nodding. "Maria and Diego were down there taking care of her sister. Gia—that was her sister's name—had some kind of terminal illness. Since their parents had been killed in a car crash several years before that, Maria was the only relative Gia had. Even when Maria got pregnant, she had no choice but to stay and take care of her sister." He paused to reach for the Scotch and water Lily was holding out to him.

"Anyway, after Gia died, Maria and Diego came back to Texas with the baby, and she worked here all those years until she had her hip surgery. I can still see Rusty running around with his Matchbox cars. He loved those stupid things."

"Enough talk about Maria," Bella interrupted. "Lily has lunch ready. She fixed my famous Beef Stroganoff recipe, and I can't wait for you to taste it, Jordan."

Jordan smiled, noticing the way Bella seemed to be the one in charge, as well as the gracious hostess. Clearly, her role at Santana Circle went way beyond personal assistant. And she left no doubt her relationship with Lucas was more intimate than simply keeping track of his records.

They all stood and followed Bella to the dining room where an elegant Southwest table with inlaid marble was set with yellow and brown stoneware. In the center a beautiful flower arrangement of large yellow daisies and orange-tipped roses complemented the décor.

"Aren't they lovely?" Bella said when she caught Jordan staring at them. "I get them fresh every week from a woman who has her own greenhouse."

"Are you talking about Karen Whitley?" Jordan asked, recognizing the large daisies.

Bella turned sharply. "You obviously get around, Jordan. First, I find out that you know Maria, and now you tell me you've seen Karen's flowers. I thought they were my own special secret."

Jordan laughed. "Flowers as pretty as Karen's can't stay a secret for very long. She sent me home with a huge bouquet a few days ago when I had lunch with Brenda Sue Taylor. They lasted longer than any flowers I've ever had."

"I'm not even going to ask how you know Brenda Sue, but I will tell you that the beef you're about to eat came from her ranch," Lucas chimed in.

"It's Wagyu?"

"Now you're scaring me," he said, narrowing his eyes and studying her. "For a girl who doesn't like beef, you sure know a lot about the stuff."

"My brother's told me more than I'll ever want to know about the beef business. I can't wait to tell him I've tasted Wagyu."

"Speaking of your brother, has he had any luck finding the thieves yet?" Bella asked.

"Not yet, but he has a few new leads."

"Anything you can tell us about?" Lucas asked.

Jordan shook her head. "I'm the last person he'd share that kind of information with."

Bella laughed. "I understand completely. I have a brother, too. I'll send you home with the leftovers, and maybe that will motivate him to get aggressive with the investigation. Marcus Taylor told me he's losing a few of his herd every month."

"Brenda Sue mentioned it. That's awful," Jordan said.

Smiling up at Bobby when he pulled out her chair, she got her first up-close look at the man who had taken over

Rusty's job at the ranch. Although he wasn't as good-looking as Rusty, "tall," "dark," and "rugged" were three words that came to mind when she stole another look.

Bobby seemed a touch uncomfortable in this social setting, fidgeting with his napkin and glaring at the silverware as if debating which fork to use first. Jordan guessed a burger and a long cold one in the bunkhouse with his buddies was more his speed than lunch at the main house with the boss.

Welcome to the club, she thought, feeling a kind of camaraderie with him.

Lily began serving, starting with something she called Layered Salad. Had it been the only dish offered, Jordan would have been quite satisfied. She made a mental note to ask Bella for that recipe, too. Next came the Beef Stroganoff that Bella had bragged about.

After her second helping, Jordan finally put down her fork. "I can't eat another bite, Bella. My compliments to your cook. This is the first time I've ever eaten stroganoff, and I'm afraid I made a pig of myself."

"I'm guessing it's the first time you've ever eaten it made with Wagyu steak. It's extravagant, I know, but we wanted you to taste the good stuff as well as the less expensive cuts of beef, so you could talk about using both to your readers," Bella explained.

"It surprises me how you maintain that great figure eating the way you do." Lucas tilted his head and studied Jordan with a sleazy grin on his face.

The afternoon had gone so well, Jordan had almost forgotten how easily Santana could make her long for a hot shower. That last remark reminded her again why she was grateful to be sitting between Bella and Bobby Carvella.

"Hope you saved room for sweets," Bella said, a touch

of annoyance in her voice. "Because Lily fixed a dessert to die for."

"I'll try a small helping," Jordan said, wondering why a woman like Bella allowed Lucas to get away with his flirtatious behavior. It had to embarrass her.

A small bowl turned into a bigger second one, and by the time she was in her car driving back into town, her stomach was about to burst, and she wished she'd worn bigger jeans. The day had turned out to be surprisingly pleasant, despite Lucas's overt flirting, especially after a few drinks. She was thankful he'd managed to keep his wandering hands to himself.

Much to her surprise, the stroganoff made with the Wagyu beef was all it was cracked up to be, and she couldn't wait to tell Danny about it. As promised, Bella had packed up what little was left and sent it home with her.

Earlier, when Bella asked about Danny's investigation, Jordan hadn't shared the fact that Rusty had been poisoned. She wondered if they'd heard about the autopsy report or the plan to bring in a toxicology expert. If they had, they didn't show it.

She speculated on how they would react when they did find out. Would their attitude toward her change if they suspected she might have poisoned him? And what if she told them there was a good possibility their friend Cooper could have had something to do with Rusty's death?

She'd been driving herself crazy thinking about this ever since her visit to Cooper's warehouse the other night. If what Danny told her about Rusty was true, that he was involved somehow with cattle rustling, there might be a whole lot of reasons for a person wanting to see him dead. Maybe a ranch owner who was fed up with losing thousands of dollars in stolen livestock decided to take justice into his own hands. Or maybe someone who'd conspired with Rusty to steal the cattle decided it would be beneficial if he was out of the picture.

Someone like Bobby Carvella, who was now top dog on Santana's ranch.

CHAPTER 11

As expected, the response to Bella's recipes was phenomenal, and once again, Jordan had been summoned to Egan's office. This time he wanted to gloat and remind her how right he'd been about her Sunday dinners with Lucas and Bella being beneficial to her column. If he hadn't been so comical, hitching his bushy eyebrows up and down after making her admit it, she would have been annoyed.

But she had to agree it hadn't been too bad. Watching Danny's expression when she'd casually mentioned he was eating stroganoff made with Wagyu was also a plus. He'd nearly choked when she'd told him, since it was probably the only time he'd ever get to try the expensive beef.

Given the beef's hundred-dollars-a-pound market value, it was definitely her last time, too. Bella had already announced that next Sunday's dinner would be something with a cheaper cut of beef, sending a message to the average

Ranchero family that you didn't have to pay a lot of money for good dinners.

Jordan looked up as Sandy Johnson approached her desk and waved. The plan was for Lola to go with them to Sandy's grandfather's house tonight, do a quick séance, and be home before eleven, which worked for Jordan. Although she didn't completely buy into the whole ghost thing, she had no desire to be in that house after midnight.

"I'm kind of nervous about tonight."

"Me too, but Lola's an amazing medium." She tapped her fingertips on the desk, relieved Sandy didn't know her well enough to realize this was something she did when she lied.

She had no idea if Lola was able to converse with ghosts or not, but she herself was a skeptic of all things psychic. Granted, some of the proclaimed spirit whisperers were gifted with incredible skills of observation, but talking to dead people?

No way!

She was reminded of one of her favorite TV shows, in which the main character had used these same abilities to scam people before becoming a police consultant to help solve crimes. Just when you thought he might really be psychic, he'd explain how he'd discovered the truth, much like a magician who reveals the "tricks" of his magic. Most of the clues came from his knowledge of body language.

When Jordan had first approached Lola for help with this, the older woman had been hesitant, saying she'd never claimed to be a true psychic. Her business was reading tarot cards and the occasional crystal ball, if the price was right. Lola had agreed to give it a shot only after Jordan reminded her that Sandy was about to lose her grandfather's house.

Jordan confirmed plans to pick up Sandy at seven. It would already be dusk, the perfect time for confronting ghosts. Though she hated that Lola would have to deceive Sandy to make her believe she was really talking to ghosts, the end result was worth a white lie—along with a little smoke and mirrors.

On the way home, she stopped at Burger Hut to pick up dinner for her and her brother. Thursday was her night to cook, and Burger Hut had a buy-one-get-one-half-off sale. Danny was sitting at the kitchen table hunched over a slew of papers when she opened the door.

Glancing up, he wrinkled his nose. "Burgers again?"

"Unless you can whip up a couple of Chicken Cordon Bleus," she retorted, a little annoyed.

Like he ever mixed up the menu. Since he was almost as broke as she was—thanks to the hefty monthly payment on his new pickup—his offering was usually a five-dollar pizza from the Pizza Palace when it was his turn to cook.

"Smart-ass! You don't even know what that chicken-corded-whatever is."

"For your information, I do know. I did an Internet search on fancy chicken dishes a few weeks ago for a recipe to use in my column."

"That doesn't count." He gathered up the papers and sauntered over to the fridge. "Diet Pepsi or beer?"

"Diet Pepsi, please. You might want to take it easy on the alcohol yourself, bro." Jordan pointed to the three empty bottles on the counter.

"Who died and made you the beer police?"

She ignored him and sat down. Opening the bag, she

pulled out a burger and half-empty bag of fries, wondering if anyone ever made it home with a full bag.

Danny sat down opposite her and shoved the Diet Pepsi her way. He made a point to set his beer bottle down on the table hard enough to get her attention, while his narrowed eyes dared her to make a comment.

Knowing he was trying to provoke her, something he always did when he drank, she snickered to herself. "So what were all those papers?" she asked, instead of taking the bait.

"Rusty's autopsy report and details on the latest theft out at the Lazy C Ranch in Collin County."

"How many did they get this time?"

"Eight. We have no clue if they stole them all at once or just a few at a time," he said, shaking his head. "If I don't make some progress with this soon, I might have to start updating my résumé."

"Is it that bad?" she asked between bites. "I told Santana you had some new leads."

"You lied," he answered, draining the beer bottle and sprinting to the fridge for another. "For the life of me, I can't figure out how they can make something as big as a cow disappear without a trace. We're checking every cattle auction held in the state of Texas, as well as the neighboring states, on a daily basis. They've got to be sending them across the border, but we haven't seen any stolen livestock showing up at the checkpoints."

"Is it possible the owners are lying about the stolen cattle? If they have insurance on their herds, which I'm sure they do, wouldn't it be to their advantage to collect the insurance money while the beef market is so depressed? Maybe get their money back on a dead or sick animal? I'm guessing no one goes out to the ranches to count cows."

She got up, gathered her dinner wrappings, and took them to the trash can.

"That might make for a great *Law and Order* episode, Jordan, but it doesn't hold water in this case. I've interviewed those ranchers about the thefts, and I can tell you, I wouldn't want to be anywhere in the county when they find the culprits." He grinned. "There are some very pissed-off cowboys out there."

"I'm just saying it's something to think about." She headed to the bedroom just as the front door opened and Victor barged in.

"I'm glad my doorbell's working," she deadpanned. "What's up?"

Victor made a beeline to the refrigerator and pulled out a beer. Popping the cap, he sat down at the table across from Danny. "The evening DJ called in sick down at the radio station, so Michael's working an extra shift. I came by to see if either of you wanted to play a round of miniature golf over at the new place in Connor."

"Can't," Jordan said.

"Why not? It's Thursday, and we all know you have no social life," Danny said.

"Oh, like you do?" she fired back. "Actually, I'm going out to Lake Texoma with Lola and Sandy."

"Sandy Johnson?" Danny asked, suddenly very interested. Since the night Sandy had gone with them to Beef Daddy's, Danny had been asking all sorts of questions about her.

"That's great," he said when Jordan nodded. "Since Vic and I don't have anything else planned, we'll go with you."

"No way. This isn't a social gathering. We're on a mission, and we don't need two guys tagging along, especially when they've been drinking."

"I only had one beer," Victor protested, holding up the bottle. "I'm watching my calories since Michael called me his butterball." He reached down and grabbed one of Danny's fries.

"The answer is still no," Jordan insisted. "Sandy is already so nervous she's about to come unglued. Besides, if you think I'm making it easy for you to hook up with my new friend, you're badly mistaken, Danny. She's so not your type."

"Who said I was interested?" Danny moved closer to her. "So what's the secret mission?"

"I never said it was secret." Jordan threw her hands in the air. "Criminy! You must be taking drama-queen lessons from Victor." She turned to her neighbor. "No offense."

"None taken. I'm proud of the fact that I'm—what's the word—demonstrative?" He waved his hand in an air Z. "Now tell us what the secret mission is."

Jordan couldn't help it and laughed. "We're trying to convince Sandy her grandfather's house isn't haunted. That way she can move out there and keep the IRS from seizing it to pay off the back taxes."

"Yeah, she told me about her money problems the other night," Victor said. "But she never mentioned ghosts were the reason she didn't live out there. I just assumed it was because of her memories of her grandfather."

"You gotta let us go with you, sis. I'm great at chasing ghosts away."

Jordan huffed. "Don't you have 'ghosts' mixed up with 'girls,' Danny boy? I seem to recall your track record for lasting relationships with the fairer sex would verify this." She took two steps toward the bathroom before turning around. "You two go play miniature golf. This is a me, Sandy, and Lola thing. Sorry." She made it to the bathroom and slammed the door behind her, shutting off any further discussion.

When she finished her shower, she found herself all alone in the apartment and was relieved Victor and her brother were no longer there to bug her about going along. She had to smile, recalling how quickly Victor and Danny had become friends that first night. It had taken longer for Danny to feel comfortable with the others. He'd been so eager to prove he was qualified to be the lone agent assigned to Ranchero, he'd acted reserved around the older residents of Empire Apartments. It was only after they'd teased him about loosening up that he'd let down his guard around them. Victor and Rosie were his clear favorites since they were as mischievous as he was.

After throwing on a little makeup and running a comb through her hair, she locked the door behind her, hoping Danny had remembered to take his key with him.

Then she knocked on Lola's door and waited.

Lola emerged wearing one of her long, flowing caftans, a scarf around her head, and hoop earrings the size of large plums. "Too much?" she asked with a grin.

"Not if you're aiming for the Carmen Miranda look," Jordan teased. She hooked her arm through Lola's. "Come on. Let's go. Sandy will be impressed, I'm sure."

"Let's hope I can convince her I'm really talking to ghosts. You do remember what I told you to do, right?"

"Absolutely. I will be the best ghost buster you know."

Lola squeezed her hand. "Make that the best ghost buster's assistant. I'm going for an Academy Award tonight."

After they picked up Sandy, the three women headed out of Ranchero just as the sun hit the horizon and dropped out of sight. Forty minutes later, they turned off the gravel road onto the circular driveway of a quaint little cottage with the largest magnolia tree Jordan had ever seen dominating the front yard.

"Wow! This is really nice." Jordan hopped out of the car and followed Sandy up the porch steps with Lola right behind her.

"Yeah, Gramps spent a lot of money fixing it up," Sandy said, unable to hide the sadness in her voice. "Come on. Let's get this over with."

Although she tried to act indifferent, Sandy looked terrified. Jordan prayed Lola could ease her fears. It would be a shame to hand this wonderful house over to the government when it meant so much to her new friend.

Walking into the small house, Jordan did a slow circle to take everything in. Decorated in rich browns and greens, the living room seemed eerily quiet, sending spurts of anxiety through her body. Scolding herself for being silly, she focused on the heavy green linen drapes that covered the windows on both sides of a large rock fireplace and the exquisite Oriental rug in front of it.

"Gramps brought that home from overseas when he was in the Marines," Sandy explained, apparently noticing Jordan's interest in the rug.

"It's impressive." She turned to Sandy. "I can see why you want to live here. It's so homey."

Sandy snorted. "It has two bedrooms, Jordan. Care to join me out here with my invisible houseguests?"

"There won't be any houseguests after tonight," Lola said, winking at Jordan out of Sandy's view. "Where shall we set up?"

"Gramps has a card table and chairs in the garage for when his buddies came to play poker. Can we use that?"

"We'll set it up on that rug over there." Lola bobbed her head toward the fireplace, then shivered. "It's cold in here."

"I'll turn up the heat," Sandy replied. "I don't want to start a fire since we won't be here that long." She adjusted the thermostat on the far wall. "First, I want to show you the lake out back, and then I'll make us one of Gramps's favorite drinks for a cold night."

As the furnace kicked in, the curtains on both sides of the fireplace fluttered, and all three of them jumped.

"Thank heavens I'm putting liquor in the drinks," Sandy said with a forced laugh. "I think we can all use it."

Jordan glanced at Lola, who was surveying the room as if deciding in which corner the ghosts were hiding. She hoped she wouldn't regret coming up with this ridiculous idea.

Jordan blew out a breath, trying to hide her uneasiness from Sandy. "Where's the liquor cabinet?"

CHAPTER 12

Jordan inhaled, filling her lungs with the cool country air as she stared at the view from Sandy's porch. With the moon shimmering down over Lake Texoma, the calm water resembled a slab of black marble covered in sparkles.

"What a view," she said, locking arms with her friend.

"There's Lucy." Sandy pointed to a big white duck on the water near the dock. "She was Gramps's favorite."

Jordan glanced in the direction Sandy had indicated, watching the lone duck glide across the water. She wondered if ducks grieved, positive Lucy had to be missing the old man who'd fed her every day.

"It always seems to be colder near the water," Sandy said, pulling away from Jordan and wrapping both arms around her chest. "Come on. Let's go make those Almond Balls."

"Almond Balls?" Jordan and Lola asked in unison.

Sandy laughed. "That's the drink I promised to make

you before we get started. I hope Gramps still has some Baileys around."

"Mmm. I love Baileys." Jordan followed Sandy and Lola inside.

As Sandy made the hot chocolate drink, Lola inched closer to Jordan. "Are you ready?"

Jordan nodded. "And you're still thinking we can get this done and be out of here in an hour, right? This house gives me the creeps."

"Don't let Sandy hear you say that. She'd never move out here. And yes, an hour tops, if all goes well."

Jordan swung around to face her. "What do you mean 'if all goes well'? I thought you said this would be a piece of cake. What could go wrong?"

"Here you go," Sandy interrupted. "Taste this, then try to convince me you've had anything as good on a cold October night."

Jordan sipped the hot drink, licking the whipped cream from her lips. "A few more of these, and we won't give a flying flip about the ghosts," she said, more to convince herself than Sandy.

They finished their drinks and set the empty cups in the sink before following Sandy out to the garage where they found the card table and three chairs. Carrying them into the living room, they set up in the center of the Oriental rug near the fireplace.

Just then, the front door flew open and all three of them jumped.

Sandy was the first to recover. "I guess I didn't shut it tight enough. The wind sure is howling out there."

"What a great way to get a séance going," Lola said. "It's the spirits' way of telling us they're around. We'll need a light-colored covering for the table."

Sandy hurried to a closet in the back hallway and returned with a pale yellow sheet. "Will this work?"

"Perfect." Lola grabbed the sheet and spread it over the table. Then she pulled a bag of white candles and a book of matches from her purse. "To summon the spirits," she explained. "The flame will burn through the veil separating the mortal world from the spirit world and will open the portals for the spirits to join us."

Jordan took a deep breath before sitting down when Lola pointed to the chair. She refused to let her imagination run wild but was aware of the fine hairs on her arms now standing at attention. The jury was still out on whether she wanted those portals opened.

"I almost forgot. Before we get started, we all need to take off our jewelry."

"Why our jewelry?" Jordan asked, getting more nervous by the second.

"Because metal repels the spirits," Lola said. "Turn your cell phones off, too." She looked up at the overhead light. "Sandy, can we turn this light off and just use the small lamp on the end table?"

Sandy stood and did as Lola instructed while Jordan reached for her purse and turned off her cell phone. Lola disappeared into the kitchen, returning a moment later with a small bowl of water.

"Water attracts the spirits and cleanses the air. Let's sit in a circle to create an unbroken ring of protection." They scooted their chairs in a circle as best they could around a square table, and then Lola continued. "Place your palms down on the table, and don't pick them up for any reason. You'll break the connection."

A few seconds later Lola began humming in a soft monotone, reminding Jordan of being dragged to her first and only Zen class by her college roommate. She hadn't liked it then, and with the candles burning in the dimly lit room, she liked it even less now.

"We sense your presence in this room, and we ask you to make yourself known."

Jordan stared at the orange flame of the candle closest to the bowl of water in the center. Her job was to exhale every time Lola asked a question and make the flames flicker without Sandy catching on.

She blew slightly and the flame moved.

This might be fun, she thought, before Lola started again.

"Make your presence known to us, oh mighty spirit, so that we can help with whatever is bothering you."

Again Jordan blew the candle.

"I call you into the room. Please give us some kind of sign when you have arrived, whether it's by tapping on our table or moving the flame."

Jordan waited, but still there was nothing. When Lola coughed, she glanced up to see her motioning with her head toward the candle.

Crap!

She had one job and she'd nearly flubbed it. Quickly, she took a deep breath and blew it out toward the candle.

"See the flame flickering? We're now joined by friendly spirits."

"Is it Grandpa?" Sandy asked, unable to hide the excitement in her voice.

"We don't know yet," Lola said. "Now let's all close our eyes."

Reluctantly, Jordan did as Lola commanded, feeling uncomfortable when the room suddenly got a little colder. In all the spooky stories she'd ever seen, that meant a dead person was in the room. She shuddered.

"As your friends, we call upon you to tell us why you're here. I can't promise we can fix whatever is troubling you, but we'll try. Come along with us, whoever you are, on a journey to let go of the past and open your arms to a new life." Then Lola began to hum again.

Without warning, she slammed her hand on the table, nearly spilling the water in the center. "Speak to us now. We mean you no harm and only wish to communicate with you, to understand why you're here."

The room was so quiet, Jordan was sure she could hear her own heart beating. She knew Lola was good at what she did, but this performance was Oscar-worthy. Despite being a true skeptic, she halfway believed Lola was actually talking to a dead person.

"There's only one spirit here," Lola continued, turning to Sandy. "It's your grandfather, and he wants to know that you'll be okay before he can leave this earth and join your grandmother."

Tears formed in Sandy's eyes. "Tell him I'm fine."

"Tell him yourself. He's in the room with us now." Lola leaned closer. "If you want to speak to your granddaughter, give us a sign." She glanced up at Jordan, nodding toward the flame again.

"It's him," Sandy exclaimed as the flame moved slightly when Jordan blew on it. "Oh, Grandpa, I miss you so much."

Jordan concentrated on the fire, her heart still racing from when Lola had banged on the table. Out of the corner of her eye, she caught a slight movement next to the fireplace, behind the drapes on the right, and she gasped.

When Lola shot her a reprimanding look, Jordan mouthed, *Sorry*.

Mother of God! She was more than a little freaked out.

"Your granddaughter's okay," Lola began before turning to Sandy. "What was his first name?"

"Douglas."

"Douglas, you can have peace now. Be gone . . ."

Just then the furnace kicked on, causing the drapes to flutter, and Jordan lost the battle with her nerves. As she screamed, she watched in horror when one side of the drapes pulled away from the wall and headed directly toward her.

Jumping from the chair, she ran for the door, glancing back only to see the other green drape chasing her, too.

Lola nearly knocked her over, trying to reach the door before the drapes attacked. Running past both of them, Sandy screamed at the top of her lungs. After pushing the door wide open, all three women poured out into the cool night air, nearly rolling down the porch steps.

Panic twisted Jordan's insides, and a scream bubbled in her throat, nearly suffocating her. When she had almost made it to the car, she tripped over Lola's caftan, tumbling across the front lawn. Struggling to get up, she felt the drape touch her shoulder, and she released a scream loud enough to be heard back in town.

"Wait."

Jordan stopped crawling away. She'd know that voice anywhere. "Danny?"

Twisting around, she saw her brother jerking the green drape off and throwing it to the ground. His cohort Victor slipped out from under the other drape.

"What in the hell are you doing out here?" Jordan hollered, restraining the urge to commit sibling homicide.

Lola and Sandy drew close, surrounding Danny and Victor, and Jordan knew if she gave them the okay, they were prepared to do the dirty work for her and inflict grave bodily harm on the two men, now sporting sheepish grins.

"Victor, have you gone mad?" Lola got right up in his face. "We could've fallen and broken a couple of bones running out of here like that. Or worse, we could have set the house on—oh my heavens! The candles!"

Danny did a one-eighty and ran back into the house. "I blew them out," he said, reappearing at the door with the remorseful expression he always wore when he knew he was in trouble.

"You guys have some explaining to do," Lola reprimanded, cradling a sniffling Sandy and guiding her through the front door, with Jordan and Victor right behind.

"It's your fault, Jordan," Danny began. "We asked you if we could come, and you said no."

"So it's my fault you and Victor decided to act like spoiled ten-year-olds?" Jordan quickly surveyed the room around her. "How did you manage to get in the house without us seeing you, anyway?"

"We hid down the street while you showered and followed you here. When we knocked, no one answered. Since the door was unlocked, we came in and saw you guys on the back porch. Rather than take a chance on being sent home, we decided to hide behind the curtains."

Victor interrupted Danny and pointed to Jordan. "When you screamed, we took off running."

"So let me get this straight. You two idiots broke into Sandy's house and hid while we had the séance? You were there the entire time?"

"Yes, and I have to tell you, Lola, that was pretty impressive," Victor said.

"Oh, shove it, Victor!" Lola said sternly, but the corners of her eyes crinkled and gave her away. "I guess you have finally come full circle. That green dress looked lovely on you."

"That particular shade has always brought out my eyes." Victor tried to keep a straight face. "Now Danny here is another story altogether. He should never even think of wearing moss green with his red hair."

"Maybe Kelly green is more your shade, Danny." Lola chuckled at her own suggestion.

Jordan laughed out loud at the image of her brother draped in Kelly green curtains. "I've seen him in that color. It so doesn't go with his red hair, either."

The tense moment gone, one by one everyone in the room started laughing, even Sandy.

"I can't wait to tell the gang how you macho men screamed like little girls when you thought the ghosts were chasing you," Jordan teased.

"Speaking of ghosts, we haven't finished," Lola said. "There's one more thing we have to do to rid the house of spirits."

"Do you really think it was Grandpa?" Sandy asked.

"There is no doubt it was him. I also believe he's satisfied that you're doing okay. Now he can ascend to the unknown in peace to be with your grandmother," Lola said.

Sandy's smile made the entire evening worthwhile.

"Then let's go finish the job," Danny said, moving closer to her. "Victor and I want to help."

"Okay, but first, you to have to hang those back up," Jordan said, pointing toward the front lawn, where the curtains lay on the ground. "You'd better hope they're not ruined."

"Deal." Victor trotted outside and gathered the drapes in his arms, singing, "We're off to scare the ghosties."

After the curtains were rehung, Jordan checked her watch. It was going on eleven. "What's next, Lola?" Even with the ghost scare as comic relief, she still felt uneasy pretending to talk to spirits.

"Okay, for this onc wc have to open the windows."

Danny and Victor complied while Lola relit one of the candles and placed it in the center of the table. "We need to get in a circle and walk counterclockwise around the room."

Jordan lined up behind Victor, and they all followed Lola in silence. "Should we chant Sandy's grandfather's name?"

"No. Now go clockwise three times," Lola instructed as she turned. "This will draw any remaining spirits out through the open windows and settle the energy in the room."

As foolish as Jordan felt doing this, she was afraid not to participate, just in case there really was energy in the room. She still didn't believe in all this occult stuff, but she wasn't about to say so out loud.

After three full turns around the room, Lola clapped her hands. "The house is now free of spirits, Sandy, and your grandfather is at peace."

Sandy ran over and hugged Lola's neck. "I know now why Jordan loves you so much."

"Let's get this place cleaned up, so we can get home before midnight," Jordan said, carrying the bowl of water to the kitchen.

Riding home in the front passenger seat, Sandy turned sideways to include Lola in the conversation. "I've been thinking. I'm going to spend next weekend at the lake." She paused to grin widely at Lola in the backseat. "If all goes well—as I expect it to—I'll call a moving company to pick up my stuff the following Saturday."

Jordan snuck a peek in Lola's direction. If only everyone's troubles could be solved with this faux-séance stuff. First on her ghost-releasing tour with Lola would be Rusty's mother. If anyone was in need of getting rid of demons, it was Maria Morales.

Thinking of Maria, Jordan vowed to finally stop talking about it and make that trip to her house the following week.

Staring out the window, she got the uneasy feeling the evil spirits in Maria's life wouldn't be as eager to disappear as Sandy's ghosts seemed to have been. And if what Jordan suspected was true, the evil spirit threatening to harm Maria probably wasn't dead.

In all likelihood, it was a living breathing person, one who was very close to the woman and doled out her medicine every day.

CHAPTER 13

"They found two stolen cows in Kansas," Danny said, shoving the last bite of the breakfast burrito into his mouth.

Jordan stopped chewing on the hash brown stick. "That's good news, right?"

"You'd think, but how they got there is a mystery."

"That's odd. How did they know they were stolen? Were they branded?" She took the remains of her Mickey D's breakfast to the trash can in the kitchen.

"Both cows were, and they have legitimate paperwork on them."

"That makes no sense. What do the people who sold them have to say?" Jordan glanced at the clock above the kitchen entrance. Already running late, she'd have to save her chocolate éclair for later.

"That's the weird part," Danny said, eyeing her pastry. "You gonna eat that?"

"Don't even think about it. You shouldn't have gobbled yours before eating your burrito."

"Oh, like you don't usually do that. Where do you think I learned that trick?" He finished his coffee and threw the empty cup in the direction of the trash can.

"You should stick with football," Jordan teased, picking up the cup and tossing it. "So back to the cows, what's so weird about it?"

"The Kansas ranchers would have never figured out anything was wrong since the cows came from the Carlyle Ranch, one of their regular suppliers. But the bill of sale listed two male Black Angus cows, and they called the Carlyle Ranch owner to let him know one was a female. Most ranchers like to keep the females for breeding, so they wanted to make sure there wasn't a mistake."

"Don't tell me," Jordan said, shaking her head. "The ranch owner said 'What cow?'"

Danny laughed. "You missed your calling, Jordan. That's exactly what he said, right before he took an inventory of his herd and found out six were missing."

"Okay, so they realized the cows had been stolen. What's so weird about that?"

He threw his hands in the air. "The cow had the Carlyle brand, and they had an authentic bill of sale written on the company letterhead. Don't you get it?"

"Obviously not."

"When the original owner checked his accounts online, it was there."

"What was there?"

"The transaction stating he had actually sold the cow to the Kansas rancher."

Jordan hurried back to the table and sat down, suddenly interested. "See, I was right. The Carlyle Ranch owner was probably going to report that cow stolen after shipping it off to Kansas for a double whammy: money from both the insurance company and the auction. Pretty clever, if you ask me."

Danny frowned. "I hate to admit it, but you might be right."

Jordan leaned across the table, her hand cupped to her ear. "What did you say? I didn't hear you. Could you repeat that last part about me being right?"

"Oh, get over yourself."

"I am right. How else could it have shown up on the books as a sale?"

"I'll find out today. I'm headed to Burleson to the Carlyle Ranch to check it out for myself. I'll be gone most of the day."

"Hope you catch the bad guys," she said, suddenly thinking about her day. "I almost forgot to tell you. I'll be gone all day, too, but I thought we could hit that great little Italian joint in Connor when we both get back. You know the one that gives you a monster-size order of spaghetti and meatballs with all the sides for under ten bucks. I was even thinking some of the gang might want to go with us."

"This is your mandatory lunch date with Lucas Santana, and you're planning to spend the whole day over there? I thought he gave you the creeps."

"Oh, please! I'm not a glutton for punishment." She pointed to the smoky gray vase on the counter filled with a colorful arrangement of lilies and gladiolas. "I'm taking those to Rusty Morales's mother after lunch."

Danny shot up from the chair. "I'll go with you. I'd like to ask Mr. Morales a few questions about Rusty, now that we know he was probably murdered."

"No way. This is a social visit, and the last thing I need

is you asking questions. Besides, aren't you off to Burleson?" Jordan wasn't about to tell her brother the real reason she was going to see Maria and decided the sooner she got his mind on something else, the better. "Hey, have they identified what killed Rusty yet?"

"They didn't find any trace of poison in the blood, but the forensics guy from Dallas says he has a pretty good idea. They're reexamining tissue samples and stomach content, and he wants to run a few more tests before releasing his findings." Danny shook his head. "The sheriff is getting antsy because we haven't made any headway on this, and he's asking for help. It ticks me off to no end that they won't give me a little bit longer to break this case before they send for the big dogs from Dallas."

"Don't take it personally, Danny. You're the new guy here, and apparently, the sheriff's getting flack from the higher-ups to put the thieves behind bars. It's starting to get mysterious, and I'd really like to be updated on this since I was with the guy when he died."

"That will cost you," he said, nodding toward her éclair.

She narrowed her eyes, mentally debating if it was worth giving up the pastry. "I'll give you half, but you'd better save me the other part."

"Done." He flashed his I-outsmarted-you grin.

She was tempted to grab the éclair and run, but she was too curious about the details of Rusty's death.

Standing in her closet surveying her wardrobe, she swallowed hard and squared her shoulders. She was so not looking forward to confronting Diego Morales.

Driving out to the Morales house, Jordan breathed a sigh of relief that her visit with Lucas and Bella had once again been pleasant. That is, unless you counted the awkward moment when he'd pulled out a brownish red scarf from a drawer. He'd winked and said he'd thought of Jordan's wild red hair and bedroom eyes when he'd seen it on the mannequin in the store window.

The anger had flashed momentarily in Bella's eyes, but she'd quickly recovered and erased any emotion she might have felt—like the dutiful wife who pretends not to notice her husband's faults. The only problem was, she didn't have the security of a piece of paper legally declaring she was more than just a nursemaid and faithful companion for all those years. Apparently, for her, living with luxury was worth the cost of putting up with the old man's disrespect.

Still, it had to have jerked her chain when Lucas brought out the expensive silk scarf. Married or not, the moron shouldn't have done that kind of thing in front of Bella. And when Jordan had refused to accept it, Bella had even insisted she would hurt Lucas's feelings if she didn't take the gift.

Like she cared a rat's rear end about his feelings—if he even had any other than lust.

Trying to put that behind her, she concentrated on the country road, praying she didn't miss the turnoff. According to Bella, Maria and Diego lived in a small house on the other side of Ranchero, almost to the Oklahoma border. As soon as Jordan made the turn and drove down the deserted road, the little voice in her head reminded her for the umpteenth time that she was taking a huge risk. Despite Brenda Sue's assurances that Diego couldn't have harmed his wife, Jordan was not totally convinced. She'd seen his temper flash when he'd spoken to Lucas at Rusty's funeral and his gentler side when he'd talked to his wife. She had no idea which Diego she'd confront inside the house.

Staring at the farmland on both sides of the driveway, Jordan almost whipped the car around and went home. With the closest neighbor over three hundred yards away, nobody would be able to hear her scream for help if she needed it.

What if Diego took issue with her questioning his wife? She remembered him as a husky man, not quite as tall as Rusty, but with arms that testified to a disciplined workout schedule. Despite his age, Diego still had a commanding presence. Even though she'd grown up taking on her brothers whenever they'd challenged her, their size and strength had always trumped her smaller stature and athletic skills.

What was she thinking, coming here? Walking up to the front door, she swallowed several times, trying to keep the butterflies in her stomach under control. She should have brought Danny with her like he'd wanted. At least he knew where she was in case she didn't make it back.

When she'd called yesterday to ask if she could visit and to get directions to the house, Diego had been hesitant, explaining that Maria tired easily. Only after she'd promised to make her visit short and sweet had he finally given in. She'd gotten the same reaction from Bella when she'd mentioned she was going to visit with Maria.

Geez! Both Bella and Diego acted like she was asking to take the old woman on a three-mile hike or something. Bella had mentioned at least twice how exhausted Maria became after her weekly visits with her. Jordan had sworn she only wanted to drop off the bouquet and say hello, purposely leaving out the part about snooping around. She had to find out if Diego was hurting Maria, even though the woman had denied it at her son's memorial service.

Jordan was still thinking about it when the door opened and Diego stared down at her, his icy black eyes sending

daggers. Mentally, she kicked herself again for not bringing Danny with her—and Ray. Even though the older man
had been retired from the Ranchero Police Department for
ten years, between regular workouts at the gym and the
extracurricular ones with Lola, he stayed in great shape
and would have been a better match for Diego if things got
out of hand.

"Maria's in the living room."

Jordan followed him to a small room off the main
entrance where Maria Morales sat in front of a roaring fire.
When she heard them enter, she swiveled the wheelchair
around.

"Hello, Maria. It was gracious of you to allow me to
come and visit with you today. I brought you these beautiful flowers from a greenhouse behind Brenda Sue's house."

At the mention of the woman she knew well, Maria
smiled and motioned for Jordan to sit in the chair closest to
the fire.

"I'll take those," Diego said, placing the vase in the center of the table. With a quick nod to his wife, he left the two
women alone.

Jordan used that time to take in the surroundings, noticing how warm the room made her feel. The worn-out carpet and the handmade afghans thrown over the faded
furniture seemed pleasantly familiar; it was almost like sitting in her grandmother's house back in Amarillo.

"I wanted to come by to make sure you were okay," Jordan said. "I know losing your only child has to have taken
a toll on you, and I wondered if there was anything I
could do."

Tears formed in Maria's eyes, and she shook her head.

"I didn't know your son well, but I spent enough time
with him to believe he was a good man." She left out the

part about how he might have been the ringleader for the cattle-rustling epidemic that was costing the ranch owners millions of dollars in lost revenue.

Maria sniffed, dabbing at her eyes with a white handkerchief that magically appeared from under the blanket on her lap.

"Brenda Sue told me all about how you raised her and how upset she was when you had your stroke."

Jordan waited for some kind of response. When there was none, she continued. *Might as well get right to the point.* "She said it was odd how the levels of medicine in your blood were so high. I hope they've adjusted the dosage so that doesn't happen again."

Again, she waited for Maria's reaction, and again, there was none. Jordan decided to press on. "Are you afraid of someone, Maria?"

Maria's eyes widened, and she glanced at the doorway before she nodded.

Just then Diego appeared with a tray filled with coffee and cookies. The look he gave Jordan when he handed her a cup made her wonder if he'd heard the last question. She reached for the coffee and took the cookie only after he insisted.

Despite the fact the cookies were definitely store-bought, Jordan decided there was no way she was going to eat it and take a chance he'd doctored it with something. Although she was certain the man had nothing to do with Rusty's poisoning, the jury was still out on whether he had overmedicated his wife with powerful blood thinners.

And right now, she was leaning toward a guilty verdict.

She decided Diego could have messed with the coffee as well, and she set her cup on the end table, untouched. When she and Maria were finally alone again, Jordan stood and walked to the fireplace. She'd forgotten to wear a sweater, and the heat felt good as she leaned in to warm her hands.

Glancing up at the rows of pictures on the mantle, she wasn't surprised most of them were of Maria and Diego with Rusty at various stages of his life. He'd been a handsome kid even in his awkward years and must've had the girls lined up as far back as elementary school.

"Rusty was a good-looking man," Jordan commented, reaching for the photo at the end. It was a picture of a very young Diego and Maria standing on the front porch with a young woman between them. It left no doubt where Rusty had gotten his good looks.

Maria had been so beautiful when she was younger. But as attractive as she was, the woman standing beside her was even more striking, resembling Eva Longoria. As Jordan turned to comment, Maria pulled out a butter knife from under the blanket and began to pound frantically on the arm of her wheelchair.

Shocked, Jordan watched as Diego ran in and rushed to his wife's side.

"What did you say to her?" he demanded, accusation lacing his tone.

"Nothing," Jordan said, shaking her head. "I only commented on how handsome Rusty had been."

Diego bent down and enveloped Maria in his arms, holding her until the pounding stopped. "I think you'd better go now, Ms. McAllister," he said, avoiding eye contact.

"I'm sorry if I upset her."

Diego released Maria and pointed to the end picture. "Did you ask about Gia?"

Again, Jordan shook her head.

He exhaled slowly, standing up straight but remaining close to Maria. "It was right nice of you to come all the way out here to bring her flowers, but now it's time for her to lie down and rest. Can you find your way to the door?"

Jordan nodded, grabbing her purse from the sofa and walking over to Maria. Just as she bent down to pat her hand and say good-bye, the woman raised her head up and mouthed, *Rusty.*

Jordan softened, understanding that Maria was still grieving. "I know. If you'll let me, I'll come back out and sit with you sometime."

Maria stared for several seconds before releasing Jordan's hand, almost in a defeated kind of way. Jordan thanked Diego on the way to the door and practically ran to her car.

That was weird! She remembered how Maria went berserk when she was looking at the pictures. And Jordan still hadn't discovered if Diego was the cause of her stroke.

On the drive back to her apartment, she decided no matter how uncomfortable visiting Maria had made her feel, she had to help the woman. For now, she'd go home and regroup.

But she would be back!

The one scene playing over and over again in her head was Maria banging on the wheelchair. Was it frustration because she couldn't speak? Or was it something else, something more critical?

Regardless, Jordan was determined to find out what had Maria so scared, and why she kept a butter knife hidden under her lap blanket.

CHAPTER 14

Jordan parked the car and slowly walked to her apartment, hoping Danny was back so they could hurry out to DiNardo's for dinner. Her stomach was already growling like a dog with a treed squirrel. Although she'd made a pig of herself on Bella's Baked Steak and Gravy, that had been hours ago. She was looking forward to a gigantic serving of spaghetti and meatballs with a salad and garlic bread. The last time they were there, she'd had enough leftover food for lunch the next two days, which was always a plus with her budget.

Even though Danny was splitting the cost of groceries, money was still tight. Her brother was turning out to be a bad influence, cooking even less than she did and coaxing her into eating out on a nightly basis. Unfortunately, while he was good at sharing Pop-Tarts for breakfast, he drew the line at bologna sandwiches for dinner. She'd experimented one night with a simple chicken recipe she'd printed in her column and ended up throwing the entire dish down the disposal. Danny still teased her about it.

There was only so much humiliation a girl could take.

The good thing was that she never had to worry about eating on paper plates or drinking from her matched set of plastic cups from the Pizza Palace when Danny was around. He didn't care what the dishes looked like as long as there was food on them.

She opened the door, glad to find it unlocked, which meant Danny was already home. She hoped he'd worked out the details with the rest of the gang, and they could be on their way to the restaurant soon. She was exhausted and looking forward to an early bedtime. On top of it all, her editor had called before she'd left work Friday, wanting to see her in his office first thing Monday morning.

That always meant he wanted something—which always meant she wouldn't like it. But she couldn't complain too much. So far, the job had been fun and seemed to have gotten easier. Or maybe it was just the fact she worried less about everyone in Ranchero finding out she was clueless when it came to cooking.

The readers had to have figured out by now that she was merely posting casserole dishes with fancy names, but they still kept begging for more. Egan had even mentioned he was thinking about having the Kitchen Kupboard run three times a week instead of two. Maybe that was what he wanted to talk about in the morning.

Danny wasn't around when she walked into the living room, but she could hear the shower running. Since his teenage years, he'd been known for his hour-long showers. And the guy would take ten of them a day if he could.

Although the thought of hot water running over her body was particularly appealing at the moment, she was far too exhausted to even think about a quick shower.

How dirty could you get sitting around all day? Besides, every time they went to DiNardo's, she came home with the pungent smell of garlic in her hair.

She flopped down on the couch, resting her feet on the coffee table and thinking if she weren't so hungry, she'd fall asleep right there. Closing her eyes, she leaned her head back to enjoy a few minutes before Danny emerged from the bathroom.

When the doorbell rang, she silently cursed having the only serene moment of her day interrupted.

Crap!

People irritated the tar out of her sometimes. It had to be someone either selling something or trying to save her from the fires of hell. Her friends usually didn't knock, never mind ring the bell.

Springing up from the couch, she blew a strand of hair out of her eyes, intent on giving whoever it was a lecture about getting their eyes checked. The sign on the front door clearly said NO SOLICITING.

When she threw the door open, she got the surprise of her life as she stared into the most dazzling blue eyes she'd ever seen—well, since the last time she'd seen them.

It had been a few months, but he was exactly as Jordan remembered. Six feet tall, wearing jeans and a UNIVERSITY OF TEXAS EL PASO sweatshirt, Alex Moreland made her heart race. His dark blond hair with golden highlights set off his Paul Newman eyes, causing her thoughts to take a sharp turn from PG into dangerously R-rated territory.

"Hello, Jordan. Did you miss me?"

Before she could lift her jaw from the floor and think of a snappy comeback, her dorky brother chose that moment to come out of the shower wearing only a towel around his waist.

"And who's this?" Danny asked, pointing to the new arrival.

"Alex Moreland," she stammered.

She watched the surprise in Alex's eyes turn to anger.

"I see you've moved on, Jordan. I guess I can't blame you." He turned to leave.

Grabbing him by the arm, she swung him around, standing up on her tiptoes to kiss his cheek.

He looked down at her, confusion clouding his eyes.

"Alex, this is my brother, Danny."

The relieved expression covering his face made Jordan want to grab him for another kiss. The man was clearly jealous. A small part of her was delighted at his reaction.

Okay, a *big* part of her.

"This is your brother?"

She nodded. "He's staying with me for a few weeks."

Danny crossed the room and extended his hand. "You must be the FBI guy my sister has been hiding from me."

"Danny!" She glared. "How did you know about him?"

"I have to protect my sources since you don't tell me squat."

"Your sources, my butt. Victor couldn't keep a secret if you wired his mouth shut." She inched closer to Alex, catching a drift of his aftershave, which somehow made her forget any earlier hunger pangs. "So what are you doing here, Alex?"

"I got a call yesterday from Sheriff Delaney down at the police station. Cattle rustling has become a real problem in this area lately, and he's—"

"What?" Danny moved so quickly toward Alex that he almost lost his towel.

Jordan didn't have to look at her brother to know his face was probably skewed with a mix of anger and disbelief. And she was not about to glance in his direction for fear she would be scarred for life if there was a sudden wardrobe malfunction.

She led Alex to the couch where they both sat down; Danny settled in the chair directly across from them.

"Why would Sheriff Delaney call the Feds?" Danny asked.

"Apparently the crime is escalating and has now crossed over into interstate fraud. Since we worked together on a case a few months ago, he requested the Bureau send me." He moved his hand behind Jordan's head and caressed the nape of her neck. "But that's only part of the reason I'm here. An old friend is working a nonrelated case for the department and asked if I could help out."

"I thought you were deep undercover. The last time we talked, you said you and your partner were finally making contacts. So how is it your boss let you come all the way back here to help with a small-town case?"

Not that she really cared why he was here. Just sitting next to him on the sofa again with his thigh touching hers, she felt a jolt of electricity through her entire body.

Alex tipped her chin and touched his lips to hers, sending goose bumps rippling down her arms. "First of all, if the thieves are crossing state lines with stolen cattle, it's no longer a small-town problem. I'm supposed to meet with the guy TSCRA sent here. I'll know more after I talk to him."

"Why wait?" Danny leaned forward and held out his hand. "Danny McAllister, field marshal for TSCRA."

Alex stopped the march of his fingers up and down the inner part of Jordan's arm and stared. He reached over and shook Danny's hand. "That's the case you're working on?"

"Yep. And I have to tell you, I'm more than a little pissed off that they'd call in the cavalry when I haven't even had a chance to really get into the investigation." He stared back defiantly.

"Trust me, this is your show, Danny. I promised Delaney I would look over the police reports. That's all. I'm really here to help with the other case."

Being this close to Alex was maddening. All she wanted to do was to lock him in her room and never let him out. She took a few deep breaths before she trusted her voice. "I still don't get it. How could they pull you away from your undercover gig when the last time we spoke you said the bad guys were finally beginning to trust you?" She leaned away from him, narrowing her eyes. "That was over two weeks ago, by the way."

His gaze dropped from her face, to her shoulders, and settled on her chest for a few seconds before he met her eyes again. "I forgot how feisty redheads can be or how quickly it can drive me to drink." He ruffled her hair. "The logistics of getting me away for a few days was a problem, since we were pretty sure the drug lord had Rocco and me under surveillance and even had our phones tapped. I couldn't use the government-issued one, because I'm sure Uncle Sam was listening there, too."

"So how did you get away?" Danny repeated, obviously still nursing a touch of anger.

"Since we knew they were watching, we staged a bar fight where the police intervened and took me and my sparring partner, another undercover cop, to jail. I've got three days in Ranchero. Then I have to head back, since that's all the time we can milk out of the arrest." He turned and nailed Jordan with a let's-not-waste-one-more-minute-with-small-talk stare.

For once, she thoroughly agreed with him. "Where are you staying?"

"My old place was vacant, and the landlady agreed to let me crash there for a few days. It cost the Bureau a little more than a hotel, but they felt I had less of a chance of being recognized there." He melted her with a sexy look. "If memory serves, I still owe you a pan of lasagna."

"That's right, Moreland. After you bragged about how you had these mean cooking skills that you learned from your Italian mother, you skipped town before I had a chance to find out if you were just blowing smoke up my skirt." She had forgotten how much fun it was to trade barbs with him.

"For the record, you went and got yourself an overnight stay at Ranchero Community Hospital on my last night in town, if I'm not mistaken. And I wasn't blowing hot air. My mother's lasagna recipe is the best."

Jordan slapped her forehead, suddenly remembering their plans for the evening. "Danny, did you ask the guys if they wanted to go to DiNardo's with us tonight?"

"Oh hell!" Danny popped up, nearly losing the towel again. Glancing at the clock, he said. "They're all coming with us. I told them we were leaving around seven. That only gives me fifteen minutes to get ready."

"DiNardo's? Is that the little dive in Connor?"

"Yes. And if you're nice to me, I'll let you come along." Jordan tried to make her smile seductive. "Unless you just want to stay and hang out here."

He pulled her into his arms and held her to him. "I can't

tell you how inviting that is, but I haven't had a thing to eat all day. All I ask is that you hold that thought."

Lowering his head, he kissed her, making her forget the rumbling in her stomach—and just about everything else, except how much she didn't want to leave the warmth of his embrace. She sighed and snuggled closer.

"Does that get me an invite to the party?"

"Absolutely," she replied. "Oh Lord, the others will be here any second, and I need a shower." *A cold one!*

Watching the gang interact with Alex as if it hadn't been almost two months since he'd left Ranchero had warmed Jordan's heart. Since Alex had taken the six a.m. flight from El Paso, he could barely hold his eyes open. Although he tried to keep up with everyone, Jordan had sent him home, convincing him he needed a good night's sleep to get ready for their date the next night.

Things have a way of working out, she thought as she made her way to her editor's office. Laughing to herself, she remembered how she'd popped Alex in the head with a skillet and knocked him unconscious a while back when she thought he might be a bad guy.

And Alex had been right. She was the one who had ruined their first big date by nearly getting herself killed and ending up in the hospital. No way she'd let an opportunity like that pass her by again. She had him for two full days, and she intended to make it impossible for him to forget about her while he was off in El Paso fighting drug smugglers.

They'd decided tonight would be lasagna night. And if Jordan had anything to say about it, dessert would be more than the chocolate cake she was picking up at Myrtle's Diner on the way over to his house.

"You can go in now," Egan's secretary said, waving toward the door.

Jordan stood and proceeded in that direction, smiling at Jackie Frazier. "Nice sweater," she said as she passed.

"Thanks." The secretary didn't even look up.

Since the very first time Jackie had summoned her to the editor's office, Jordan hadn't been able to get the woman to utter more than a few words in response.

Inside the office, Egan was on the phone reading someone the riot act and motioned for her to sit down. Slamming the phone in the cradle, he leaned back in the chair, his hands behind his head.

"Idiots! We're getting bombarded with bigger orders from the 7-Elevens, and the incompetents at the distribution center can't seem to get off their asses and make it happen. It's like they have no clue we're in an economic crunch and fighting for every newspaper sale we can get." He stopped and released a frustrated sigh.

"Is that why you wanted to talk to me?" Jordan tapped impatiently on the arm of her chair.

Only two more hours until quitting time. Three more until she was on her way to Alex's apartment. And hopefully, only a couple more after that and all her fantasies from the past few months would finally come true.

"Of course not. What could you do about it? We can fix a lot of things, but we can't change stupid." Egan straightened up in his chair and pointed to an envelope on his desk. "Know what that is?"

She shook her head, not sure if she wanted to find out.

"It's a big fat check from Lucas Santana. Apparently, your column with last week's beef recipe is making a pretty significant difference in his profit margin. At least for this month, he's cashing in on the increased sales and has doubled his ads." He slapped the desk. "I gotta hand it to you, Jordan, I wasn't sure you could pull it off."

"Does that mean I get a bonus?" She thought about the extra money she had already spent this month on takeout alone. "Because I sure could use it."

"Yeah, yeah. So could the rest of the world. I have a different kind of bonus for you."

Her interest piqued, she leaned forward, resting her elbows on his desk. "More Cowboys tickets?"

The editor laughed out loud. "I knew you had spunk from the moment I first saw you." Shaking his head, he continued. "I'm talking about only running the personals two days and jacking up the culinary column to three times a week."

"And that's your idea of a bonus? I work twice as hard getting recipes and talking about food than I do just copying someone's desperate attempt to hook up. So, no thanks."

"And you get to sit in the press box with Jim Westerville at the Cougars basketball game against Wichita Falls in three weeks."

She jumped from her chair and leaned across his desk. "For real?"

"Did I not promise you that way back when? It's my way of saying thank you for a job well done so far." He shrugged. "Of course, I had to bribe Westerville before he'd agree."

She didn't care what he'd had to do to get her a pass to sit with the sportswriter for the *Globe*. A picture of the big man falling down the steps of the bleachers flashed in her head, and she quickly blinked it away.

Okay, the more Christian thing would be to wish he only sprained his ankle, so she could take over his job for a few weeks. She wouldn't have to plan a trip to the confessional that way.

"Before you gush all over my desk, get out of here and get back to work." He patted the envelope with the check from Santana. "For now, we'll hold on increasing your column an extra day. You'd better hope you live up to the hype with another good recipe this week."

"I'm using Bella's Baked Steak and Gravy recipe. I can personally tell you it will have the people of Ranchero begging for more."

"You're cocky, McAllister, but I like it. Now go make some money for the newspaper."

Jordan grabbed her notebook on the way out and stopped at Jackie Frazier's desk. "Have a great night, Jackie."

The secretary didn't even flinch.

"Or not," Jordan mumbled under her breath. She pushed the elevator button, so totally happy with her life, it didn't matter that she'd been snubbed yet again.

What did matter was she was one step closer to her dreams. Jordan McAllister was going to watch a Grayson County College basketball game from the press box!

CHAPTER 15

Jordan picked up the dessert at Myrtle's Diner and headed east toward Connor. Alex's rental house was located on the southern tip of Ranchero, and although she'd never been there, it was easy to find.

Tucked behind a row of evergreen shrubs that lined a white picket fence, it was the perfect house for someone like Alex. He'd been raised with three sisters, and Jordan knew he would appreciate the quaintness of the tiny sea-foam green house with the wraparound porch.

It must be nice to have a place like this and have some-one else pay the bills. She parked her car by the curb and made her way to the front door.

Before she could maneuver the dessert box to free up a hand to knock, the white, colonial-style door, dressed up with a Texas bluebonnet wreath, swung open.

Alex leaned against the doorjamb and grinned like the proverbial Cheshire cat up to no good.

Which was fine with her.

"Hey, gorgeous, did you make this especially for me?" He grabbed the box from her and made a sweep with his empty arm, beckoning her to enter.

"Oh, yeah. Myrtle and I whipped it up when I got home from my forty-hour-a-week day job—right after I gathered the eggs and milked the cow out back. I almost didn't get the butter churned because I had to sneak in a pedicure and shave my legs." She smiled, already anticipating spending time alone with this man. "I'll bet you're worth the extra effort, though."

Okay, she had shaved her legs and did wish she'd had time for a pedicure. That much was true. She leaned in to kiss his cheek. "Ooh, something smells good."

"Grandma Serafina's Lasagna." He took a step back and looked her over from head to toe. "In those tight black jeans you deserve the best," he said, giving her another once-over. "Come on. I've got another treat. There's a glass of homemade sangria waiting for you."

Here she was, alone with a guy who made George Clooney look like just another dude, and all she could think about was how much her readers would love the new recipes.

What did that say about her?

She took the glass from him, not about to confess that she usually drank wine only in small doses. Not only had she never acquired a taste for it, but she usually paid a high price with a monster morning-after headache. She preferred margaritas, especially the ones with a little sangria swirled through them like the ones she'd had last week at Santana Ranch, though they tended to give her a headache as well.

Just to be nice, she sipped the drink and was surprised

by the pleasant fruity taste. Licking her lips, she looked up at him and realized he was waiting for the verdict. "You made this, too?"

"It's the recipe you printed this week in your column. Are you impressed yet?" He set his glass on the table and came around behind her to nuzzle her neck with his lips.

As an electric current shot up her spine, she tilted her head forward to give him better access.

Abruptly, he stopped. "Aha! I knew the sangria would render you helpless against my charms."

She turned, ready to hit him with some smart-alecky comeback but began to laugh when she saw the comical expression on his face. "Geez, Moreland, I wouldn't brag about that if I were you. Bet your cop buddies would love to hear how you have to ply a girl with homemade cocktails to get her interested." She bit her lip to hide the smile and finished off the wine.

"That's a valid point, but let's see what you say after tasting my lasagna. You *will* be defenseless, McAllister."

"Promises, promises. Now feed me before this wine goes to my head." She handed him her empty glass. "This time, fill it all the way to the top."

An hour later, they finished Myrtle's Better Than Sex Cake and were still teasing each other about everything from their childhoods to their jobs. Just as Alex predicted, the lasagna was fantastic, and he promised to get a copy of the recipe to her the next day. After yet another glass of sangria, Jordan was feeling pretty mellow.

"I had a long meeting with your brother and the sheriff this morning. We mapped out how Danny's going to approach the cattle-rustling problem. He's the lead, and I'm only going to be a consultant." He paused to shove his dessert plate away. "Your brother's a smart guy, Jordan."

"He said the same thing about you," she replied. "I mean about being smart. He mentioned you were going to work with a forensic toxicologist from Dallas who's trying to figure out what kind of poison was used on Rusty."

Alex nodded. "That's the real reason I'm here. Dr. Maldonado and I worked a case in Dallas a few years back. The symptoms were very similar, with signs of asphyxiation and seizures right before death. Both of those autopsies came up empty as far as something in the blood or the stomach contents. For the Morales case, the plan is for Dr. M. to come up with the poison, and I'll figure out how and when it got into Rusty's body."

"Has he found anything yet?"

"He's about eighty-five percent sure he knows what it is, but that was only after reexamining a lot of tissue samples. Even then, he found only a trace of the suspected poison. Luckily, knowing the results from the other two cases, he was able to test for the specific toxin in the organs."

"What was it?" she asked.

"Aconitum napellus. It's extremely deadly and works almost instantly."

"I've never heard of it."

"Most people haven't. It isn't that common even though it's relatively easy to acquire."

"That's kind of scary." She wrinkled her nose.

"Danny said you were sitting next to the dead guy all night. Did you know him well?"

Jordan noticed the twitch that started on the side of his mouth as he waited for her response. The mischievous part of her would have loved to tease him for a while longer about her relationship with Rusty, but this was too serious to make light of.

"I only met him that night. I went to the Cattlemen's

Ball so I could write a review about it in my column." She
didn't mention that Rusty had been an arranged date, or
how hot he was, sure that wouldn't make for good pre-
pillow talk.

A look of relief flashed in Alex's eyes. "What about the
other people at the table? Did you know them?"

"No, that night was the first time I'd met any of them."

She lowered her eyes, not willing to tell Alex that she
suspected Cooper. Since it was obvious his fiancée was
still in love with Rusty, it might have been a good motive
for wanting to see him harmed.

Might have been a good motive for wanting to see him
dead.

And then there was Bobby Carvella, who now held
Rusty's job at Santana's ranch. But he hadn't been at the
hotel in Fort Worth that night.

"Aconitum napellus roots are the deadliest, but they
have a horrible taste. It would be hard for someone to put
that into food without the victim knowing. However, the
powder form, aconite, could have been slipped into his drink
or even sprinkled on his food," Alex said, gathering up the
dishes.

When Jordan stood up to help, he pushed her back in the
chair gently. "Sit. You're my guest tonight. I'm just going to
rinse these off and load the dishwasher. You can talk to me
while I work."

"Holy cow, Moreland! I need to talk to your mother and
get her to write a book about raising a son. A girl could
really get spoiled by all this."

"My intentions exactly. A pampered woman lets down
her guard."

"You wish," she said, trying to be playful, but her thoughts
were still on Rusty. "You know, I never saw anything

suspicious that night, Alex. Rusty ate the same thing I did, and his drinks were delivered by a waiter who had a tray full of them. I can't imagine how that acanat, or whatever you called it, could have been slipped into something Rusty ate or drank."

"Aconite," he corrected. "It's also known as wolfsbane because it was thought to be potent enough to kill werewolves, according to ancient lore. It's been said some hunters even put it on the tips of their arrows and used it to kill real wolves."

Jordan's mouth dropped and her eyes widened. She wasn't aware a sound had escaped her lips, but it must have, because Alex was kneeling by her chair in a flash.

"My God, Jordan! What's wrong?"

She took a calming breath, then another, before she turned to him. "Is this the same poison that can be used in homeopathic remedies? The one that's produced from monkshood?"

It was his turn to look surprised. "How do you know about that?"

She pointed to the bar stool. "Hand me my purse." Her heart felt like it would beat its way out of her chest as she remembered the conversation in Karen Whitley's greenhouse two weeks before.

Taking her handbag from Alex, she reached in and grabbed her phone. After a few seconds of scanning she found what she was looking for and handed it to Alex.

"What's this?" he asked, puzzled.

"Monkshood," she replied. "It's growing in the greenhouse behind Brenda Sue and Marcus Taylor's ranch house over in McKinley. Brenda Sue and Rusty once had a thing, and I believe she was still in love with him."

Alex studied the picture of the plant with the purple and

yellow blooms. "Do you think her husband knew how she felt about Morales?"

Jordan nodded. "He definitely knows." She covered her mouth with her hands. "Ohmygod! They were both at the ball that night. She seemed really distraught when the policeman told us Rusty was dead. Marcus, on the other hand, looked angry."

"Send me this picture, Jordan," he said, handing her phone back and reaching for his own. "I have to call Danny. We need to get a warrant and drive out to that ranch."

For the next ten minutes, Alex made plans over the phone for the McKinley police to get the warrants and meet him and Danny at Taylor's Wagyu Ranch to search Brenda Sue's house as well as the greenhouse behind it.

Grabbing his coat, he bent down and kissed Jordan, who was in the kitchen finishing up with the dishes. "Leave those. I'll do them when I get back." He studied her wistfully. "Looks like our big date will have to wait one more night. I'm sorry, Jordan, but we really have to do this now."

"I know. Get out of here." She gave him a hug and nudged him toward the door. "I'm going to stay and clean these up before I go home, so don't argue. Our date can wait. I have to be at the newspaper super early in the morning, anyway."

"Tomorrow will be fantastic, I promise."

She narrowed her eyes. "You have your work cut out for you, Alex. I won't be so easy without chocolate to soften me up."

"Then I'll have to bring some. Hell, I'll drive into Dallas and visit the Ghirardelli store at the Galleria if I have to." He tipped up her chin and gave her a long delicious kiss before pulling away. "Hold that thought." And then he closed the door behind him.

"Bummer!" she said aloud. She'd been so close to being in his arms, and now she had to wait one more day. Time was ticking for them, and if they weren't careful, Alex would be on a plane back to El Paso before they ever got to have their big date.

Not if I can help it, she thought before her mind wandered to the task at hand for Alex and Danny.

Was it possible that Marcus Taylor poisoned Rusty that night? He certainly seemed cold enough the few times Jordan had seen him. In his defense, it must be hard watching your wife lust after another man right in front of you.

Jordan froze, letting the hot water run over the dishes. What if Brenda Sue was not so sweet and innocent? What if underneath that adorable southern drawl, she had a killer mean streak?

The old if-I-can't-have-you-no-one-else-can adage was a powerful motive.

She reached for the last plate, which still had a small piece of cake on it, and wondered how anybody could leave chocolate. Popping in into her mouth, she closed her eyes, enjoying it all the more because she knew it was Alex's.

Myrtle's Better Than Sex Cake should have a patent on it.

But she'd have to wait another twenty-four hours before she could vote on whether or not it lived up to its name in this case.

CHAPTER 16

Despite being called back to Egan's office the next day, Jordan couldn't keep the smile off her face, knowing she and Alex would finally get to have a real date that night. After she'd finished the dishes at his house the previous evening, she'd hung around awhile, hoping he would return, but she'd eventually headed home, eager to know whether he, Danny, and the McKinley Police Department had successfully served the warrant at the Taylors' ranch.

By the time Danny had gotten home, however, she was already asleep, so she'd had to wait until the morning to find out what went down. She'd been surprised to find Danny already dressed and ready to leave for the police station when she woke up. Quickly, she'd dressed, grabbed a Pop-Tart, and walked out to the car with him.

As she'd expected, they'd found the monkshood in Karen Whitley's greenhouse, but so far, they had uncovered nothing to implicate Karen, Brenda Sue, or Marcus Taylor in Rusty's murder.

They were waiting to see if there was anything suspicious on the computers they'd confiscated from both the greenhouse and Brenda Sue's house. Danny had mentioned how Marcus Taylor had lost his temper during the search and had to be restrained by three cops.

Now, there was a surprise—not!

Although Karen processed the monkshood into a fine powder used to make the aconite she sent all over the country, the homeopathic concentration wasn't enough to kill a big man like Rusty. That is, unless he had ingested a boatload of it. Given how quickly his symptoms had appeared and how he'd stopped breathing within such a short time, both Danny and Alex thought it unlikely that Karen's monkshood was the cause of Rusty's death. However, the toxicologist was running tests today to verify that theory one way or another.

As soon as Jordan got off the elevator, Jackie Frazier tilted her head toward Egan's office, a signal that he was waiting. When she entered the room, he motioned for her to sit down.

"McAllister, I know I don't have to remind you where Longhorn Prime Rib Steak House is located, right?"

Jordan nodded, wondering where this conversation was going. It was the second time in two days she'd been called to the editor's office. This couldn't be good.

"I just got off the phone with the new owner, a man named Hiro Tamaki, who's interested in buying advertising space on a weekly basis."

Jordan braced herself, knowing from past history that the next thing out of Egan's mouth would involve her doing something she'd rather not.

He didn't disappoint.

"He's turned the old Longhorn into Tamaki's Hibachi Grill and Sushi Bar and wants you to come by there tonight for the grand opening. Then you can write about it in tomorrow's column."

She jumped up from the chair, shaking her head. "No way!"

Egan eyed her suspiciously. "You misunderstand me, Jordan. That isn't a request."

She eased back down, resigned to the fact this was his playground and she'd have to play his game of choice. She decided to try a little diplomacy. "Any other night would be fine. Just not tonight, please."

The corners of his eyes crinkled with mischief. "Got a big date planned?"

The man had no boundaries. "Yes, and he's leaving town in the morning. I don't know when I'll see him again."

"Then take him with you." Egan rested his chin on his hand. "The *Globe* is picking up the tab, since we're trying to convince Tamaki to spend his advertising dollars with us. I'm sure he won't mind the bigger check. He's anxious to get the word out about his restaurant, so it's a given he'll treat you good. And you don't even have to worry about writing a review. Simply have a good time tonight and mention it in your column if you like the food. If you don't, then tell it like it is and chalk it up as a free meal for you and your boyfriend."

Jordan sighed. Although she hadn't planned on spending the night anyplace other than Alex's house, they had to eat, didn't they? "It's a Japanese restaurant?"

"Yeah. One of those places where they chop up the food and cook it right in front of you. The good news is, besides steak, they also have chicken and shrimp. Nothing should end up in your purse like the duck did the last time you reviewed a restaurant."

Jordan grimaced, remembering how that incident had nearly gotten her killed the night she'd reviewed the steak house that used to be at that location—the steak house whose owner now sat in a federal prison somewhere in Texas. "And both Alex and I can eat free?"

"Oh, so mystery man has a name?" Egan chuckled. "I think I can spring for one more meal. I'll call and make a reservation for two at eight. That will give you plenty of time to say your proper good-byes to—what was his name again?"

"Alex," Jordan answered, not sure she wanted to go there with her boss.

If she really thought about it, though, she'd have to admit it would be nice to enjoy a delicious meal with Alex without having to fork over any cash. That would still allow them to spend time alone at his place.

She stood. "I'll do it, but make the reservation for seven. And I want tomorrow morning as my half day off." She headed for the door, positive she heard the man snicker.

She didn't care if the whole world knew about her date tonight. It was anyone's guess when Alex would be able to get back to Ranchero, and they'd already given up one night in the name of law and order.

After Jordan made her way back to her desk, she picked up the phone and dialed Alex's number. Just hearing his voice made her pulse quicken. "Danny told me you were out pretty late last night. You should have slept in this morning."

She heard him laugh and would have given her entire stash of Ho Hos to see his face right now.

"I'll have plenty of time for sleep when I get back to El Paso tomorrow. What's up? Do you miss me already?"

She reached into the drawer for one of the chocolate treats. She should never have thought about them. "How would you like to take me to a Japanese restaurant tonight? I'll even spring."

"Seriously, Jordan, like I would even consider letting you pay for a meal."

Jordan's insides turned to butter, totally convinced that if his mother did write a book about the correct way to raise a son, it would be an instant best seller.

"So, is that a yes?"

"I love Japanese food. What time should I pick you up? And where is it?"

"The reservation is for seven, and it's the old Longhorn Prime Rib."

He laughed. "I know it well. Okay then, seven it is."

"And you won't be paying, either. My boss wants me to show up for the grand opening, and he's picking up the tab for both of us."

"So I'm part of your assignment?"

"You're dessert," she blurted, her hand shooting up to cover her mouth.

"I like the way you think, Jordan. Nothing tastes better than free food." He paused. "And delicious dessert."

Before she could respond, he said, "Hold on."

She heard his muffled voice explaining about the restaurant, which gave her cause for concern. She hoped whoever he was telling hadn't caught the subliminal message in their dessert banter.

"Sorry. Your brother's here and wanted the details. Since we can't really connect the monkshood from the greenhouse to Rusty's killer, we're working on what our next move should be. Gotta run. I'll see you around six thirty."

She hung up and unwrapped the Ho Ho she'd taken from the drawer, deciding it would be lunch for the day. With free food on the line, it would be a sin to go to the restaurant any other way but starving. She loved Japanese food. The visual of just the two of them finally alone and maybe even drinking a little sake while their very own chef prepared chicken fried rice in front of them was enough to get her through the rest of the day.

"Isn't this fun? All of us together for your last night in town?" Victor held up his drink and the others followed suit. "To good friends and free food."

Jordan stole a glance toward Alex, and he responded by squeezing her knee under the table. She'd be the first to toast good friends and free food.

Just not tonight.

"Hey, Jordan, this was a great idea," Danny said. "Don't you think so, Sandy?"

Sandy nodded as Danny leaned in closer to whisper something in her ear. Apparently it was funny, because Sandy actually giggled. Watching her brother at work with the opposite sex was not high on her list of favorite ways to spend an evening.

With his hand now massaging Jordan's knee, Alex turned to Michael. "So tell me again how you managed to get a free meal out of this?"

"KTLK FM. I knew my job would come in handy one of these days." Michael and Victor fist-bumped.

"Even if the owner took out an ad, I still don't get how you wrangled gratis meals for—" Jordan stopped to count. "Six people."

"It's not an ad, Jordan, that's how. Instead of him paying

hundreds of dollars for a thirty-second spot tomorrow, I'm going to talk about how I ate here and how I liked the food."

Victor slapped his partner on the back. "That's freaking brilliant, Michael. Aren't you glad our Rosie thought of it when Danny told her that Alex and Jordan were coming here tonight?"

Jordan shot Rosie a look that said she'd deal with her later.

So much for a nice romantic dinner for two. But she still had high hopes for the after party. Surely, the gang wasn't planning a sleepover at Alex's tonight.

Her thoughts were interrupted when the chef appeared to cook their meal, with the waiter on his heels, carrying another round of drinks. Given her history with alcohol, she'd already decided she would be a teetotaler tonight. She wanted to remember every single detail in the morning. Glancing toward Alex, she wondered if he was thinking the same thing. He'd barely touched his first drink and waved off a second.

She'd waited long enough for some alone time with him, and there was no way she would ruin it by falling asleep before they even made it back to his place.

She jumped as a huge flame ignited in the middle of the cooking surface at the center of their table, and her eyes focused on the onion volcano in front of the chef that had everyone cheering.

For the next twenty minutes, the chef entertained them with culinary skills she'd give up her Ho Hos to have. When they were finally eating the delicious meal, the owner stopped by to introduce himself to Jordan and Michael.

Unlike the last time she'd reviewed a restaurant, Jordan

didn't have to pretend she liked the food. "Honestly, Mr. Tamaki, this was so much fun tonight. And the food was first class. My readers will be flocking here in droves after I mention this."

"And my listeners will be right behind them," Michael added.

For a second, Jordan thought the man was going to tear up, and he bowed several times.

After he left, Danny stretched his legs under the table and pushed his plate away. "I can't eat another bite. It was the best steak I've ever eaten."

"Speaking of steaks," Ray said, leaning around Lola to talk to Danny. "How's your investigation coming along? Catch any cow thieves yet?"

"No, but I will."

"Did you ever figure out how those stolen cows they found in Kansas ended up with a legitimate bill of sale? Can the owner explain how that happened?"

"You know we can't talk about an ongoing case, Ray." Danny chugged what was left of his drink before continuing. "I will tell you this much. The guy still swears he never sold those cows to the rancher. When he investigated further, he had several Wagyu missing from his herd, too. Sooner or later, someone is going to make a big mistake, and we'll send them all to jail where they belong."

"Maybe they already have made a mistake, Danny. Did you ever think of that?" Jordan asked.

He dismissed her comment with an am-I-stupid look, then turned to Alex. "That reminds me. Did you bring the pictures you got off Delaney's computer down at the station?"

Alex pulled out his cell phone and handed it to Jordan, who took a quick peek at the first photo and then did a double take rather than pass the phone to Danny. "Wait, I know him."

Danny scrambled out of his seat and came around to see what she was looking at. "Who is he, sis?"

"I don't know," she said, shaking her head. "He just looks familiar. Alex?"

"He's one of six guys with rap sheets who work at Taylor's Wagyu Ranch."

"What are you talking about?" Ray asked, stretching across the table as he tried in vain to get a look at Alex's phone.

"Sorry, Ray. As much as I'd like to bring you in on this, I can't." Alex retrieved his phone and shoved it back into his pocket. "Well, guys, it's been fun, but I want to have Jordan to myself for a few hours before I hop on that plane in the morning."

"Sandy and I will ride with you."

Jordan turned to her brother and glared. "No, you and Sandy will not ride with us. You came with Ray—you're leaving with him."

Danny narrowed his eyes, then laughed. "Okay, okay. I can take a hint." He turned to Alex. "I don't know when I'll get to see you again, but I hope it's sooner rather than later."

"Me too." Alex shook Danny's hand, then reached for Jordan's. "Come on. We have a lot of good-byes to say." He nudged her toward the door.

Jordan giggled, then scolded herself for acting like a teenager. She was twenty-eight years old, for God's sake. She said good-bye to her friends and made a face at Victor when he whispered in her ear, "The man makes those jeans look like they were made for his tush."

She decided Victor had perfect eyesight when Alex

walked away and she had the opportunity to see for herself.

On the ride to his house, they were strangely quiet, as if neither of them knew what to say.

Finally Alex broke the silence. "I have no idea when I'll see you again."

Jordan took a deep breath, afraid to meet his gaze, afraid she wouldn't be able to hold back her emotions. She didn't know if she loved this man or not, but she was positive she'd never felt this way about anyone else. Not even her love affair with her college sweetheart compared to this, and she'd followed him all over Texas after graduation, fully intending to marry him.

Of course, that was before she found out his intentions were a little different and involved a petite blond weather girl. The gold digger had used him to move up the ladder and then dumped him for the station manager.

She couldn't help but appreciate the poetic justice.

It had always been about Brett back then, and although she still loved him on some level, she'd never felt for him what she felt for Alex.

"What are you thinking about?" Alex asked.

She sniffed, cursing her female hormones. "How much I'm going to miss you." Gulping a few times, she finally trusted her voice. "You scare me and excite me all at the same time."

He threw back his head and laughed. "Welcome to my world, Jordan McAllister. I've faced the worst criminals in the world, seen the most heinous human behavior imaginable, yet in my heart, I know that after tonight, nothing will ever be the same." He glanced her way for a second. "And trust me when I say that scares the hell out of me."

She moved closer, swiping at her eyes. "That's exactly

what I wanted to hear, Moreland. Now, put the pedal to the metal and get me back to your place before I really give you something to fear."

"Yes, ma'am."

Jordan rolled over in bed and reached for Alex. When she came up empty except for the cold sheet, she called his name. Hearing no response, she sat up, noticing the light on in the living room through the slightly ajar door. Swinging her legs over the side of the bed, she reached for the button-down shirt Alex had worn to the restaurant that was now lying in a heap on the floor along with the rest of their clothes.

As soon as she put her arms in the sleeves, the smell of his aftershave, a pleasant, musky scent, wafted up, bringing memories of the last couple of hours. She felt a rush of warmth travel through her body when she opened the door and saw him on the sofa staring at his phone.

As she entered the living room, he glanced up and grinned, patting the sofa next to him. "I don't think I'll ever wear that shirt again without thinking of you."

She sat down beside him, unable to hide the concern she knew must be all over her face. "Is something the matter, Alex? Did you get bad news?"

Outlining her lips with his fingertip, he held her eyes captive, sending chills up her arms. "Nothing like that. I'm just taking a final look at all the information we have on the poisoning, that's all. I hate leaving my doctor friend without anything to go on."

She leaned in and pressed her lips against his. "You're not. If it weren't for you, the police wouldn't have discovered all that monkshood at Karen's greenhouse."

"That was because of you, not me," he interrupted. "I just wish I had a little more evidence for him to go on."

She snuggled closer and looked at the phone where the same photo she'd recognized earlier flashed by in a slide show with several other faces.

"Go back," she shouted, waiting until he came to the picture again. "It's the guy that I said looked familiar at the restaurant. It's killing me that I can't remember where I've seen him before."

"His name is Jake Richards. He hauls cattle for the Taylors." He showed her the rest of the pictures. "These are the only six employees at the ranch who have records."

"Geez! Why would a smart guy like Marcus Taylor hire someone with a record?"

"Everyone deserves a second chance, Jordan. We discovered Marcus himself could have ended up with a different life had it not been for a wealthy cattle owner who saw something good in him and gave him another opportunity."

She huffed. "My money's on a past that included assault and battery. And he's so jealous and control—" She gasped, pointing at his phone. After staring at the phone for several seconds, she was sure.

"What?" he asked, watching her intensely.

"This guy was at the Cattlemen's Ball. I remember noticing his crooked nose and wondering if he was a boxer. He was the one who served our drinks."

CHAPTER 17

Still thinking about the good-bye kiss Alex had given her on his way out the door that morning, Jordan nearly collided with Sandy, who greeted her as soon as she walked into the newsroom.

"I had a great time last night, Jordan. Your friends made me feel so welcomed." She giggled. "Especially Danny."

"Yeah, he's a real gem." Jordan bit her lip to hide a grin. When she'd returned to her apartment before coming to work, there had been no sign of Danny. Either he'd already been out and about, or he'd enjoyed some *dessert* of his own. Considering that his damp towel wasn't littering the bathroom floor as usual, her money was on the latter.

"He's such a sweetheart," Sandy gushed. "Even went out and brought back my favorite doughnuts for breakfast."

Bingo!

As much as she and her brother constantly teased one another, Jordan was glad he had finally hooked up with a girl their mother wouldn't have to scare off with stories about his childhood. Jordan could still remember how mad he'd get at her, but it had worked every time. Sylvia McAllister could run off even the most persistent bad girl.

"Jordan, did you hear me?"

She blinked a few times, willing her mind back to the present. "Sorry. I was thinking about how happy it would make my mother to see Danny with a sweet girl like you. What were you saying?"

"I tried to spend the night at the lake house the other day, and I just couldn't do it."

"Did you hear the knocking again?" In her head, Jordan was already planning another séance, but this time she'd make sure her brother and Victor didn't show up and ruin it.

"No, but my imagination got the best of me, and I couldn't make it to my car fast enough. I was gone by eleven." Sandy swallowed, obviously trying to stop the tears from forming in the corners of her eyes. "I might as well resign myself to the fact that I won't be able to save Grandpa's house."

Jordan patted her arm. "Don't give up so easily. You said there was no pounding. That's a start."

"Not really," the girl said, sniffing. "I usually hear it around two or three in the morning and only on the weekends. But I can't go back out there. What if Lola didn't get rid of the ghosts? What if she only made them angry and they take it out on me?" Her entire body began to shake.

Jordan drew her close. "That's not how ghosts work. They're just ordinary people like you and me who need closure before they can enter the spirit world." She closed her eyes remembering *Poltergeist*. The ghosts in that movie were anything but good spirits.

"I still can't go back." Sandy sighed, pulling away. "I'm

going to call the bank this afternoon and start the paperwork on the foreclosure. No sense delaying the inevitable
any longer. Maybe then I can quit worrying about paying
the back taxes and get on with my life. Let someone else
deal with the ghosts."

"Don't do that yet. Isn't it worth one more try before you
throw in the towel?"

Sandy shook her head. "I wish I were as brave as you,
Jordan, but I'm not."

"What if I spend Friday and Saturday night out there
with you? Together, we'll scare the ghosts away once and
for all."

Sandy's eyes lit up. "You'd do that? You're not afraid?"

Jordan laughed. "Terrified, but we'll team up and send
those poor lost souls back to where they can be at peace.
We can leave directly from work Friday and head out
there." She saw a smidgeon of hope forming in Sandy's
eyes. "It'll be fun. I'll even bring some games, and we can
stop for wings or something on the way out."

Sandy threw her arms around Jordan and squeezed.
"You're such a good friend, Jordan. Gramps has a fishing
boat and several bicycles. The house sits on a cove with a
great bicycle trail, plus I can give you a tour of the lake in
the boat."

"I can't wait," Jordan said, remembering the view of
Lake Texoma from her table facing the water the last time
she ate at Longhorn Prime Rib.

Watching Sandy walk back to her own cubicle, Jordan
concentrated on coming up with a good lie to tell Danny,
so he wouldn't show up this time. Maybe she'd say she was
going to spend the weekend with a friend, and without
naming names, give him the impression that friend was
Brenda Sue Taylor.

She frowned. That idea had one major flaw. Brenda Sue was no longer speaking to her after her house had been ransacked by the police in the middle of the night. Jordan could still hear her usually soft voice shouting obscenities in that cute southern drawl, accusing her of befriending her only so she could spy for her brother.

That wasn't true, of course. The real reason she'd gone out to Brenda Sue's house was to find out about Maria and Diego, but somewhere along the way, Jordan had discovered she actually liked the woman. It was highly unlikely they could ever be friends now. Danny knew that as well since he'd been in the living room when Brenda Sue called and had made no attempt to cover up his overt eavesdropping.

Her thoughts wandered back to Sandy and the upcoming weekend. Jordan really didn't believe in ghosts, but Sandy was so convinced they were there, even thinking about it made Jordan uncomfortable. Despite putting up a brave front for her friend, she was more than a little squeamish about actually spending the night in that house. As always, her mouth had opened before her brain had time to filter her thoughts. She'd popped off about spending the weekend out there with her friend, and now she'd have to go through with it.

But not without liquor.

She decided she'd stop on her way home and pick up a bottle of Baileys just in case they'd depleted Sandy's supply making Almond Balls the last time. The expensive liqueur would put a huge dent in her budget for the month, but it definitely qualified as one of those rainy-day emergencies.

Despite her plan to drink more than her fair share, Jordan had no illusions about getting any sleep out there. She'd run over to Lola's apartment when she got home and borrow one of her bazillion paperback mysteries. On second thought, Jordan decided that might not be such a great idea. She'd better stick to a romance novel.

She still remembered reading Stephen King's *Salem's Lot* one night when she was all alone in her apartment. Not only had she slept with all the lights on, but she'd also clutched a bottle of garlic salt in one hand and her rosary in the other.

The kicker was, she had no idea where the garlic salt had come from, but it was now hidden in a secret place just in case she was ever dumb enough to read another novel that left her staring at the window to make sure blood-sucking vampires didn't come for her.

Blowing out a breath, she concluded the only good thing about spending the weekend at the lake was she'd have the perfect excuse for cutting short her visit with Lucas and Bella on Sunday. Who could argue against her need for sleep after a girlie weekend?

Looking at it that way, a couple of sleepless nights was a small price to pay.

"Why are you packing a bag, Jordan?" Danny asked the next day, popping his head around her bedroom door.

"I'm spending the weekend at Santana Ranch," she lied, hoping he didn't catch the stammer in her voice.

He walked into the room and flopped down on the opposite side of the bed. "An entire weekend with Lucas Santana?" He laughed, shaking his head. "That ain't happening anytime soon. Where are you really going?"

Shoot! She'd have to go to Plan B. That was the problem; there was no Plan B.

"That's none of your business," she said, hoping something would come to her quickly.

"You're going to Sandy's, aren't you?"

She turned her back to him, pretending to rummage in her drawer so he wouldn't see the surprise on her face. When she had recovered, she turned back, throwing her pajamas into the bag and cursing the fact that she was a worse liar then she'd thought. "Why would I go there?"

He slipped off the bed and scrambled around to her side of the room. Spinning her around, he studied her face. "Yep. You suck at lying. That's why you were always the one Mom interrogated when she suspected trouble."

"Okay, I'm going to Sandy's," she blurted. "But you can't come. Really, Danny, it's just going to be Sandy and me."

His eyes widened. "The lake house? You're kidding, right? How in the world are two sissy girls going to fix her ghost problem?"

Jordan huffed. "There's no ghost problem, you nimrod. It's only in Sandy's mind." She shoved her thumb and forefinger in front of his face. "She's this close to letting the bank foreclose on her grandfather's house, and I can't let that happen. At least not without a fight."

"Why can't I come? I want to help, too."

They both turned when they heard the front door open.

"Yoo-hoo. Where is everyone?" Rosie called out.

"We're back here," Jordan hollered, seconds before Rosie swung the bedroom door open and sauntered in.

"What's with the overnight bag?"

"Jordan's going out to the lake with Sandy and won't let us go."

"Us? When did it become plural?"

"Why not, Jordan?" Rosie asked, flopping down next to Danny and jamming the pillow behind her head.

Jordan explained Sandy's dilemma again. "I'm going

out there so she can see there's nothing to be afraid of. We all know there are no such things as ghosts, but she's still jittery."

"Which is why we all ought to go," Rosie said. "We could take our Friday night card game out there and keep her mind off things that go bump in the night."

Danny high-fived Rosie. "Behind that dyed hair and those sexy eyes is one very smart lady." He nailed Jordan with a lost-puppy-dog look. "So what do you say? We could pick up some pizzas and meet the two of you at the *Globe* tomorrow afternoon."

Jordan quit packing, mulling their suggestion around in her head. In all truthfulness, it was probably not a bad idea to have a lot of people around at least until after their card game, when they would head back to Ranchero, leaving her and Sandy alone in the house. Sandy had mentioned Friday was the night she usually heard the pounding, and as much as Jordan didn't want to believe in ghosts, having everyone out there for half the night might be comforting, just in case she was wrong.

"Okay. If Sandy agrees, we'll meet out in the parking lot at five o'clock, and make it crunchy chicken sandwiches instead of a pizza. Wendy's has them on sale for ninety-nine cents this weekend." She closed the suitcase and set it on the floor, praying she wasn't going to regret this decision.

"All right! A road trip, a deck of cards, and plenty of liquor." Rosie paused, wrinkling her eyebrows. "There will be liquor, won't there?"

"I'm picking up a bottle of Baileys, and if you guys bring a couple of six-packs of beer and a few Cokes, we should be good."

"I gotta go tell Victor," Danny said, already halfway to

the front door. "He loves that old magnolia tree in Sandy's front yard."

The next day at work, Jordan glanced at her watch eighty thousand times. Her feelings about the trip to the lake house were extremely muddled. On the one hand, she did not believe in ghosts, so she knew she should have nothing to fear on that score. On the other hand, the house gave her the creeps anyway, although she didn't quite know why. And on the third hand, she was comforted by the thought that there was safety in numbers, even though having the whole gang along for the evening could lead to complications. With these confused musings rattling in her head, Jordan found it hard to focus on her column, but eventually she was able to push them aside and actually do a little newspaper-related work.

She kept busy researching the free translation website for a suitable name for Bella's Baked Steak and Gravy recipe, finally settling on Boeuf Cuit au Jus de Viande. She wondered how much longer she could get away with this charade of posting casserole recipes and slapping fancy names on them.

At five fifteen, she and Sandy couldn't get out the door fast enough to make their way to the parking lot where everyone was waiting in Ray's Suburban. Since she was staying out there until Sunday, Jordan decided to leave her car in the *Globe* parking lot and ride with her friend.

Grabbing a couple of chicken sandwiches from Rosie, they hopped in Sandy's car and started the trek to the lake with the Suburban following close behind. Half an hour later they piled out of both cars and walked up the steps to Sandy's front porch.

Once inside, Sandy turned up the thermostat while Ray and Michael dragged in the folding chairs from the garage and placed them around the kitchen table. Jordan couldn't stop glancing toward the green curtains every few seconds. With everyone here, she wasn't as nervous as she would have been if only she and Sandy had come, but she knew that something as innocent as a sudden movement could set her off. God forbid Danny and Victor tried a repeat of the drapes stunt they'd pulled the night of the séance.

All her misgivings evaporated as soon as the card game got underway, and the laughing and teasing took over. Watching Sandy interact with her friends, Jordan was pleased to see the evening had turned into a kind of a tranquilizer for the girl, decreasing her anxiety—at least for the moment.

At ten thirty when the last drop of Baileys was gone, they called it a night. By eleven everything was cleaned up and put away, and the Empire Apartments gang was on their way back to town. Watching the car roll down the gravel driveway, Jordan glanced quickly toward Sandy, already noticing the signs of panic returning to her face.

"Don't worry about it," she reassured her. "We'll get through this, I promise."

Sandy exhaled loudly, then walked over to her purse and pulled out a bottle. "My doctor prescribed sleeping pills. She didn't want to, but after I explained why I needed them, she agreed to give me enough for two days. That's why I only had one drink tonight." She shook one of the pills into her hand and then handed the bottle to Jordan. "You can use the other one so you'll get a good night's sleep, too."

Jordan laughed. The one and only time she'd taken an over-the-counter sleep aid, she'd been like a zombie the entire next day. "No thanks, I'm good. Save that second one for tomorrow night, although I'm pretty sure you won't need it."

"Suit yourself." Sandy swallowed the pill with a sip of water. "Are you ready for bed?"

"Absolutely. I've had a busy week, and I'm exhausted. I don't think I'll have any trouble getting to sleep."

"I'll stay in Grampa's room, and you can take the full-size bed in the guest bedroom."

"Sounds good." Jordan yawned.

After hugging Sandy, she went to her room and changed into a T-shirt and running shorts. Within minutes she was fast asleep, dreaming of her last night with Alex and totally forgetting the house might be haunted.

Jordan rolled over and pulled the covers up to her neck, shivering. It was freezing in the house.

Then she heard it!

The sound of someone pounding was faint but definitely audible. As the scream bubbled up in her throat, she shot up in the bed, glancing all around the room.

"Whoever you are, go away," she said, her voice almost a whisper.

The pounding stopped.

Slowly, she slid out of bed, eyes darting to all four corners of the room, waiting for the sound to return or for some kind of movement. When there was neither, she yanked off her T-shirt and shorts and quickly redressed in the jeans and sweater she'd worn earlier.

Inhaling deeply, she made her way to the door, then stood there with her hand on the knob for a few minutes before finally summoning enough courage to open it. Half expecting to see the room filled with moving objects and flickering lights like in the movies, she was almost disappointed when it looked exactly as she and Sandy had left it before they'd gone to bed.

The pounding started up again, startling her, and she jerked her hand up to cover her mouth.

There are no such things as ghosts, she repeated to herself over and over as she stood perfectly still, afraid to move.

"Is anyone out there?"

When there was no answer, she made her way to the master bedroom and slowly opened the door, ready to fight off any evil spirits if they were messing with Sandy.

But there were none.

Sandy was snoring softly in her drug-induced slumber, blissfully unaware the pounding had begun. Jordan did a quick sweep of the room to make sure she hadn't missed any white-sheeted guests, then smacked her forehead for being so ignorant.

She decided not to wake her friend, not that she could, anyway. The last thing she wanted was to have Sandy freak out before they could figure out what was going on. Walking back into the living room with a renewed sense of bravado, she was determined to deal with the spirits once and for all.

Listening, she pinpointed the sound as coming from the kitchen. For a split second, the visual of a bunch of ghosts drinking Almond Balls flashed in front of her, and she stifled a giggle.

Get a grip, Jordan, she reprimanded herself.

When she walked into the kitchen, the pounding grew louder. Remembering how Lola had opened the windows to allow the ghosts to float out to wherever the hell ghosts go, Jordan ran to the back door and flung it open, gasping when the night air took her breath away.

"Be gone," she said, just as Lola had at the séance. Then her eye caught a slight movement down at the dock, and all her bravado disappeared. She wrapped her arms across her chest to stop the shaking.

Stepping out onto the back porch, she stared down toward the water. Under the glow of the perfectly round full moon, the dock was outlined as if it were decorated with Christmas lights. She let out a whimper and sucked in a gigantic gulp of air when she realized what had caught her attention was only a white sheet of paper or something blowing around in front of the dock.

Laughing out loud, more in relief than anything else, she concluded the knocking noise must be Sandy's grandfather's boat hitting the side of the dock in the gusting winds. She turned and walked back inside, wrapping her arms around herself to keep out the chill. She was just about to close the door behind her when the pounding returned.

She twirled around, hoping to catch Danny and Victor and read them the riot act for scaring the bejesus out of her, but she froze as the realization hit hard. It wasn't the boat rocking against the dock making the noise.

The pounding was coming from the middle of the lake.

CHAPTER 18

Jordan ran back into the house and locked the door behind her. With shaking hands, she quickly turned off the kitchen light, so no one could see inside. Sliding down to the floor out of sight, she took several calming breaths, trying to slow her racing heart. For a long time she sat there, wondering what to do next.

The good news was that the racket in the middle of the night definitely was not the work of lonely spirits waiting to enter the netherworld. She had no idea what it really was, but that didn't matter. Now she could look her friend in the eye and tell her with confidence the house wasn't haunted.

So why was she still acting like there was a boogeyman out there?

Finally brave enough to stand, she peered out the window at the calm water. When the pounding started again, she quickly slumped to the floor before remembering that whatever was making all that noise was too far away to hurt her.

She'd share her discovery with Sandy in the morning, and after lunch maybe they could take that tour around the lake Sandy had been promising and see for themselves if there was anything bobbing in the water.

On the other hand, she hadn't really discovered anything except that the sound was coming from the lake, and she wasn't even sure about that. Sandy would never believe there was something out there in the water banging into a floating object at the same time every week.

Who would? Jordan shook her head, knowing the only way her friend would ever feel comfortable living in her grandfather's house was if they could pinpoint the exact cause of the noise. According to Sandy, the pounding only occurred at night, and only on Fridays. After thinking of a zillion reasons why she should go back to bed and discuss it with her friend in the morning, Jordan decided, terrified or not, she couldn't wait. She would walk down to the dock and see for herself while it was happening.

Slowly, she stood up again and leaned against the door. She remembered Sandy going to the kitchen for a flashlight earlier when Ray had to run out to the car to get the cards. Rummaging through the drawers, she finally found it and checked to make sure it actually worked. After retrieving her coat from the hall closet, she opened the back door and walked out onto the porch.

The cool night air slapped her in the face, and she breathed in deeply. She could smell the unmistakable odor of rotting leaves and fish. Looking down at the dock, she was relieved to see nothing had changed during the time she'd huddled on the kitchen floor. She had no idea what she'd expected to be different and scolded herself for being so fearful.

Giving herself a quick pep talk, she summoned up the courage to start down the porch steps and made her way to the dock. Halfway there, the pounding stopped, and she came close to hauling her butt back to the house. Knowing this was the only way to help her friend, she forced her feet to keep moving forward.

Close to the dock, she pointed the flashlight beam across the wooden structure, slowly surveying the area. Just as Sandy had said, there was a boat suspended above the water on a lift and a Jet Ski in the next stall, also above the water.

When the pounding started up again, Jordan jerked around and flashed the light toward the center of the water. Lake Texoma was huge, with limited visibility across its expanse, but she was able to determine the noise was coming from the other side of the cove to her left. Though she could see all the way to the shoreline under the glow of the moon, her first glance didn't pick up anything clanging together in the water.

Disappointed, she made another scan of the area. She had to find out something—anything—so Sandy could live out here without the fear of unwanted houseguests.

Making a spur-of-the-moment decision she knew she would probably live to regret—assuming she did live—she turned the switch on the wooden column separating the boat from the Jet Ski. With a loud cranking sound, the lift holding the Jet Ski began to descend. When it was low enough, she jumped on before common sense had time to veto what the crazy side of her brain was already planning to do.

She thought back to her adolescent years when her family

and their friends used to camp on Lake Amarillo in the
Texas summer heat. Someone always brought Jet Skis, and
she remembered how the keys would be stored in the front
compartment. She wondered if Sandy's grandfather had
done the same. With adrenaline racing through her body,
she opened the box below the steering column. A wave
of disappointment, mixed with a flurry of relief, surged
through her.

There was no key.

Leaning back, she closed her eyes. What was she thinking? Even if she could get it started, she'd freeze out there
with the chilly water spray soaking her. Despite her jeans
and jacket, the cold would be unbearable. And what if the
Jet Ski stalled in the middle of the lake? Or worse, what if
there really was something out there waiting for her?

She snorted, thinking Victor wasn't the only melodra-
matic one at the Empire Apartments. What did she think
was out there—the Loch Ness monster?

Sliding off the seat and jumping back on the dock, she
flipped the switch to raise the ski back up, taking one final
look across the water. On her way back to the house, Jordan resigned herself to the fact she might never discover
the source of the pounding. She just hoped the screeching
of the pulleys elevating the Jet Ski hadn't awakened Sandy.
Then she realized that the chance of that happening with
Sandy happily in la-la land, thanks to the sleeping pill, was
about as unlikely as a toddler refusing candy.

As soon as she entered the house, Jordan went straight
to the master bedroom to make sure Sandy was okay. Seeing her friend sound asleep and totally oblivious to her
close encounter with the Lake Texoma Creature, Jordan
began to relax. They'd have a good laugh about all of it in
the morning.

Back in the kitchen, she fixed a cup of hot chocolate, wishing they hadn't polished off the Baileys earlier. Craving a Ho Ho after all her excitement, she accepted that the warm mug of chocolate would have to do. Still shivering from being outside in the cool air, she kept her coat on as she stood by the sink and sipped the drink.

Even with her insides finally warmed from the cocoa, she was still too wound up to sleep. She decided to dig out the romance novel she'd borrowed from Lola. Maybe a little escape from reality with a Highland warrior would settle her nerves. Plopping down on the couch, she opened the book.

Though she tried to concentrate, halfway through the first chapter, she was still thinking about Sandy and the lake house. What a great place this was, now that it no longer gave her the creeps. Situated in an isolated cove, it had everything you needed for fun—the boat for fishing, the Jet Ski for playing on the water, and even bike trails around the cove for exercise.

Holy cow, Jordan! Can't you just sit here and enjoy the stupid book?

Why'd she have to go and start thinking again? Why couldn't she just let it go, knowing things happen for a reason? Maybe if Sandy stayed in town and wasn't reminded of her grandfather at every turn, her grief over his death might not be so traumatic. Maybe this was all for the better.

That was bull and Jordan knew it. Sandy loved this place and might never get over it if she didn't do everything in her power to keep it in the family. Losing her grandfather's legacy was something she would regret for the rest of her life.

Rats!

Jordan laid the book on the end table and bounced up

from the couch. Why did she have to go and think about the bike trail right at this minute? Why couldn't she just give it a rest?

With the little voice in her head reminding her that she was an idiot, she went to the garage door and turned on the light. She spotted the bikes tucked in the far corner and secretly hoped the tires were flat. A closer look verified that the gods were not with her on this one. Both bikes were in pristine condition. Staring at them, she knew what she had to do even though every brain cell in her head screamed for her to go back to the romance novel and the great-looking Scottish guy in a kilt on the cover.

Choosing the newer-looking bicycle, she guided it out the side door of the garage and into the cool night air. She wrapped her scarf around her mouth and nose, thinking, for once, Lucas Santana had done her a favor by giving it to her.

As Jordan made her way to the bicycle trail Sandy had pointed out earlier, her eyes darted from side to side. She'd lived in Texas all her life and knew the critters came out at night to play.

And to hunt.

Peddling at a medium pace and wondering what if anything she would find on the other side of the cove, Jordan breathed in the wonderful aroma of country night air. The path was wide and the moon provided just enough light. Further from the water now, the fish odor wasn't as strong. Even though the leaves had already fallen from the trees, the earthy smell of wet vegetation reminded her of midnight hayrides back in Amarillo with everyone bundled up in heavy blankets.

Times like these made her miss living closer to her family, but not enough to entice her to actually move home.

She had no desire to live her life with the constant meddling of overprotective brothers.

The loud chirping of the crickets along with the sporadic call of a hoot owl worked like a Ho Ho, calming her nerves and strengthening her determination to resolve this noise thing once and for all. More than likely, she'd find a farmer with sleep issues on the other side of the cove using this time for handyman chores or something equally innocuous.

Or was that wishful thinking?

When she lifted her face to the sky, enjoying the way the wind blew her hair and tickled her ears, her scarf slipped down around her neck. Touching the silky brownish red fabric, she decided Santana must've spent a small fortune on it. She could still picture the anger on Bella's face when the old man had blurted out that he'd bought it because of Jordan's red hair and bedroom eyes.

Bedroom eyes, my butt! Neither her eyes nor the rest of her would ever be anywhere near Santana's bedroom. Once again Jordan wondered why a woman who looked like Bella stayed with a man like Lucas Santana.

Was she hoping to get her hands on his money? Lucas had never mentioned any family. Maybe Bella was biding her time, waiting to recoup the losses of basically wasting her twenties to play nursemaid to a pervert like Lucas all these years.

Bella had mentioned she'd been twenty-four when Lucas had nearly lost his leg. She'd been his nurse at the hospital, and when he was discharged, he'd insisted he would make it worth her while if she'd come home and take care of him. Worth her while must've cost him a pretty penny, and now, some ten years later, Jordan wondered if

Bella still thought the benefits of life with Lucas out-weighed the sacrifices.

Or maybe Bella really did love the old guy. Santana's wife had still been alive when Bella moved in. She had probably turned a blind eye to her husband's outrageous behavior back then just as Bella did now. She'd bet money on it, convinced she would never truly understand the rules of attraction.

Her attention was diverted as an armadillo crossed the bike trail ahead followed by four younger ones. She braked and watched as the little animals hurried to catch up with their mama. Knowing armadillos always gave birth to four identical babies of the same sex, Jordan wondered if these were girls or boys. Another oddity she didn't understand.

When they were safely across the trail, she began pedaling and nearly crashed as the pounding started up again. But it wasn't a soft sound muffled by the lake now. This was a loud and unmistakable thump every few seconds.

And whatever it was, it was right around the bend.

She wanted to turn back but couldn't. For Sandy's sake, she had to find a rational explanation for the noise. Jordan prayed whatever was around the corner fit that category.

Rounding the curve, she saw what looked like stadium lights in the distance, off the main road about a hundred yards from her. She approached the turnoff to get there and saw headlights coming directly toward her from the opposite direction.

Gasping, she quickly moved into the shadows of the thick underbrush at the side of the road. As the headlights drew closer, she decided the smart thing to do was to stay hidden. Moving deeper into the brush, she could only hope there weren't any animals nearby who might be thinking a redheaded Irish girl sounded delicious.

With the full moon shining above, Jordan was able to identify the vehicle as a dark-colored pickup. When it slowed to turn down the gravel road toward the tall lights, she caught a glimpse of the driver, and she bit her lip to keep from screaming out in surprise.

What in the world was Cooper Harrison doing out here in the boonies? Watching the pickup stir up dirt and gravel as it raced toward the lights, she covered her mouth to stifle the cough from the dust.

And why was he hauling a cattle trailer?

She pulled out her cell phone to call Danny, then suddenly closed it. What would she say to her brother? "Hey, Danny, I know it's two in the morning, but I just saw Cooper hauling a cattle trailer." In this neck of the woods nearly every pickup had a trailer hitch and hauled either boats or animals. Maybe there was a horse in the trailer behind Cooper's truck.

She pocketed the phone, thinking there was no way she was going to give her brother that kind of ammunition. She'd have to listen to Danny whine about being awakened for at least a week or two, all because Cooper wanted to ride his stallion in the middle of the night.

Okay, maybe that was a little far-fetched, but Jordan couldn't think of any other logical explanation for Cooper's being here, now. Letting her curiosity get the best of her, she wheeled the bike out of the bushes and followed Cooper down the road. Once again, the pounding abruptly ceased, jacking up her anxiety level another notch.

Ten minutes later, she pedaled into a medium-size parking lot with a large warehouselike building on the right. She spotted Cooper's navy truck parked close to what looked like a loading ramp. Taking a deep breath, she was instantly sorry because the smell nearly wiped her out.

Glancing at the sign that read NORTH TEXAS BEEF DIS-TRIBUTORS, she realized why.

This was Carole Anne's company where they processed and packaged beef.

She jumped when she saw Cooper and another man appear at the back of the trailer. Scrambling off to hide behind a tree, she hoped they hadn't seen her.

Cooper opened the back of the trailer, and the other guy walked up the ramp and disappeared inside. A moment later, he reappeared, leading a cow down the ramp. Cooper hopped up into the trailer, and after a few minutes, he came out, leading another animal. Safely hidden in the shadows, Jordan was mesmerized as the two men led the cows around the side of the building and out of sight.

Cooper offloading cows at a meatpacking plant in the middle of the night could mean only one thing. Since he didn't raise cattle himself, and he certainly didn't need to moonlight for extra cash, Jordan realized she was probably witnessing Cooper and the other man in the midst of cattle rustling.

Though stunned, she didn't hesitate. With shaking hands, she reached for her cell phone to call her brother. He could inform the local police and have them out here in thirty minutes or less.

Crap! There were no signal bars on her phone.

Praying that Cooper and his friend were still on the side of the building, she hopped off the bike and held her hand out as far as she dared without exposing herself.

Still no signal.

She knew she should hightail it back to Sandy's house and use the landline to call Danny, but her curiosity and the urgency of the situation beat out her better sense. She had to find out what they were doing before they climbed back into the truck and disappeared. If the operation was as slick as Danny and Alex had insinuated, there was a good chance there would be no physical evidence to incriminate Cooper by the time the cops made it out this way.

It took all of two seconds for Jordan to make a decision she hoped wouldn't be her last one. She had to get pictures so that it wouldn't matter how much Cooper denied being there. She'd have the evidence that proved he was a liar, and it would no longer be her word against his.

Cursing the full moon she'd been grateful for up until now, Jordan scrambled from her safe spot and took off in a dead run toward the pickup before she lost her courage. The closer she got to the truck the more unbearable the stench became, and she pulled the scarf over her nose. Stopping every few steps to make sure she hadn't been spotted, she was prepared to bolt if necessary. If what she suspected was true, the critters hiding in the dark were probably a whole lot less dangerous than the criminals who'd arrived in the truck.

When she'd made it to the pickup without setting off some major alarm, she slowed to catch her breath. Glancing up, she noticed security cameras on several of the steel poles in the lot and wondered if someone was watching her every move—waiting for her to get close enough so that escape would be impossible.

Puffing out white smoky breaths into the nippy Texas air, she knew she had to take that chance if she was going to get a photo of Cooper in the act. Besides, if they were watching her, wouldn't they have already sent someone out to intercept her?

Finally, she talked herself into moving away from the truck and toward where Cooper and his friend had taken the cows. She heard his voice as soon as she got close to the corner of the building, and then there was silence. She inched closer and spied the cows in a large pen, but there was no sign of Cooper or the other guy.

Taking a few steps forward, she was careful to stay in the shadows in case they suddenly reappeared. When she was almost to the pen, she realized they must have gone into the packing plant through a side door. Moving to a window, she took a quick peek.

The large room was empty except for several rows of hanging carcasses off to the left. She figured Cooper and his friend must have gone into a room in the back. Pulling up the scarf to cover more of her nose, she turned back to the pen and snapped several pictures of the cows.

Satisfied she had enough, she decided to head back to the front to hide out in the shadows again and wait for Cooper to come out. That way she could catch him before he got back into his truck. As she turned away, her scarf caught on a nail sticking out from the side of the window and ripped.

Crap!

She'd just found the perfect place to snap a shot of the rustlers that would include the NORTH TEXAS BEEF DISTRIBUTORS sign above the door when she heard the distinct sound of a gunshot, followed by another.

Swallowing a scream, she turned and ran as fast as she could back to the tree where she'd hidden the bike. When her scarf blew off halfway there, she was too frightened to stop and pick it up. Glancing over her shoulder, she saw Cooper running from the building and heading for his truck. For a split second their eyes met.

Out of breath, she collapsed in the bushes next to the bike, feeling like her heart was about to thump out of her chest. When her hands finally stopped shaking, she climbed onto the bike and made a mad dash in the opposite direction of Cooper's pickup, which was now rumbling down the main road, kicking up dirt and gravel.

Taking a quick glimpse back, she watched the truck's tail lights disappear down the road, and then she pedaled like there really was someone chasing her. She had to get back to Sandy's before Cooper decided she'd seen too much.

She shivered just thinking about that. Had she really seen anything worth silencing her over? Was it possible Rusty had stumbled onto this and was killed because he, too, had seen too much? What if the gunfire was standard operating procedure in places like this where the meat was processed in the dead of night and Cooper was running because he was simply in a hurry to get out of there?

If so, then why had he driven away like he'd actually seen the Loch Ness monster?

CHAPTER 19

By the time she reached Sandy's house, Jordan was out of breath, and her nose was so cold she could barely feel it. Guiding the bike back through the side door of the garage, she put it in the corner next to the other one, then raced into the house to see if her cell phone worked.

There were two bars.

She quickly dialed Danny's number, glancing up at the ornate fish-shaped clock on the wall. It was almost three. After five rings, he finally picked up.

"Danny, you have to come to Sandy's house now. I saw Cooper with stolen cows, and then I heard gunshots." She stopped to take a breath.

"Jordan? What the hell are you doing calling me at three in the morning?"

"Didn't you hear what I just said?" She flopped down on the couch and grabbed the blanket from the back of the sofa, wrapping it around her legs.

"I don't hear so good when you babble on like that. What's so freaking important that it couldn't wait till— say, ten?"

Jordan repeated the information.

"First, how do you know the cows were stolen?"

She heard excitement creeping into Danny's voice as the information finally registered. She pictured him jumping up from the couch and reaching for his jeans.

"Ouch! Hold on. My foot got caught in my pants and I darn near wiped myself out." A minute later he began again. "Are you and Sandy safe, or do I need to call the Texoma security patrol and have them get over there ASAP?"

"We're safe right now," Jordan said, popping up to recheck the locks on all the doors just in case. "I can't be sure, but I think Cooper may have seen me."

"Jesus! Make sure the doors are locked. I should be there in about thirty-five or forty minutes with the Ranchero cops. They have jurisdiction in that cove."

Jordan hung up and slumped back onto the couch. It didn't make any sense to wake up Sandy until the last minute, and even then, it was probably not going to be easy.

What a waste of a good sleeping pill! Jordan thought, tapping her foot on the carpet while she waited.

She reached for the romance novel on the end table, but after five minutes of staring at the same word, she decided it was a losing battle. If only she'd thought to bring a crossword puzzle to occupy her mind, but then, she sucked at those kinds of things, anyway.

The earlier scene kept playing over and over in her mind. She wanted to believe there was a logical reason for Cooper to be hauling cattle to a processing plant at this time of night.

One that didn't involve theft and possibly murder.

She straightened up when a more ominous thought occurred to her. Cooper had been alone when he'd run from the building and driven away. What happened to the man who had arrived with him? Had he been on the other end of a bullet? For a second, a flash of guilt creeped over her. She should have stayed to find out if anyone needed help, especially after she saw Cooper leave.

But she'd been too frightened, and she wasn't totally convinced the gunfire meant someone was even hurt. What if she'd walked into the plant right in the middle of a crime going down? Just thinking about it made her shudder.

No, she'd done the only thing she could: hauled butt and called her brother. It was comforting to know he was on his way.

Her thoughts wandered back to Cooper. Given the very real possibility he had just killed his partner in the cattle-rustling ring, his involvement in Rusty's death was looking more and more probable. He'd been close enough to Rusty at the Cattlemen's Ball to slip him the poison.

When she'd first suspected he might be Rusty's killer, she'd assumed the motive had been Carole Anne. Cooper had flirted with Jordan outrageously that night, yet she remembered the way his nostrils flared and his eyes flashed anger every time Carole Anne looked Rusty's way, though he'd pretended not to notice. Now it seemed there might be a less passionate reason for murder than the proverbial green monster.

Money could make the most honest of men do strange things. Maybe Cooper wanted to be the one calling the shots and decided to take matters into his own hands.

Deep in thought, Jordan nearly jumped out of her skin

when Sandy appeared in the doorway, wiping the sleep from her eyes.

"Why are you still up?"

"I don't have time to explain," Jordan said, wishing her nerves would quit acting like hamsters on speed. "Get dressed, Sandy. Danny and the cops will be here any minute."

Sandy's eyes widened. "The cops?"

"Hurry, there's not much time before they arrive. I'll fill you in after you change clothes."

Before Sandy finished dressing and came back into the living room, Jordan heard the wail of sirens nearby. She raced to the window and peered out from behind the thick green curtains just as Danny's car pulled into the gravel driveway. Rushing to the door, she flung it open and waited while her brother climbed out of the car. Two police cruisers pulled up behind him, their sirens still blaring.

She waited at the door, and as Danny and four Ranchero police officers entered, she recognized two of them from a few months earlier when her apartment had been ransacked.

"Tell us the whole story, Jordan," Danny prompted, sitting down next to Sandy, who still looked half-asleep.

Jordan recapped the events of the night.

"And you say this all took place at the North Texas Beef Distributors plant across the cove?"

"Yes," Jordan said, turning to Sandy, who seemed instantly alert. "That's probably what you hear every Friday night. They were processing the beef in the wee hours."

Her face lit up as tears formed in her eyes. "You mean it isn't ghosts?"

"It's definitely not ghosts. Now you can move back out here without worrying."

Sandy grabbed Jordan and squeezed. "Thank heavens, it's finally over."

"Okay, let's get on over that way and take a look," the policeman Jordan remembered as Officer Rutherford said. His demeanor left no doubt he was in charge. "I had the captain wake up a judge who lives a few miles from here. I've sent a uniform over there to get the signed warrant, and he'll meet us at the meatpacking plant."

"Stay here," Danny said to the two women. "This may take a while, but I'll come back afterward to let you know what we found." He focused on his sister. "You should probably pack your bag and come back into town with me, Jordan. There'll be a lot of questions for you once we sort out what's going on."

"I'm coming, too," Sandy said matter-of-factly. "No way I'm staying out here by myself."

"Good idea," Danny said, reaching into his jacket for something.

Jordan's mouth dropped when she saw the shoulder holster. "Since when do you carry a gun?"

"I've always had it, but I keep it hidden. Knowing you the way I do, I figured you might shoot me if you knew where it was." He opened the front door. "Let's go, guys. Make sure everyone's wearing a vest. Unless my sister's hallucinating, there's been recent gunfire over there."

Jordan locked the door behind the departing officers, and both she and Sandy packed their bags. Then there was nothing left to do but wait.

"Want to watch a little TV?" Sandy asked. "We have satellite out here, and I'm sure we can find something we both like."

"First, I need another hot chocolate. My insides feel like they're frozen."

Huddled together under a blanket watching an old *Charlie's Angels* rerun, Sandy fell asleep again. As tired as she was, Jordan knew sleep would not come that easily for her.

Not until her brother was safely back in Sandy's house.

Jordan heard the sirens a good five minutes before she saw two ambulances fly past the house on the way to the other side of the cove. She said a quick prayer that no one was seriously hurt, but two speeding ambulances wasn't a good sign.

She must have nodded off finally and woke up shortly before hearing the emergency vehicles again. A check of the clock told her Danny and the police officers had been gone for about forty-five minutes.

She was going crazy wondering what was happening over there, worrying that Cooper's partner in crime had been shot. She'd never been a patient woman, and tonight was no different. By the time she heard a car approaching, she'd nearly walked a bald circle in the living room carpet.

When Danny finally walked in, she pounced. "Was anybody hurt?"

Danny glanced toward Sandy, snuggled in the blanket, blissfully unaware of her surroundings. "Is she okay?"

After Jordan reassured him she was only sleeping off a sedative, he continued. "That's good. Hey, it's frickin' freezing out there. Got any coffee?"

Knowing she'd get no information until he warmed up, she pointed to the kitchen. "All she has that's hot is cocoa."

"Perfect." He nudged her toward the kitchen. "Come on. I'll tell you what went down while you're fixing it."

Jordan reached for a cup, filled it with tap water, and

then put it in the microwave before turning back to her brother. "You're killing me, Danny. If you don't start talking, I swear I'm going to wring your neck."

His eyes flashed their signature mischievous glare before he obviously decided it wasn't the time or the place to verbally spar with her. "A man we identified as Johnny Lorenzo was lying in front of the doorway with a bullet in the back of his neck. We think he was trying to get away when he was shot."

"Oh no!" Jordan said, taking the hot water out of the microwave and adding the chocolate mix. She was afraid to ask the next question but was unable to stop herself. "If I had gone back, could I have saved him?"

"According to the Grayson County ME, who, lucky for us, lives only about fifteen minutes away, the bullet probably severed the man's brain stem. So, no, nothing would have helped him."

Jordan released a long sigh of relief. She wouldn't have been able to live with herself if she thought the man was dead because of her inaction.

"I think you should sit down, Jordan."

The relief of not being responsible for a man's death quickly vanished, and a burst of panic raced through her body. "Why?"

Danny led her to the kitchen table and waited until she was seated. "There was another body there."

She gasped. Two shots—two kills. She wasn't sure she wanted to know who the other victim was but had to ask, anyway. "Who was it?"

"Diego Morales."

Her heart sank, tears welling in the corners of her eyes. "Oh my Lord, what will Maria do now?"

"I knew you would be upset. The preliminary exam shows they were probably both shot with the same gun, a forty-five, but we'll have to wait for ballistics to confirm it."

"Diego was the night watchman," she said, wondering why she hadn't remembered that before. She recalled hearing Lucas Santana talk about how stupid Diego had been to walk away from his job at Santana Circle Ranch and take the lower-paying job at the meatpacking plant.

"That may be true, but working security wasn't the only thing he did out there—at least not tonight. He was processing beef when he was killed and was still wearing his bloody apron."

"Maybe that was part of his job," Jordan said, more concerned with what would happen to Maria now that both Diego and Rusty were gone.

"We checked with the owner. Diego's only job was making sure the premises were secure on the weekends."

"You spoke to Carole Anne?"

"Her dad. He has no idea why Diego was cutting up meat."

"Do you?"

Danny rubbed his chin, his eyes thoughtful. "I have a theory, and if I'm right, it would explain why the cattle rustlers have been so hard to catch. I knew someone would slip up and give me the break I needed to solve this case."

Jordan thought it through but was unable to follow his reasoning.

Danny leaned forward, his eyes animated with the possibility he might have a positive lead. "I'm thinking Cooper and the dead guy stole the cattle last night and took them directly to the packing plant where Diego was waiting to process the beef. By the time anyone could figure out they were missing livestock, the meat would already be wrapped in white butcher paper and hidden away in Cooper's secret meat locker."

Jordan nodded. "That's actually very clever, but that means Carole Anne and her father must be in on it, too."

"Not necessarily," Danny said, shaking his head. "What if Cooper was using the beef exclusively for his barbecue business? That would certainly save on operating costs and line his pockets with extra cash." He paused. "And it might explain why the food is so good at Beef Daddy's. The livestock we found in the pen outside the plant were Wagyu cows." .

A flashback to the night Cooper had invited them all to his warehouse after he'd treated them to a free meal at his restaurant brought some clarity to the whole theory. Excited, she asked, "Remember when we were at Cooper's warehouse for dessert and he nearly mauled me in his private office?"

"Yeah, but I still think you overreacted."

"Maybe so, but I remember his office being in the back of a smaller refrigerated room." She made a gun with her finger and pointed it at him. "And while I was overreacting, I noticed the room was filled with nothing but packaged Wagyu beef."

Danny chuckled. "I think I love you, sis. My guess is Cooper either stole them from Marcus Taylor, or old Marcus and his southern belle wife, Brenda Sue, are up to their necks in a scam to double dip on profits from their stock."

"By getting a kickback for the cows and then filing insurance claims saying they were stolen?" Jordan slammed her hand on the desk, and both of them turned when Sandy mumbled something.

Satisfied her friend was still asleep, Jordan continued,

but this time in a much softer voice. "I suggested that after they found those cows up in Kansas with a legitimate bill of sale. You pooh-poohed me, remember?"

He had the good sense to look sheepish under her glare. "Okay, maybe I was wrong. Either way, I'll definitely be having another talk with the Taylors tomorrow to test out my—your—theory and see their reaction. And there's an APB out on Cooper. I'm betting he can be persuaded to shed some light on all this."

Jordan was unable to bask in the compliment because of the sadness that suddenly gripped her. "Brenda Sue was practically raised by Diego and Maria Morales. There's no way she could have been involved in his death."

"What if she didn't know he was going to be murdered? What if Diego and Cooper got into an argument over something and cooler heads didn't prevail? Or what if Cooper was hell-bent on claiming the number one spot in the rustling ring and eliminated the competition? That might explain Rusty's death, too."

Jordan shook her head. "You might be jumping the gun here, Danny. You don't even know for sure that Rusty was involved in the theft ring."

"No, but I promise I'm going to find out. This latest lead is too good not to yield results. I hate to say this, kiddo, but you may have given me just what I need to show my bosses I know what I'm doing."

"Not on purpose," she teased.

"Who cares that you stumbled onto this because you're forever sticking your nose into other people's business?" When she frowned, he added, "Just kidding. If this pans out, I'll owe you one."

"What about the security camera I saw? Were you able to identity Cooper on it?"

"The tape was gone along with the murder weapon."

"So now you think Cooper might've killed Rusty, too? What about the Taylors? The last I heard you were leaning toward Marcus as the perp."

Danny laughed out loud. "Just because I said you might be right about this one little thing, don't go trying to impress me with your Dirty Harry lingo." His face turned serious. "It wouldn't surprise me in the least if we find out Cooper and Taylor were in cahoots for whatever reason. A couple of uniforms are knocking on Cooper's door as we speak, and my guess is, he'll open up like a yellow rose under the hot Texas sun."

The flower analogy reminded Jordan of Karen's greenhouse and the monkshood. "Did you ever talk to the waiter who served our drinks at the Cattlemen's Ball?"

Danny stared, confusion on his face. "I thought I told you about him."

"No, you didn't. Were you able to link him to the poison that killed Rusty?"

"He wasn't in his apartment when we served the warrant, but we found a vial of white powder that tested out as aconite. We're pretty confident he was the one who slipped it into Rusty's drink. We just don't know why."

"He won't talk?"

"He can't," Danny said, finishing his drink and carrying the cup to the sink before turning back to face her. "That's another thing I forgot to tell you. They found his body in an isolated wooded area close to the Oklahoma border last night."

CHAPTER 20

After lowering the thermostat and closing up the house, Danny had insisted Jordan drive Sandy's car home since she was still so groggy from the sleeping pill. He followed in his own car. Five miles down the road, Sandy had already fallen back asleep, and Jordan was left with only her own thoughts to keep her awake.

Danny had mentioned before they'd left the lake house that he'd made plans with Officer Rutherford to meet at Taylor's ranch around ten fifteen that morning. Jordan was already anticipating another call from Brenda Sue later in the day to ream her out again.

Staring out the window at nothing in particular, Jordan couldn't stop thinking about Maria Morales. She'd assumed the older woman's fear had been for her own safety, but now she wondered if Maria had sensed Diego was in danger.

But why tell me? Did she think I could make it go away?

Jordan had no idea how expensive home health care had become now that Rusty was no longer around to help with the cost, but she guessed it was not easy making ends meet without the extra cash. With his lower-paying job at the meat-processing plant, Diego had probably had to supplement his income with a little butchering on the side. But he had to have suspected something was illegal about the whole operation. Why else would Cooper and his friend show up on Friday nights with cows and ask a night watchman to process them?

Thinking about Cooper, Jordan wondered if he'd recognized her when their eyes met for a brief moment as they were both running away from the gunshots. Although it had been dark, the moon had illuminated the parking lot enough so she had identified him, and common sense told her he must have ID'd her, too.

She shivered thinking about it, remembering how uncomfortable she'd felt around him even before she knew he was a thief—and possibly a killer!

A million questions ran through her mind. What if being top dog in the theft ring hadn't been the motive, and Rusty had really been killed because he couldn't keep it in his pants? What if the waiter that night secretly had a thing for Brenda Sue? He did work at the Taylors' ranch and may have been tired of watching Brenda Sue throw herself at Rusty.

Or maybe he just hated Rusty because he seemed to have it all. She figured they'd never know since the waiter was now on a slab at the county morgue.

Jordan was still thinking about that after she'd parked Sandy's car and made sure Sandy was safely inside her apartment. She hurried to Danny's pickup and climbed in.

They were almost to the city limits when Danny finally broke the silence.

"What are you frowning about?"

"Was I frowning?" When he nodded, she shrugged. "I was thinking about the waiter. What if he had no connection to the cattle rustling?"

Danny pulled the car behind the Empire Apartments and slid into one of the empty spots. After he opened the door and got out, she followed suit, waiting beside the car for his reply.

"What other motive could he possibly have?" he finally asked after giving it a lot of thought.

Again she shrugged. "I don't know. Jealousy? Hatred, maybe?"

"Whoa! What's going on under that mop of red hair, Jordan? How did you come up with that?"

"Brenda Sue still loved Rusty. I saw it the minute she touched his arm that night. What if she and the waiter had a thing, too?"

"Guess that could be a reason, but my money's still on him being just a hired gun—or in this case, a hired poisoner."

Jordan smirked. "That's not even a word, but you're probably right. It seems a logical choice that Marcus Taylor was the one writing the check."

They'd just started across the parking lot to the apartment building when a slight movement to her left caught Jordan's eye, and she shrieked, grabbing Danny's arm.

"Sheesh! You're going to give me a heart attack." He pointed to a calico cat making its way from the garbage cans to the alley behind the building. "Although I have to admit that is one ferocious-looking kitty."

"Shut up." She gave him a shove, wishing she wasn't so jittery. "Guess my nerves are shot."

"You should be reveling in all the good you did today. First, you solved the mysterious pounding thing at the lake house, and because of you, Sandy will be able to keep the house out of foreclosure. Plus, you handed me the biggest lead yet in my investigation." He playfully punched her shoulder. "I should have this wrapped up by the end of the week and be on my way back to Amarillo by next weekend."

"I *will* miss you, you know."

He laughed. "Yes, you will, but don't bust out the champagne just yet. I suspect you'll be seeing a lot more of me in the next couple of months."

She crossed her arms and arched an eyebrow as his meaning sunk in. "Danny McAllister, are you saying you might be falling for Sandy?"

"Oh, hell no. Don't go getting crazy on me, Jordan. I like Sandy, and I wouldn't mind exploring the possibilities, but that's all." He unlocked the door and allowed her to walk into the apartment ahead him.

"I think she'd like that," Jordan said, turning to plant a quick kiss on his cheek. She didn't recognize this man who opened doors for her and talked about a woman without saying he'd like to serve her breakfast in bed. But she liked the new persona. "I can barely hold my eyes open. I'll see you in a few hours." She made her way to the bedroom.

As tired as she was, she couldn't stop replaying the events of the past twelve hours. They were missing something. She had no idea what, but since everyone seemed to be dying, there was a good possibility they would never find out what it might be.

Before she fell asleep, she thought she heard her cell

phone ring, but when she got up to check it, there was no missed-call message. She figured her nerves must still be on overdrive.

Just when she'd thought she'd worked past the jitters, a scary feeling settled over her as another thought crossed her mind. She'd seen Cooper running away from the two murders at the beef-distributing plant earlier, and he was still out there.

Was he looking for her? Did he even know she was there when the shots were fired?

For the second time that night, Jordan was thankful for her brother, who was asleep on the couch with a Glock under his pillow.

Danny had already left the apartment by the time Jordan woke up. With only four hours of sleep, she decided to put a late afternoon nap on the day's agenda. Since she'd planned on spending her Saturday on Lake Texoma with Sandy and sleeping over one more night, she now had nothing scheduled for the day.

Polishing off a quick Strawberry Milkshake Pop-Tart, she picked up the phone and dialed Bella, proud that she'd gotten part of her daily requirement of both milk and fruit.

Bella picked up on the fourth ring, and without bothering to say hello, began to speak. "Have you heard the news?"

"Danny told me." Jordan stopped before mentioning she'd actually been there when it happened. Bella would find out sooner or later and have a million questions. Right now she wasn't in the mood to relive the terror of the night before.

"The police left a few hours ago. They think Diego

might have been involved with the cattle theft. And they said Cooper was definitely involved. Do you believe that?"

Jordan hedged. "I only know what Danny told me. I guess we'll learn more soon enough, but that's not the reason I'm calling."

"Is something the matter?"

"I'm worried about Maria. Do you know what's going to happen to her now?"

Jordan heard Bella sigh. "The poor woman is beside herself, as you can imagine. I went over there as soon as I heard and helped the night nurse pack her things."

"Pack her things? Where's she going?"

"Since the only family she has left is an elderly aunt in Mexico, social services took over. With no one to care for her, they moved her to a nursing home in Connor early this morning. She'll be there for a few days until they can arrange around-the-clock care for her at home or a place at an assisted living facility that allows wheelchair patients. I'm heading over there as soon as I make sure Lucas is okay."

"What's the matter with Lucas?"

"Nothing to worry about. The last few days he's been really fatigued, and his blood pressure's up. He says he can feel his heart pounding in his chest and his ears. The doctor upped his beta blockers, but if he isn't feeling any better by tomorrow, I'm going to drag him into Connor to see the cardiologist so they can make sure his blood thinners don't need to be adjusted."

"Let me know if there's anything I can do." Jordan hoped the impatience in her voice didn't travel across telephone wires. It wasn't that she was heartless. It was just that right now she was more concerned about Diego's widow. "So where did they take Maria? I'd like to go see her, too. She must be hurting and feeling so alone right now."

"I didn't realize you knew her that well. Hold on while I get that information." After a moment Bella returned. "She's at the Connor Center for Continuing Care off Texas Parkway. When are you planning to visit?"

"Probably tomorrow," Jordan answered quickly before remembering her mandatory luncheon with Bella and Lucas.

After a brief silence, Bella replied, "It might not be a bad idea to cancel your visit tomorrow with Lucas feeling so weak. He'll be disappointed he won't get to see you, though."

"Maybe I'll drive out that way to say hello after I run over to Connor." Jordan crossed her fingers, hoping God wasn't keeping track of her lies. She had no intention of swinging by to see Lucas if she didn't have to.

"He'd like that," Bella said. "He thinks a lot of you."

Jordan was absolutely positive she detected a hint of frostiness in Bella's voice despite the cheery delivery. Maybe the woman was finally tired of the old man's antics with other women.

Good for her.

Jordan glanced up just as Danny sauntered into the apartment, looking like he hadn't seen a bed in days. The cowlick he fought every morning had definitely won out over his hair products today.

Without a word, she muted the TV and walked to the kitchen to fix him a cup of coffee.

Slumping down on the couch beside him, she handed him the cup, careful not to spill it. "What'd you find out at

the Taylors'? Did Marcus admit to hiring the waiter? What
was his name again?"

"Jake Richards, and no, neither Marcus nor Brenda Sue
knew the guy very well, or so they said. Seems all the hiring at the ranch is done by David Whitley, the husband of
the woman who has the greenhouse out back. Whitley
oversees the ranch for the Taylors. He hired Richards, your
fake waiter, about a year and a half ago."

She snapped to attention. "How convenient that his wife
just happens to grow and sell the exact powder that was
used in the killing. Does David Whitley have a motive for
wanting Rusty dead like it seems the whole rest of the
world did?"

"None we could find. We talked to his wife alone to feel
her out—see if maybe there was something going on with
her and Morales since he seemed to be irresistible to every
woman who laid eyes on him."

Jordan harrumphed, thinking there was a real possibility her name might have been added to Rusty's list of con-
quests if she'd been able to get to know him better. The
man had definitely been eye candy and could probably
charm the pants off a nun.

"Anyway," Danny continued, "the only thing we got
from Karen Whitley is that she had a complaint from one
of her regular customers last month. Seems an order of
aconite was shorted by one container. Karen said she had
no idea how that could have happened since she packs the
powder herself and personally carries it to the post office to
ship to the pharmaceutical companies."

"Who else had access to the poison before it shipped?"

"That's the interesting part. Karen is really the only
one who deals with the stuff, except for the workers who
help her process it. I had Rutherford send a couple of

black-and-whites out there to interview them, but most can't even speak English and wouldn't have been at the hotel where Rusty was killed."

"That's true, but they could have stolen it for someone more than willing to pay a pretty penny for it," Jordan interrupted.

"A definite possibility. Hopefully, they can rule that out when they get them in a room alone. Here's another tidbit to add to the puzzle. When I asked Karen if she ever strayed from her normal routine with the aconite, I was not surprised by her answer. At first she said no, and then she remembered being interrupted about a month ago right in the middle of packaging the powder. Seems she heard her dog barking frantically and thought maybe a pack of coyotes had him cornered. So she grabbed a shovel and ran out to see what all the commotion was about."

"So either Brenda Sue or Marcus could have sneaked into the greenhouse and lifted just enough poison to do the job."

"Or maybe it was Jake Richards," Danny said. "Karen said she found her dog stuck in the shed. Somehow the door had jammed, and the poor guy was howling bloody murder. At the time, she didn't think it was strange and had assumed the stupid mutt had trapped himself. You know how Labs are. They're wonderful dogs, but they sometimes eat their own poop."

"By itself, the dog getting stuck in the shed would just be a funny incident, but when you factor in the possible missing poison from her shipment, it's too much of a coincidence to overlook. Did Karen see anyone hanging around the greenhouse when she returned?"

"My thoughts exactly, and no, she didn't see anyone. When I questioned her about whether Richards had access to her greenhouse, she confessed she didn't keep it locked during the day. Anyone could have lured the dog into the shed and then trapped him there while they waited for Karen to rush out and rescue him."

"When did this happen again?"

Danny flipped open his notebook. "The middle of last month."

"That means if the killer stole her drugs that day, he had about three weeks to figure out how to slip it to Rusty." Jordan shook her head, grateful she wasn't the one investigating the murder. It was turning out to be a lot more complicated than she'd imagined.

"Assuming she hadn't just screwed up the order and shorted the customer—maybe all this had nothing to do with Jake Richards serving drinks at the Cattlemen's Ball. We're still not even sure that's how Rusty was poisoned. It might all be a big coincidence that Richards was even at the hotel on the night Rusty died."

She tsked. "There's that coincidence again. I don't believe in them."

"Neither do I. That's why I had the department send over Richards's phone records so I could go over them with a fine-tooth comb."

Jordan stiffened. "And?"

"And there were several calls made to Rusty's home phone over the past two months. One as recent as the night before he died."

"But why would Richards be talking to Rusty?"

"That, my dear, is the sixty-four-thousand-dollar question. Unfortunately, both Morales and Richards are no longer with us, so we can only assume they were cohorts in the cattle-rustling business."

"Bummer." She yawned. "What do you say we go back to bed and sleep until tomorrow?"

Danny checked his watch. "Let's run out first for fast food, then crash. The only thing I've had less of than sleep in the past twenty-four hours is food, and I'm starving." He grinned. "I'll even treat."

"Who are you and what have you done with my brother?" Then before he changed his mind, she clicked off the TV and jumped up. "I'll get my purse."

"Oh, by the way, do you remember Officer Rutherford, the Ranchero cop who was out at Sandy's last night?" When she nodded, he continued. "He called me when I was on the way back from the Taylors'. Cooper Harrison is on the lam."

CHAPTER 21

Jordan sat in the nursing home parking lot, staring at the entrance. She'd rather be doing anything else, be anywhere else right now. What do you say to a woman who's lost both her son and her husband in a matter of weeks? Jordan didn't have a clue, but she did have a soft spot in her heart for the woman and wanted to comfort her in some way, even if it was only by being a familiar face.

From the moment Maria had grabbed her arm and mouthed "Help me" at Rusty's memorial service, Jordan had made the decision to do what she could. Whatever Maria had been afraid of then couldn't come close to what she must be feeling right now, facing a future more bleak than anything Jordan could imagine. It must be frustrating to want so desperately to communicate your thoughts and not be able to.

She switched her phone to vibrate. It would be awkward enough facing the poor woman, knowing there was nothing she could do to help, without her phone blaring "Girls Just Want to Have Fun" in the middle of a tender moment.

With every horror story she'd ever heard about nursing homes playing in her brain, Jordan took a deep breath and slowly exhaled before opening the door. Expecting dingy gray walls and dreary-looking hallways reeking of urine, she found herself pleasantly surprised. A pale shade of blue decorated the walls and was complemented by window treatments adorned with little yellow flowers on a background of coordinating blue. She braved it and took a deep breath, delighted when the visual of a garden after a spring rain crossed her mind instead of a men's room at a roadside park.

"May I help you?"

Jordan turned to find a smart-looking, middle-aged woman with a smile that matched the soft voice. "I'm looking for Maria Morales. I believe she came in yesterday."

The smile disappeared. "She's in room 104 down the hallway to the left. Since she's arrived she's been inconsolable, and nothing we do seems to help. Maybe you can comfort her." She extended her hand. "I'm Sophia Bradley, the assistant administrator here."

Jordan reached for her hand and shook it, immediately noticing the strong grip in direct contrast to the soft voice. "Jordan McAllister."

Recognition flashed in the administrator's eyes. "The Kitchen Kupboard's Jordan McAllister?"

Jordan would never get used to people saying her name in the same breath as her column. "Guilty. I'm flattered you recognized the name."

"The residents here love your recipes. Last week, the chef made the Beef Stroganoff, and now they're insisting we make it a weekly thing. We didn't use that expensive cut of beef, of course. They love the Potato Chip Chicken dish, too."

Jordan hoped her cheeks didn't crack from smiling. Hearing things like this made her appreciate the opportunity she'd been given, even if she still yearned to be on the sidelines at sporting events. "I'll share that with my boss."

The administrator laughed. "No need. At least fifteen of the residents have personally telephoned the newspaper to rave about the column."

"Let them know I appreciate that," Jordan said, wondering why Egan had kept that little tidbit to himself. Then she smirked as it came to her. She knew exactly why the cheapskate hadn't shared the compliments. God forbid if her fan base—or her head—got too big. Her editor might have to dip into the old piggy bank and bump her salary up a notch.

She smiled once again at the administrator, then headed down the hallway. Maria's was the last room on the right. Hesitating only briefly, Jordan pushed through the door and saw Maria sitting by the window staring out. She didn't even bother to look up when Jordan approached. It was heartbreaking to see the woman's state and know how much pain she must be in.

"Maria?"

Startled, Maria jerked her body around. For a second, Jordan thought she saw a smile crinkle her eyes before she plunged her hand under the blanket on her lap. Pulling out a picture frame, Maria held it out to Jordan, pointing repeatedly to the photo it held.

Reaching for it, Jordan realized it was the same one she'd seen on the mantle when she'd visited Maria at home. It was also the photo that had upset Maria so much that

Diego had practically kicked her out of his house for asking about it.

"This is a lovely picture of you and Diego and your sister," Jordan began cautiously.

Maria leaned forward and banged on the photo with her hand, all the while uttering sounds that could have been mistaken for the cry of an injured animal. With each thump on the glass, her voice escalated. It was obvious she was trying to convey something important, but for the life of her, Jordan couldn't tell what.

She decided to get right to the reason she'd come all the way over to Connor in the first place. "I know you're sad because Diego was killed. I'm sad, too, Maria, but this looks like a lovely place."

Are you freakin' kidding me? The woman has just lost her husband and her son, and here I am insinuating everything will be okay because the place didn't stink.

Seriously! It was like saying, *Too bad your world has just crumbled around you and everyone you love is gone, but hey, how about that nice firm mattress on your bed!*

Somebody should write a book about stupid things *not* to say to a grieving person.

As if to emphasize how incredibly dumb her last statement had been, Maria violently shook her head from side to side, then pounded the picture again.

Jordan concentrated on the photo. "This is your sister, Gia, right?"

An excited look crossed Maria's face as she nodded as aggressively as she had shaken her head minutes before.

"You must miss her, too."

The older woman's face took on a frantic look, and tears welled up in her eyes.

Great, Jordan. Your comforting skills are matched only by your cooking talents!

Maria grabbed the picture from her and shoved it back under the blanket. With one hand she spun the chair around and wheeled herself away from the window, totally dismissing Jordan.

Unable to make any sense of it, Jordan eased down into the chair beside the bed, hoping for some miracle that would help her figure out how to comfort the poor woman.

Fifteen minutes later, she decided that was not going to happen, at least not today. Discouraged, she walked over and gently touched Maria's shoulder. "I'm going now, but I'll come back to visit, if it's all right with you."

Hoping for some sign that she would be welcomed, Jordan was disappointed when there was none. Maria remained trancelike, humming to herself in a low monotone.

Feeling totally inadequate, Jordan walked to the door before turning one last time to try to communicate with Maria. When it was obvious the woman was in a world of her own and unaware—or uninterested—that anyone else was in the room, Jordan left, her heart heavier than when she'd arrived.

On the ride back to Ranchero, she felt her own tears forming, unable to stop thinking about Maria. Life wasn't fair sometimes, and the woman she'd just left at the nursing home was a perfect example of how cruel it could be.

She was startled when her cell phone vibrated, and she figured it was Danny reminding her to pick up lunch on the way home.

Without looking at caller ID, she answered. "Hey, Danny, I should be home in about twenty minutes."

"Jordan?"

It was a good thing she was stopped at a red light, or she might have swerved across the road at the sound of that voice. She glanced in her rearview mirror to make sure he wasn't behind her before she spoke. "Where are you, Cooper?"

"That's not important. I know you were at the warehouse the other night. You're the only one who knows I didn't kill anybody."

She spied a Methodist church ahead and pulled into the empty lot. Without switching off the ignition, she scanned the surroundings, making sure Cooper hadn't followed her.

Satisfied he was nowhere to be found, she relaxed a little. "I did see you, Cooper. I know you were stealing cows, but I saw nothing that convinces me you didn't kill Diego and your friend."

"I swear I didn't. And you're right, Johnny Lorenzo was my friend," he interrupted. "We stole cows, yes, but that's it. You have to believe me. Can you meet me somewhere, so I can prove it to you?"

"How stupid do you think I am?"

"I swear, Jordan. I may be a cattle thief, but I'm not a killer. I figure whoever killed Johnny and Diego was looking to put out my lights, too. That's why I was running for my life when you saw me. Johnny must have gotten a look at Diego's killer."

"Tell that to Maria Morales," she blurted, unable to hide her anger over the anguish he'd caused the woman. "You took away both Rusty and Diego."

"Rusty? Why would you think I killed him? He was my bread-and-butter."

"So he really was the brains behind the cattle-rustling ring?" Even as she said it, she didn't want to believe her brother had been right all along.

"I wouldn't call him the brains, but he was the one who came up with the idea right after the old woman had her stroke. It was the perfect setup with his father working at the plant on the weekends."

Considering the astronomical cost of around-the-clock nursing care, it made sense, but it still didn't explain why Cooper had murdered three people, and possibly four, if you counted the waiter from the Cattlemen's Ball.

"If you're innocent, why don't you turn yourself in? Then you can clear your name once and for all. I could call my brother Danny and have him meet—"

"No," he shouted. "No cops. I won't be hanging around long enough to convince people I'm not guilty, anyway. This time tomorrow I'll be in the wind, and you and your brother will never hear from me again. That's why it's so important that you meet me now."

"So you can tie up all your loose ends and kill me, too?"

"You're talking crazy, Jordan. Why would I kill you?"

"Oh, I don't know. Maybe because I'm the only witness who can place you at the North Texas Beef Distributors on Friday night. The only one who can positively identify you as the guy running from the building after you killed Diego and Lorenzo."

"You have it all wrong." He paused. "Time's running out, Jordan. Are you going to meet me or not?"

God help her, she was about to do something she hoped didn't come with too high a price. "Where?"

"In the parking lot of Hearth and Home off Texoma Parkway."

She glanced down at the clock on the dashboard. "It's one thirty, and I'm in Connor right now. It will take me about thirty minutes to get there."

A minute passed before Cooper responded. "If you're not there by two, I'm gone."

She heard the phone go dead and immediately dialed her brother.

After listening to her repeat the conversation with Cooper, Danny said, "Hurry up and get to the 7-Eleven just past the Connor-Ranchero border. I'll meet you there and hop into the backseat."

"Bring Ray," she said, remembering the last time she went by herself to meet someone she thought might be dangerous. If nothing else, it had taught her never to be that stupid again.

"I'll do more than that," Danny responded. "I'll bring the whole damned police force."

"No," she shouted. "He won't show if he suspects the cops are nearby. He made that perfectly clear."

"He'll never even know they're around. Just hustle and get to our meeting spot."

Somehow, knowing the Ranchero Police Department was coming didn't instill any confidence in her. Alex had once dubbed the two that had investigated the break-in at her apartment as Dumb and Dumber. She had to agree. But it was too late now to argue about it.

Just past the WELCOME TO RANCHERO sign, she saw the 7-Eleven up ahead and Danny and Ray standing beside Ray's Suburban. They hurried to her car when she pulled in, even before she could come to a complete stop.

"Let's go. We've only got seven minutes left," Danny said.

When they were close to Hearth and Home, both Danny and Ray slumped down in the backseat.

"Do you see him, Jordan?" Ray asked.

She scanned the nearly full parking lot. "It's packed. I'll have to drive up and down the aisles."

"Check out the ends closest to the highway first. I'm sure Cooper wouldn't be comfortable jammed in between cars where he couldn't make a quick escape."

At that moment, Jordan saw a police cruiser pass by on the main road, followed by two others close behind.

So much for no cops allowed.

"I don't see him."

"Call him."

Jordan pulled into an end slot and redialed the number Cooper had used earlier. She was immediately connected to voice mail. "Cooper, where are you? I'm waiting in the parking lot." She disconnected and shrugged. "Now what?"

"Nothing to do but wait," Danny said. "Got any food? I'm starving."

"I'm sure you can find a few French fries on the floor." Teasing her brother made her relax a little, and she leaned back into the headrest.

At three, after several more calls to his cell phone went unanswered, they decided Cooper was not going to show. Danny phoned Officer Rutherford and called off the operation.

"If I saw the cops, trust me, Cooper did, too. I told you not to get them involved, Danny. Now we may never find out anything."

"You're probably right, but there's not much else we can do right now. We still have an APB out for him and his car. Asking you to meet him here might have been just a ruse to throw us off about where he is right now. That would give him more time to make his getaway. I'll call the Border Patrol and have them on the lookout, just in case he isn't already in some villa drinking a margarita with some young senorita."

Knowing Cooper might be long gone didn't calm her fears, and she scanned the lot one last time before pulling out. "Now what happens to you? Will you hang around until they find Cooper and bring him in?"

"Probably not," Danny answered. "It looks like the cattle theft ring has been shut down, at least for now, and my boss needs me back in Amarillo. I'll let the police deal with chasing down Cooper and prosecuting him for murder."

"We can't let you go without a party," Ray said, patting Danny's back. "We'll all miss you, kid."

"I—" Danny's voice cracked before he laughed. "I'd be an idiot to turn down a party."

Jordan dropped Ray off at the 7-Eleven to get his Suburban, and she and Danny headed to the apartment, stopping only long enough to pick up a bucket of chicken. There was still no word from Cooper, although Jordan must have checked her phone a dozen times to see if maybe she'd missed the call.

By late afternoon, her thoughts were already off Cooper and back on her visit with Maria. It bothered her that she couldn't understand what Maria had been trying to say.

And why did the photo of Diego and her sister upset her so much? That had to be the clue.

CHAPTER 22

With the response to Bella's Baked Steak recipe keeping her busy, the week flew by for Jordan. For the past two nights, she'd gone straight to Sandy's from work to help pack up the apartment. Although a couple of off-duty firemen were scheduled to move the heavy stuff on Saturday, Jordan and her friends were pitching in to help transport the rest of Sandy's things.

The week had also been busy for Danny. Between wrapping up his investigation and getting ready for the trip back to Amarillo, he hadn't spent much time at the apartment. Cooper Harrison was still at large, and they figured he was probably holed up in some tiny village in Mexico. Although they'd found an offshore account in his name, surprisingly, it hadn't been touched in days.

While cattle rustling in North Texas remained a problem, Danny's bosses were convinced they had dealt it a crippling blow by putting Cooper out of business. Following a hunch, Danny had carried out a search warrant against Cooper's friend, Blake Graham, Cooper's accountant and computer expert.

The police discovered Blake had hacked into the files of Buddy's Barbecue Pit and stolen Buddy's secret, world-famous recipe for barbecued beef. Additionally, they'd found evidence linking the computer expert directly to the cattle-rustling ring. A paper trail revealed he'd hacked into the private accounts of several Texas ranches, as well as a few from out of state.

By placing legitimate bills of sale in their accounting files, Blake had made it appear as though the very ranchers who were victims of the theft were guilty of double-dipping. It was genius, actually, since proving they hadn't sold the cows themselves and claimed the losses on their insurance policies had been nearly impossible.

Blake's computer led the police to North Texas Beef Distributors where they'd uncovered even more evidence of the fraud. Apparently, he had also been manipulating the files there to show invoices for the stolen meat that was subsequently sold as legitimate. No wonder the company was doing so well.

When Carole Anne Summerville found out that Cooper had killed Diego and was on the run and that Blake was awaiting formal charges, she cut a deal with the DA's office faster than they could spout off her Miranda rights. To avoid being charged as an accessory to the murders, she'd squealed like a baby pig in a hog-tying contest, leading them to several other cowboys who'd been involved in the operation. Jordan wasn't surprised to see that Bobby Carvella, the ranch hand who had succeeded Rusty Morales as Lucas Santana's right-hand man, was at the top of the list.

She was proud of her big brother, especially when he was given a public commendation for his work in bringing the thieves to justice. She'd taken off Thursday afternoon, and the gang had all descended on City Hall to watch the presentation. As the youngest boy in her family, Danny had always worked harder to prove himself. He deserved every bit of glory the city of Ranchero poured on him.

By the time Friday rolled around, Jordan was more than ready for a nice relaxing evening with her friends. At quitting time, she couldn't get out of the office fast enough, stopping at Piggly Wiggly on the way home to pick up Danny's favorite, German chocolate cake.

Although she was anxious to get back to a normal routine again, she'd miss her brother. It'd been nice having him around, even if they still fought like they had when they were younger. It was little comfort to know she'd see more of him now that he was sweet on Sandy.

When her apartment was quiet again, she would do more research on the latest treatments available for stroke patients with aphasia. The image of Maria pounding on the picture frame still tugged at her heart, and she was determined to do whatever she could to help, even if the results proved to not be completely transformative. To that end, she'd placed a call to a doctor in Dallas who specialized in stroke victim rehabilitation. Unfortunately, he was out of town and wouldn't be able to return her call until Monday.

Danny wasn't at the apartment when she got there, and she used the alone time for a power nap, which usually refreshed her. But this time she still felt exhausted when Danny got home and began banging things around.

She watched him pull out his suitcase and fling it on the couch. Tonight would be the last time she'd see him for a while. After the get-together, he planned to spend the night with Sandy and head out of Ranchero bright and early from there.

Slowly rising from the recliner, she walked over to where he was adding the finishing touches to his packing. Slamming the suitcase shut, he set it on the floor.

Reaching around him with her arms, she hugged him from behind. "You know how much I'm gonna miss you, right?"

"Yeah, I'll miss you, too." He turned and hugged her back. "I know I don't always show it, but I love you, sis."

Jordan swallowed hard, feeling the same way. "I'm going to remind you of that the next time you're acting like a jackass."

He laughed. "You wouldn't want it any other way. Admit it."

She would rather hang upside down from a tree the way he'd forced her to do sometimes when they were kids than admit it to him, but he was right.

Pulling away before they both got too sappy, she said, "I get the bathroom first. We only have a half hour before showtime at Rosie's. You know how antsy the gang will be if we're not there on time. I'm convinced they all have timers in their bellies that go off right at seven."

"I talked to Sheriff Delaney today. With all the circumstantial evidence pointing to Cooper as the killer, he's closed the case," Ray said. "He told me it couldn't have happened without you, Danny."

For the first time since they were kids, Jordan saw a slight blush creep up Danny's face. "Yeah, yeah. I had a lot of help, but it still looks damn good on my résumé."

"Any chance we can talk you into moving to Ranchero

permanently?" Victor asked. "I have a feeling you and I could get into a lot of trouble together, bro."

Danny laughed. "I'm sure we could, but after the curtain debacle at Sandy's, I think my sister would kill me if I lived any closer than the Panhandle."

"She'd have to get in line behind me," Lola said playfully. "For a minute out at the lake, I actually thought I had summoned up the spirits." She paused, obviously realizing from the look on Sandy's face that the girl still believed she'd said good-bye to her grandfather that night. "Forget I said that, darling."

Jumping in to rescue her friend from that slip of the tongue, Rosie pointed to the kitchen. "So, who's hungry?"

When they all shouted in unison, she added, "I thought since beef was the reason Danny's here with us in the first place, it should be his parting meal. We're eating Steak and Gravy, Jordan's recipe."

"Bella's," Jordan corrected. "Her recipes are the one good thing that came out of my Sunday visits at Santana Circle Ranch. They were a big hit with the people of Ranchero."

"How much longer do you have to keep doing that?" Michael asked, grabbing a plate and heading for the kitchen.

"I think I'm through. Lucas wanted to get more people buying steak, and he's accomplished that. The last time I was in Egan's office, he showed me a report that confirmed a nearly twenty-five percent increase in local beef sales since I started publishing Bella's recipes."

"You'd think they'd want to continue with it if he's already getting those kinds of results in just a few weeks," Lola said.

Jordan grabbed her own plate and followed Michael.

"The deal was for me to go out there four times, but I'd be surprised if I have to continue doing that. Technically, I have two to go, but with Lucas under the weather right now, I seriously doubt they'll hold me to it."

"What's the matter with him?" Rosie asked, dishing out the food.

"Palpitations or something. Bella said he's already taking blood thinners for atrial fib or some problem with his heart, so they lowered the dosage."

Jordan sat down at the table and waited for the rest of the gang to do the same.

After a quick prayer, they began to eat, and all chatter stopped while they made pigs of themselves.

"I can barely move," Lola said, pushing her plate away. "Rosie, you outdid yourself with this one."

"Does this mean you don't have room for dessert?" Rosie asked.

"Oh, hell no, darling. Did you get a look at the chocolate cake Jordan brought?"

"Oh yeah. I'll get the coffee brewing. I even bought a bottle of Kahlúa and a can of whipped cream so we can have a proper sendoff for Danny."

For the next hour, the talk centered on plans to help Sandy with her move the next day. Danny was leaving around five, hoping to be on the road before the sun came up. Jordan tried to talk him into sleeping in and leaving after breakfast, but he held his ground, wanting to get on the highway before it got congested with travelers trying to get home before Monday. Knowing he wouldn't get much sleep, she prepared herself for an all-day worry fest until he called to say he was home safe.

"Ray, are you ready to tell everybody the news?" Michael asked.

All eyes turned to the retired cop, whose face lit up. "Lola and I are taking a cruise." He shot his lady a look that promised more than a boat ride.

"I hate you, but that's awesome," Rosie said. "I've always wanted to go on one of those but never could afford it. When are y'all going?"

"In two months," Lola responded when she finally broke eye contact with Ray. "We're actually part of the hired help." She turned to Michael. "Tell them about it."

Michael leaned forward as if he was about to reveal a secret. "I'm sure you guys have heard about the Caribbean Cook-off we've been advertising over at the radio station?"

"Who hasn't? That's all you've been talking about for the past three months," Rosie said before turning to Ray. "And you and Lola have hired on?"

"Yep," Ray said. "Michael approached me last week and said the head of security for one of the big celebrity judges has to fly to a godforsaken village in Chile. Seems one of his kids is getting married and he won't be available. They were going to cancel the trip, but Michael threw my name out there to Beau Lincoln's people. I sat down with the powers that be yesterday and worked out all the details."

"The Beau Lincoln who's the head of Sinfully Sweet?" Rosie didn't wait for a reply. "I absolutely love their brownies."

"Yep, that Beau Lincoln," Michael replied. "Lucky for you, he's bringing some of his famous fudge on the cruise."

"Ooh, chocolate," Jordan said, licking her lips. "What makes his so special?"

"Alcohol, darlin'," Rosie explained. "Every kind imaginable."

"I'm all over that," Jordan said before turning to Ray.

"So why would a rich guy who makes fudge need a security detail?"

"Good question. I guess my job will be to police the buffet lines to keep him from overeating." He chuckled before he got serious again. "I'm thinking it's more like making sure nobody interrupts his dinner for an autograph or some jealous person doesn't see the cruise as an opportunity to throw him overboard or something."

"Wayne Francis, Michael's boss, went to school with the guy and said he wears a lot of expensive jewelry. Maybe that's why," Victor said, clapping his hands. "And I'm going, too. Michael convinced them I would be terrific with the entertainment. You know, leading the games by the pool, trivia in the bars. Since they're expecting a big crowd, they needed the extra help."

Rosie turned to Lola. "And you?"

Lola grinned, patting Ray on the knee. "I'll be doing fortune-telling and psychic readings. Too bad Danny isn't coming along. He and Victor would make for great visual effects." When everybody laughed, she continued. "Seriously, I'll be offering classes on tarot card and palm readings, thanks to Michael."

"How long will you guys be gone?" Jordan was already thinking how much she'd miss them.

"Seven days," Michael said. "I'm signed on to oversee the contest. There'll be wannabe chefs from all over Texas competing, and the winner gets a contract with a mega talent agent from New York to do a million-dollar ad campaign with a big gourmet food conglomerate. It's really a big deal, and the cruise has been sold out for weeks. If everything goes as planned, the bigwigs at KTLK are already talking about making this an annual event."

"Too bad you and Rosie aren't going," Victor said, pooching out his lower lip in an adorable pout.

"Like either of us could afford it," Jordan said, trying to stay enthusiastic for her friends but feeling left out.

"Bloody hell, Michael, you have to tell them," Victor exclaimed. "Jordan is about to cry." He giggled.

"Tell us what?" Rosie asked.

Michael turned to her, mischief in his eyes. "After I told my boss how unbelievable you are with casseroles, he couldn't wait to talk to you."

Rosie squinted her eyes. "Why would they want to talk to me?"

"Seems with all the fancy food the contestants will be dishing up at night, they wanted to have simple home-cooked meals for lunches for the celebrity judges and the radio personnel. What better way to feed the masses than with your mouthwatering dishes?" He paused to look at his watch. "Matter of fact, you have an appointment to discuss this with my boss in about two days and twenty hours, but just between you and me, you're already a shoo-in. I gave him part of your leftover Potato Chip Chicken from last week, and after one bite, he was ready to hire you on the spot."

She jumped up and hugged Michael. "I'm actually going on a cruise to the Caribbean?" When he nodded, she hugged him even harder.

It was hard watching her friends celebrating and laughing about how much fun they'd have on the cruise, knowing she wouldn't be there with them. She loved them all and wished them the vacation of a lifetime, but she didn't know what she'd do by herself for seven days.

"Why the pouty face, doll?" Victor asked. "Will you miss us?"

She tried to smile. "Of course, you ninny. How could I not?"

"Then I guess it's a good thing you won't have to," Michael said.

When his meaning sunk in, Jordan jumped up from the chair. "What do you mean I won't have to? Please tell me you got your boss to give me a job with housekeeping or something." She was already planning on how she would approach her editor with the request for a whole week off.

Michael threw his head back and laughed. "I tried to sell him on the idea of your being Rosie's assistant, but he would have none of it after I told him your idea of a home-cooked meal was a peanut butter and jelly sandwich."

"Oh, for Pete's sake, Michael. Look at that face. Tell her now or I will," Victor said.

"Okay, okay." Michael reached for Jordan's hands. "Right now, your boss is working out the details with the radio station executives to send you on the cruise with us. They want Rosie cooking the recipes that you've printed in the newspaper, along with more of her own." He grinned. "I didn't tell them most of them were from her recipe file, anyway."

Jordan screamed. "Are you playing with me, Michael?"

The mischief was still in his eyes. "Sweetie, I wouldn't do that to you."

"What would I be doing?"

"Here comes the really funny part. You, my dear, will be judging the contest with George Christakis, the legendary chef from the Cooking Channel, and Beau Lincoln."

CHAPTER 23

After five trips to the lake in Ray's Suburban crammed with boxes, the gang decided Jordan and Victor should pick up meatball subs while the others stayed behind to start unpacking and to hook up Sandy's washer and dryer.

A few miles from the lake house, Jordan's cell phone rang, and she fished it out of her purse.

"Hey." Not bothering to check caller ID, she fully expected to hear Rosie with a request to add a few turnovers to the food list. The woman had a sweet tooth that could put a toddler to shame.

"Jordan, this is Bella."

"Is everything okay?"

"Not really," Bella responded. "Lucas seems to be getting worse instead of better. For the past two days he hasn't even been out of bed. That's why I'm calling."

"I'm sorry to hear that."

"He wants to talk to you," Bella blurted before Jordan could add the standard *Is there anything I can do?* that usually followed news like that.

"Me? Why does he want to talk to me?"

"He didn't say. Can you swing by sometime today?"

Jordan lightly banged her head on the window, causing Victor to turn her way and nearly crash Ray's car. She'd thought her visits with Lucas and Bella were over.

When his eyes questioned her, she waved him off and lifted the cell phone back to her ear. "I don't know, Bella. I'm helping a friend move today, and I'm dirty and sweaty."

"Your friend who lives out by the lake?"

"Yes," Jordan said, racking her brain, trying to remember when she'd mentioned Sandy to Bella.

"That's perfect. The ranch is on the way to her house. You can stop in for a few minutes." When Jordan didn't respond, she added, "He really wants to see you today."

Crap! All the guilt she'd learned from the nuns in Catholic grade school compelled her to nod, even though she knew Bella couldn't see her.

"Jordan, did you hear me?"

"Yes, I heard." She glanced down at her watch. "I can run by right now for a few minutes, but that's all the time I can spare. It will be dark soon, and we have one more load before we call it a day."

"I'll tell Lucas you're on the way."

"What did you get us into now?" Victor asked when she'd closed the cell phone.

"Apparently, Lucas needs to see me for something. It's on our way. Do you mind if we stop for a few minutes before we go to Guido's?"

"Are you kidding me? I've wanted to get a look at that ranch and those two ever since you first told me about them. Lead the way, woman."

Ten minutes later, Victor pulled into Santana's circular driveway, and they both got out.

"Wow! This is some kind of spread," Victor commented, turning a complete circle to take it all in.

Walking up the steps, Jordan whispered, "If we're not out of here in ten minutes, excuse yourself and go to the bathroom. Then call me so I can say we need to leave."

"Okay." Victor reached into his shirt pocket. "Dang it! I laid my phone on the table when we moved the heavy bedroom set out of the master suite. I was afraid it might get crushed."

Jordan blew out a frustrated breath as she rang the doorbell. "Figure something out. If I give you the look, use your love for drama to get us out of there."

"Drama I can do." He smiled just as the door opened.

Jordan heard his sharp intake of breath as he got his first look at Bella. The tight pair of Levi's she wore had the kind of holes at the knees that came with a high price tag. And the aqua and purple turtleneck sweater capping the outfit showed off a body that would make a much younger woman green with envy. Apparently used to getting that kind of reaction, Bella smiled back.

Jordan made quick introductions.

"Come in. Lucas is waiting for you," Bella said.

Victor was still staring at her like an awestruck teenager with his first peek at the centerfold of a Playboy magazine. Knowing her friend preferred hairy-chested men with five o'clock shadows over beautiful women, Jordan couldn't decide if his mouth hung open because Bella was train-stopping gorgeous today in her jeans and sweater, or because he wanted her outfit for himself. He loved anything with purple.

They followed her up the winding staircase and down the hall to the master bedroom. The stunning cherrywood four-poster bed was nearly swallowed up in the massive room decorated with a definite masculine touch.

"Good heavens, is this a Victorian Eastlake?" Victor asked, thoroughly impressed. "I love the marble topped dresser and washstand."

Bella nodded. "It belonged to Lucas's grandmother. You have a good eye."

Victor beamed. "I own Tomorrow's Treasures on the square downtown. You should stop in someday. And if you ever want to sell this furniture . . ."

Bella laughed. "The only way that bed is ever leaving this room is over Lucas's dead body." She moved closer to the bed, and Jordan and Victor followed.

Propped up with huge pillows, Lucas didn't look anything like the towering, obnoxious man Jordan had met that first night in the limousine. With dark circles under both eyes and a hollowed face from visible weight loss, he tried to smile but didn't quite pull it off.

"The doctor doesn't want him to get too excited until we can get the palpitations under control," Bella explained. "He gave him a mild sedative before he left earlier."

"Jordan," Lucas whispered, motioning with his hand for her to move closer.

"I'm sorry you don't feel well, Lucas. I . . ." She winced in pain as he grabbed her hand and squeezed, cutting off the rest of her sentence—and her circulation.

"I think I'm dying."

How do I respond to that?

"You'll be back to your old self soon, Lucas," Jordan

said, mentally slapping herself. They both knew it probably wasn't true. "Why did you want to see me?"

The old man looked confused. "I wanted to see you?" he asked in a raspy voice.

She turned and shot Bella a questioning look before the woman moved closer to the bed and pried Lucas's fingers from Jordan's hand.

"Jordan has to go now, Lucas. Ring the bell if you need me." She gently nudged Jordan toward the door. Victor was already in the hallway ahead of them.

"I'm sorry. He gets so confused. I think he just wanted to ask if you could thank your brother for putting the cattle rustlers behind bars."

He couldn't have done that over the phone? Jordan thought but said instead, "No problem."

When they were downstairs, Bella asked if she could get them something to drink.

"Actually, we have to be on our way. They're waiting for us to bring back dinner, and they have no idea we even made a stop," Jordan said.

Bella eyed the two of them before she finally asked, "That was something else about Cooper, wasn't it?"

"Yes."

Jordan thought Bella was probably desperate to have a conversation with another human being after being holed up for a week with a sick man, but she was in too big a hurry to discuss Cooper with her. Her stomach was already growling, not to mention that the others were going to kill her and Victor if they didn't get back soon with dinner.

"Did you actually see him kill Diego?"

Jordan froze. At Sheriff Delaney's request, the *Globe* had deliberately left out her name when they reported the murders at North Texas Beef Distributors. Since she had been the only witness, he'd cautioned about the very real possibility of Cooper coming after her—which he'd already done.

But how did Bella know this?

"What makes you think I was there?" Jordan blurted before she could stop herself.

She was getting an uncomfortable feeling, especially when Bella glared at her through narrowed eyes as if reading her mind. No one except her friends knew she'd been there that night. The only way Bella could have that information was if—Jordan gasped—if she'd been there herself and *had* seen her.

"We have to go now," she said, grabbing Victor's sleeve and practically running to the front door. She'd call Sheriff Delaney as soon as she got to the car. He could deal with it after that.

As her hand gripped the door knob, she heard a click.

"I wouldn't do that if I were you," Bella said, her voice strangely ominous.

Both Victor and Jordan turned. At the sight of Bella with a gun in her hand pointed directly at them, Victor's inner drama queen finally surfaced, and he threw both arms above his head. "Oh my God, woman, put that big-ass gun down before you blow somebody's head off."

Although there was a smile on her face, her eyes remained hard, and she didn't bother to respond, instead turning to Jordan. "You're too smart for your own britches. Unfortunately, that's what will get you killed."

"I have no idea what you're talking about." Jordan prayed she could pull this off. "I did see Cooper kill Diego that night, but that's all I saw."

Bella smirked. "I never figured you for a liar, Jordan. I saw your face a minute ago and knew you'd put two and two together." She backed up to the hutch and opened the drawer, then pulled out Jordan's scarf and threw it at her. "Pick it up and look at it," she commanded.

Jordan bent down and picked up the scarf, fingering the tear from the nail it had caught on right before Cooper ran out of the building that night.

"As you can see, it's the one you lost the night you saw me kill Diego. So don't try to play innocent with me. We both know Cooper didn't do it. In fact, he was lucky he made it out alive himself." She chuckled. "Well, maybe not so lucky."

Thinking Bella might have been there, and actually hearing her admit she was the one who had committed the two murders were two different things. The only reason Bella would confess to her and Victor was if . . .

"I asked you to come here for two reasons. I needed to find out if you'd seen me, and I wanted you to be able to say how sad it was that Lucas's health had deteriorated so rapidly. Then when the poor man dies in a few days, you could say you witnessed firsthand how I did everything in my power to help him."

Jordan stared, hoping that didn't mean what she thought it did. "What makes you think he's going to die this week? I thought you said the doctor was treating him."

The cold laughter that came out of Bella's mouth sent shivers up Jordan's spine. There was no doubt she and Victor were in deep trouble.

"Because the pathetic man is going to bleed out while he sleeps." She shook her head, pasting a phony sympathetic look on her face. "Honestly, he's been so confused lately that he must have taken too many of his blood thinners. And since the doctor prescribed potassium for his palpitations, it won't be a shocker when they find high potassium levels in his blood, too." The sympathy transformed into an evil grin. "Pretty clever, don't you think?"

A horrible thought crossed Jordan's mind and she couldn't keep it to herself. "Did you have anything to do with Maria Morales's overdose?"

"You are sharp. I'll give you that. That was really one of my finer moments. Everyone thought Diego accidently gave his wife too many pills. Nobody bothered to find out Lucas took the same medicine. Maria didn't have a clue I was dosing her coffee every day. She was too busy being flattered that I took the time to sit down and talk to her when she arrived for work." She tsked. "Sometimes people are so hungry for attention, they don't use their God-given brains."

Victor finally found his voice. "Why would you want to hurt her? What did she ever do to you?"

Bella's eyes drilled into him. "That's none of your business. You should be worrying more about what's going to happen to you since your friend dragged you along with her today." She pointed to the door with the gun. "Give me your cell phones and let's go."

"Our friends know we're here, and they'll come looking for us," Jordan blurted.

"Are you forgetting you've already mentioned you didn't tell them?" She reached for Jordan's cell phone and grabbed the torn scarf from her. "Now go before I have to kill you right here. I'd hate to ruin this expensive Oriental rug."

Bella followed behind and directed them to Ray's car.

"You drive, Victor, and Jordan will get in the passenger side."

When Victor started the ignition, Bella instructed him on which way to go. Soon they were heading down a dirt road in a heavily wooded area of the ranch.

Jordan stared out the window, frantically searching for a ranch hand or someone who would notice the Suburban, but the road was too isolated. Her hope that this whole ordeal would somehow have a happy ending was fading quickly.

Finally, she got up the nerve and asked the question she wasn't sure she wanted to know the answer to. "Where are you taking us?"

"Lucas calls it Hunter's Haven. He used to camp out here several times a year and hunt. It's where most of the animals on the den wall came from. Rusty used it occasionally, but for the most part, it's gone unattended and has become overgrown with brush since Lucas's car accident. He keeps threatening to have it plowed so he can put wild horses back here."

At the mention of Rusty Morales, Jordan shot up in the seat. The last thing she wanted was to make Bella more irritated than she already was, but she couldn't resist. If curiosity did in fact kill the cat, she was about to be one dead feline.

"Why kill Rusty, Bella?" She knew it was fishing, but one way or another, she was going to find out.

"See, Jordan, this is why you're wasting your talent posting recipes at a podunk newspaper like the *Globe*. You have a nose for investigative reporting."

Jordan wasn't ready to let it go. "Were you and Rusty lovers?"

Bella laughed. "We had a fling at one time, but that ended when we decided we were much better as business colleagues than bed partners."

Victor, who had been unusually quiet up until now, spoke up. "You were a part of Rusty's cattle-rustling ring?"

Bella leaned forward and pressed the muzzle of the gun

against the back of his head. "Let's get something straight, gay boy. It was never Rusty's cattle-rustling ring, although we operated out of his house behind the ranch. He was too busy chasing every skirt in town. He answered to me."

"And that's why you killed him?" Jordan figured if she and Victor were going to die, at least they could find out the whole story.

"Rusty has only Maria to blame for his death."

Jordan whirled around to face Bella, then turned back to the front when Bella jerked the gun from Victor's head and poked it into her face.

"You came this close to eating a bullet, Jordan."

"What did his mother have to do with it?" Victor asked, shooting a quick glance Jordan's way. It was obvious he was looking for her to come up with some sort of plan, but she had nothing.

After a moment, Bella leaned back against the seat. "Since neither of you will walk out of here alive, I guess it wouldn't hurt to tell you why I had to kill him." She chuckled. "But I like the idea of your not knowing. It will give you something to think about when you meet your friends."

Jordan caught her breath as a glimmer of hope battled the fear. "We're going to see our friends?"

"New ones who can't wait to crawl all over you."

Jordan had no idea what she meant, but she decided the smart thing to do now was to keep Bella talking. If they could distract her from her present course of action, maybe they could somehow get the gun away from her.

Remembering that Bella's house had been filled with fresh flowers from Karen Whitley's greenhouse every week, Jordan went with a hunch. "How'd you get the waiter to slip the poison you stole from Karen Whitley into Rusty's drink?"

She snorted. "Jake Richards didn't need much persuading. He would've poisoned his own mother for the right price. But to answer your question, it seems Rusty had a thing with Jake's sister years before, and she blew her brains out after he broke her heart. I think Richards would have paid me for the opportunity."

She paused when Victor hit a bump in the road, and they all went airborne, hitting their heads on the top of the car.

"Slow down," she hollered, her voice getting even more agitated.

Victor eased up on the gas pedal, and she began again. "I called in a favor with David Whitley, the man who does the hiring for Marcus Taylor. We needed an inside man at the Wagyu ranch to help us move the cows. Plus I knew sooner or later the cops would figure out where the poison came from. You have to admit, Jake looked guilty as hell."

"Not after the police found him in a deserted field with a bullet in the back of his head," Victor fired back.

"Yeah, well, I hate loose ends."

"So Marcus and Brenda Sue were in on this, too?" Jordan asked.

Bella snorted. "They didn't have a clue that Jake was personally directing us to every new hiding place on the ranch. It was quite a setup. Too bad Jake had to go."

They'd been on the dirt road for about fifteen minutes when Bella instructed them to turn left.

Victor maneuvered the car through the heavy brush until they came to an opening. To the right a hunting tree stand stood sentinel, overlooking miles of open acreage. A sudden shiver skittered up Jordan's spine when she realized this was where Lucas had towered above the land, picking off the helpless animals, all in the name of decorating his walls.

And now she and Victor were about to become Bella's helpless prey.

As that realization hit her, she hung her head, wishing she'd gone to church more often. She made an on-the-spot promise to God to remedy that if He got them through this ordeal. Her heart sank, knowing The Man probably heard so many of those empty promises every day, He was probably shaking His head right now saying, *And I'll bet you have some ocean front property in Arizona to sell.*

"Stop the car and get out slowly," Bella ordered from the backseat. "Keep in mind I'm a marksman and can shoot the tail off a rabbit at a hundred yards."

Victor and Jordan complied. When they were standing side by side with their backs to Bella, Jordan reached for his hand and found he was shaking.

Bella pointed to a path to their right. Jordan grasped Victor's hand tightly and they began to walk.

"At least tell us why you killed Rusty," Jordan said one last time.

"I told you, his parents were the reason."

"Were you really so angry at Diego and Maria that you would kill the only thing that meant anything to them?" Jordan knew she was taking a big chance making Bella talk about it. The woman wouldn't hesitate to shoot her in the back. Jake Richards was proof of that.

"Yes, I was, but not for the reason you might think. Diego had been blackmailing me for the past few years. His demands increased after Maria's stroke. When he figured out he could suck more and more money out of me, he made a fatal mistake. He threatened me, and I snapped. I knew he'd never stop seeing me as a cash cow—no pun intended—as long as Rusty was alive."

"Blackmailing you for what?" Victor asked. "And what

did Rusty being alive have to do with anything? You were all involved with the cattle theft, so why did he have to die?"

"If I tell you, I'll have to kill you."

Bella's sarcastic laugh sent more shivers skittering up Jordan's spine.

"Since the day Lucas brought me to the ranch ten years ago, I have gone far and above to be a good wife to the man."

"But you weren't his wife, Bella," Jordan interrupted. "And what does that have to do with Rusty's death?"

Bella jammed the gun into Jordan's back. "You talk too much, you know? And just so you understand, I am Lucas's wife, at least according to Texas law. We registered our informal marriage at the courthouse years ago. Without a will, everything goes to me when he dies this week. I wasn't about to let that be jeopardized by another whore."

Both Jordan and Victor stopped walking, and Bella nearly ran into them.

"Do that again, and you'll wish I had killed you back at the house," she barked.

"Another whore?" Victor finally asked when they closed in on a circular area of dead branches and leaves.

Bella laughed, a sickening, twisted sound that made Jordan's skin crawl. "Every single woman who has ever paraded half-naked in front of Lucas, including you, Jordan." Bella's voice escalated with mounting rage. "No red-blooded man can resist that kind of temptation, and Lucas was no different." She poked Jordan with the gun. "Stop right here."

They were on the edge of the circle, and even though she had no idea what would come next, Jordan knew it was not going to be pleasant. She had to keep Bella talking until she and Victor could wrestle the gun from her.

"Is that why you've been mad at Maria all these years? Lucas had his eye on her?"

Bella snorted. "I take it back about you being smart, Jordan. Maria thought of me as her best friend and confided in me before the stroke. She would never do that to me." She stepped closer. "This is where Lucas used to trap the animals. He called it the Prey Pit. The two of you are going to jump when I tell you, or I'll shoot you in the back."

"Oh shit!" Victor said, loud enough to startle Jordan.

"You don't have to do this, Bella. We won't tell a soul what you said, we promise. Just don't do this," Jordan pleaded.

"Get ready, get set, jump."

When neither of them moved, Bella fired a warning shot, close enough for the foliage between them to slap Jordan's leg.

Still, they didn't move.

Jordan's heart was beating so fast, she thought it would burst from her chest. When Bella fired another shot and Victor cried out, she squeezed his hand and both of them jumped.

CHAPTER 24

Jordan landed with a thud and immediately grabbed her right ankle. It felt like something had exploded on the inner side of her leg, and for a second, she thought she might pass out. She tried standing when she heard Victor moan beside her, but she immediately collapsed. Twisting toward him as far as she could, she said a quick prayer, terrified that he was badly hurt—or worse. Facing away from her, he was slumped over, a dark red stain spreading across his sleeve. When she touched his back, he screamed.

"Victor, talk to me. Are you okay?"

She heard him blow out a breath. "The bullet grazed my upper arm, and it hurt like hell when I hit the ground. Otherwise, I think I'm fine. Unfortunately, I can't say the same for Cooper Harrison."

"What?" She leaned forward, straining to see around Victor. Cooper was lying on his back with his head in a weird position, his eyes open and staring grotesquely. "Is he dead?" she asked, even though she already knew the answer.

"I'm pretty sure he is," Victor responded, before poking him to double-check. "Yep, he's a goner. It looks like he has a bullet wound to his head. He can't have been dead too long, though. Even with the cooler temperatures, he would be getting ripe if he'd been here longer than a day or two."

"I'm beginning to understand what Bella meant when she said we'd see our friends," Jordan said. "But I don't get the part about them crawling all over us."

Victor moved closer to Jordan and farther away from the dead body just as another bullet rang out and the dirt immediately in front of him flew up in the air. It took a moment for Jordan to realize Bella was still up there and had no intention of leaving their fate to chance.

She grabbed Victor's shoulder, eliciting a scream of pain from him. "Press your back as far as it will go against the wall and tuck your legs under you. Hopefully, Bella won't be able to get a good angle on us." She prayed there was some truth in her words, though she'd said them only to keep him calm.

After another couple of shots hit the ground in front of them, there was silence before they heard Bella's evil laughter from above.

"You think you're so smart. Well, I have news for you. Nobody ever comes out this way since Lucas gave up hunting. How long do you think you're gonna last down there with no food or water and all your little friends welcoming you?" She cackled again, and then they heard her footsteps crunching the leaves as she walked away.

Jordan glanced toward Victor and put her finger to her lips so he wouldn't speak. It would be just like Bella to be up there eavesdropping, trying to figure out a way to finish them off. When they finally heard Ray's Suburban drive away, she let out the breath she'd been holding.

"Do you think she's really gone?"

Jordan turned toward Victor and nodded, noticing the fear in his eyes. She smiled, hoping he bought into her fake bravado. Then she noticed that Cooper's body had shifted, leaning more toward Victor, and she scooted so that he could move farther away from it.

She wondered how Bella had lured Cooper to the ranch in the first place, but then remembered his saying he hadn't seen who'd killed Diego and his friend.

He had told Jordan that when he heard shots fired and saw his friend go down, he raced back to his truck like a gazelle with a tiger on its tail. Because he'd had no idea who the shooter was, she knew he wouldn't have thought twice about coming when Bella called, especially if she offered to help.

"Jordan?"

"Yeah."

"I was just thinking about all the things in my life that I haven't done yet," Victor said, his voice breaking.

"Quit talking like that, Victor. It won't be long before our friends realize we've been gone way too long and come looking for us."

"They don't even know we're here." He sighed. "I never did make it to Paris. That was my lifelong dream, you know."

"I didn't know, Victor, but you need to quit worrying about your bucket list. It isn't doing you any good to get so morbid, and you're freaking me out."

She wrapped her arms around her chest, wishing she hadn't thrown her sweater in a corner at Sandy's house. Even though there was still an hour of daylight left, it was chilly in the hole. As she breathed in the smell of wet dirt and rotting leaves and listened to the sounds of what must be a quadrillion birds in the trees surrounding the pit, she thought back to what Bella had said.

"What do you think Diego had on Bella that he was using to blackmail her?" she asked, deciding she'd better get Victor's mind on something other than dying.

"I don't know. If I had to guess, I'd say he knew something about her past that she didn't want revealed. That's usually how it works in the movies."

"Yeah, or maybe he threatened to tell Lucas about her affair with Rusty."

"That sounds more like it, since her goal was to inherit the old man's money."

"I guess we'll never know," Jordan said. She turned toward him, wincing when pain shot up her leg. "I'm so sorry I got you into this mess, Victor."

"Hush now, Jordan. I was the one who wanted to check this place out." He tried to smile. "What I wouldn't give to be eating cold meatball subs with Michael and teasing him about his new haircut right about now."

When Jordan heard him sniff, she reached over and patted his leg. "We'll be out of this stupid hole soon, Victor. But instead of cold subs, I want a pizza with sausage, pepperoni, green peppers, and extra cheese."

"Yum. That does sound good." He was silent for a moment. "Do you honestly think we'll make it out of here alive? I can't bear the thought that the last thing I'll ever see before I bite the bullet is a dead man."

"I'm positive we will," she replied, hoping he didn't hear the desperation in her voice.

Bella had said no one ever ventured out this way anymore, and they hadn't seen a single person on the ride over.

For a ranch the size of this one that employed a lot of people, that seemed odd. Where were all the workers?

"I hope you're right," he said.

"I promise I'll . . ." She paused to listen, hoping what she'd just heard wasn't what she thought it was.

But when she heard it again, she realized her worst fear had come true. It wasn't a sound you ever wanted to hear if you were stuck in a pit with no way out. She'd heard that rattle enough times hiking with her brothers in the woods behind their house in Amarillo to know exactly what it meant.

When her peripheral vision picked up a slight movement across from them, she jerked her head around and whispered, "Don't move, Victor."

"Why?" He sat up straight and followed her eyes. "Oh, sweet Jesus! Is that what I think it is?"

She couldn't take her eyes off the biggest rattlesnake she'd ever seen, and she'd seen a lot of them in West Texas. "Be still. They have heat seeking receptors below their eyes. It's already aware that we're here, but we don't want to make any sudden moves."

The rattler had been coiled in the dark and was now staring at them menacingly, all the while flicking its forked tongue. When it began to slowly slither forward, Jordan spotted two smaller snakes that had been under their mother, and she nearly cried out.

Placing her hand on Victor's knee to stop the shaking, she whispered in his ear, "Don't go crazy on me, but there are a couple of baby rattlers behind the big snake. That might explain why she might be more aggressive than usual, although rattlesnakes aren't known for their mothering skills."

"Oh shit!"

"Whatever you do, don't let the babies near you. I was always told their venom is much more concentrated than an adult's and gives you a bigger bang for the buck. I've since learned this probably isn't true, but still, use caution."

"You're a cowgirl, Jordan. Do something," Victor shouted.

With Victor's voice echoing in the hole, the snake once again rattled its tail. Quickly, Jordan searched the ground with both hands, finally settling on a clump of dirt. Grabbing it, she flung it toward the reptile, causing another warning rattle before the snake hissed and slithered back to protect her babies.

When she thought it was safe to breathe again, Jordan exhaled noisily. "That was close."

"Do you think that's what killed Cooper?" Victor whispered, never taking his eyes off the snakes.

"I don't know. Rattlesnakes inject a hemotoxic venom that destroys the blood cells. It's strong enough to stun smaller prey so they can swallow them whole. It's usually not fatal to a fully grown human if they can make it to a hospital quickly and get the antivenom."

"Obviously, Cooper didn't get it."

"Judging by the hole in his forehead, I'd say the rattlesnake was the least of his worries," Jordan said.

"Can that rattler reach out and strike from where it is?" Victor asked, sliding so close to her, she imagined she could feel his heart beating.

"They can only extend about two-thirds the length of their bodies. We have a little room to play with, but let's not chance it. Just be still and don't startle her. They normally only attack when they're after food or they sense danger. Still, I wouldn't want to mess with any mother and her offspring."

Just then a shot rang out, and both Jordan and Victor

screamed as the snake flew up in the air and landed several feet in front of them. Two more shots were fired in succession, killing the babies.

"Don't touch it, Victor," Jordan screamed when he leaned toward the dead snake. "Their biting reflex remains intact even after they die."

"Are you okay down there?" A masculine voice called out.

Both Jordan and Victor hollered at once before Jordan clamped her hand over her mouth. What if it was one of Bella's henchmen here to finish the job?

She leaned closer to Victor and whispered, "Push back again. Let's not make it easy for whoever's up there to pick us off like sitting ducks."

"I'm dropping a rope down. Grab on to it, and I'll use my vehicle to pull you out, one at a time."

Victor's eyes lit up. "Why would someone go to all the trouble to rescue us then kill us once we're out of this hole?"

In her mind, Jordan recited all the reasons why they should take their chances with the dead snake rather than risk facing a live one with a gun, which was way more deadly than a hemotoxin. She was still debating what to do when the heavy rope descended.

Victor grabbed it and pushed it her way. "Ladies first."

"Maybe we should go up together because of your arm."

"I'm okay, really."

She hesitated momentarily, then grabbed the rope, murmuring to herself, "Okay, God, it will be Sunday masses for me from now on if there's a good guy waiting up there." She took a deep breath and one last look at Victor before hollering, "I'm ready."

Slowly she was lifted up the twenty-foot wall until she was over the edge. Only then did she make eye contact with the man who had just rescued her.

"Farley?"

The smile that crossed the man's face could have lit up a room. "You're that reporter girl, aren't you?"

Her return smile faded fast as pain shot up her leg when she tried to stand and couldn't. The man she and Danny had met the day of Rusty's memorial service jumped down from the three-rowed golf cart and was by her side in a flash. He scooped her up as though she were lighter than air and carried her to the cart, positioning her sideways to elevate her right foot on the seat.

"That looks like a nasty sprain," he said, taking a moment to examine her ankle.

Jordan glanced down to see that it was now swollen to double its normal size. "How did you find us?" she asked.

"First things first. I need to get your friend out of that pit in case there's another snake I might have missed."

"I only saw the three you shot," Jordan said. "One of Bella's bullets grazed my friend's shoulder, but he says he can make it."

Farley threw the rope down in the hole for a second time, then raced back to the cart and slowly drove it forward after Victor gave the okay. Jordan's eyes were glued to the edge of the pit, and when she saw Victor's smiling face, she burst into tears.

Farley stepped down and moved to the other side to help Victor into the cart. Once he was situated in the seat behind Jordan, Farley started off.

"You can't take us to the ranch house, Farley. Bella will kill us."

Instead of looking surprised, the old man merely

lowered his head and nodded. "I know. I saw what she did to you."

"How?"

"When I noticed a car driving toward the hunting area, I figured it was a couple of good old boys with a cooler full of beer and an array of high-powered rifles trying to sneak in a little hunting. Although Lucas has made it perfectly clear the area is off-limits, I still have to scare off trespassers every now and again."

"Where were you? We didn't see anyone on the road."

"There's a twenty-foot length of fence over yonder that I've been meaning to repair for weeks. With everything that's happened, I never could seem to find the time. Fortunately for you, I finally made it out there today and spotted the SUV. When I didn't recognize it, I jumped in the cart and followed. I was almost to the hunting stand when I saw Bella following you two with a gun. Before I could confront her with my own shotgun, I heard the shots and saw you both jump."

"You can't possibly know how grateful we are to you," Jordan said, finally getting her tears under control.

"You can bet your sweet one that I'm coming back in a day or so and get that big-ass snake," Victor said. "After all I went through, that mama owes me a man purse."

Both Farley and Jordan laughed. It was great hearing Victor cracking jokes again.

"You're not going to be laughing so hard when I tell you what Bella did to your car. I saw her drive it to the lake several hundred yards from the hunting area, and she let it slide in. It bubbled a few times, then disappeared."

Jordan twirled around and giggled. "Ray is gonna kill us."

Farley chuckled as he turned down a gravel road and pulled up to a small house.

Turning around, he handed Jordan his cell phone. "There's a strong signal here. You'd better call 911."

CHAPTER 25

The next few hours were chaotic. When the police arrived at the ranch, they found Lucas semiconscious with a feeding tube down his throat. Apparently, when he was no longer able to swallow or refused to, Bella had decided to use her nursing expertise to speed things up. They arrested her and whisked him off in an ambulance, along with Jordan and Victor.

After X-rays confirmed Jordan's ankle wasn't broken, the ER doctor wrapped it and fitted her with crutches. Victor fared better with only a bandage on his shoulder and a prescription for antibiotics. Once cleared and allowed to leave the hospital, he'd insisted they take him to Jordan's room while she waited for the physical therapist to stop by and give her instructions on how to walk with the crutches.

When the gang arrived and surrounded her bed, Jordan finally got the scoop on Bella. After the police discovered Lucas near death, they'd obtained a search warrant. In a

drawer next to Santana's bed, they'd found several empty
bottles of potassium and blood thinners as well as the gun
used to kill Diego, Cooper, Cooper's friend, and Jake
Richards.

"And you had no clue Bella might be the killer?" Lola
asked, squeezing her ample bottom in between Michael
and the bed.

"None," Victor answered for Jordan. "I still don't know
how Jordan figured it out." He leaned over the bed rail.
"Well?"

"She asked if I'd seen Cooper kill Diego that night."

"What's wrong with that?" Michael asked.

"When the newspaper reported the murders, they didn't
mention there'd been a witness."

"Aha!" Michael exclaimed. "You knew there could only
be one explanation for her knowing you'd been there."

"Exactly. The reason I never play poker is because one
look at my face and you know what I have in my hand.
Bella knew immediately I was onto her. When I grabbed
Victor and tried to get out of there to call the cops, she
pulled out the gun."

"Holy cannoli," Rose said. "You must have really been
scared."

"I don't know about Jordan, but I came this close to
needing an underwear change," Victor deadpanned, holding his thumb and forefinger up about an inch apart. "And
I didn't even connect Bella to the killings when she pointed
the gun at us. If I had known what was going on in Jordan's
head, I would have embarrassed myself for sure."

"She threw a scarf at me," Jordan added. "And immediately, I knew it as the one Lucas had given me the last time
I was at the ranch. I'd torn it on a nail outside the warehouse, and when I ran across the parking lot after hearing

the shots, it blew off. I was too frightened to stop and pick it up."

"That must be how she knew you'd been there," Lola said.

"It is, plus she saw Jordan on the security tape from the warehouse." They all turned as Ray walked into the room and stood at the end of the bed. "The police found the tape at the ranch. It shows Jordan sneaking across the parking lot."

He snickered. "A cat burglar, you are not, Jordan. Anyway, I just had a conversation with my old partner's kid, Paul Rutherford. He said Bella confessed to killing Diego and the other two men when ballistics linked the gun they found to the murders. Apparently, she's denied having anything to do with Rusty's death, though."

"She admitted killing him to me and Victor," Jordan said. "Mentioned something about it being Maria's fault that he had to die. Never in her wildest dreams did she picture us climbing out of that hole to tell anyone, which is probably why you're not viewing us on a slab in the morgue right now."

"She must have thought the snakes would do the job for her," Victor said. "And they almost did."

"Lucky for you that old ranch hand was around." Rosie held a glass of water with a straw up to Jordan's lips.

"I'm not helpless, Rosie." She closed her eyes after she took a sip. The truth was, she could get used to the TLC from her closest friends in a hurry. Shortly after the ambulance had brought her to the ER, it had finally registered how close she and Victor had come to dying.

If it wasn't for Farley . . .

She couldn't even think about it without tearing up.

"We may never know who actually paid the waiter to

kill Rusty or if he acted alone," Ray said. "When they investigated his death, the police discovered he had a sister who committed suicide a few years back."

"That's true," Jordan said. "Bella told us that's why it didn't take much to persuade him to do the deed. But she was still the one behind Rusty's death."

"It's a moot point, anyway, since she'll most likely spend the rest of her life behind bars without a chance at parole for the other four murders," Ray added.

"Make that five if Lucas dies," Jordan said, unable to keep the sadness out of her voice. "Has anyone heard how he is?"

Ray grinned. "Here's why it pays to be nice to cops. Paul said Lucas is still in ICU, but he's coming around slowly. They managed to get his potassium level down and hope it won't be too much longer before his blood clotting is back to normal. Unless something unexpected happens, Paul said the prognosis looks good."

Jordan exhaled in relief. Although she never wanted to spend time with Lucas Santana again, he was just as much a victim as she was.

"How long do you have to walk around on crutches?" Michael asked. "The cruise is coming up, you know."

"Don't worry. It will take more than a little sprain to keep me off that ship." She pointed to her ankle, now elevated on pillows. "You know the old RICE routine—rest, ice, compression, and elevation for the first forty-eight hours. The only time I'm allowed up is when nature calls. The doc said I could get rid of the crutches when it doesn't hurt to put my weight on it anymore."

"That settles it. I'm moving in with you for a few days," Rosie announced.

"I'll be okay," Jordan said. "I appreciate the offer but I'll—"

"No arguments. Knowing how much you hate fancy food, I'll need to fatten you up before the cruise, anyway. With all those wannabe chefs cooking up dishes we can't even pronounce, you're probably the only person on this planet who will lose weight on a cruise ship."

When they all laughed, Jordan caught Rosie's eye and mouthed, *I love you*.

"Back atcha," Rosie said.

"Okay, then it's settled. Rosie will stay with Jordan for a few days. Now then, there's another problem that needs our attention. Who's going to call Alex and tell him we almost lost her again?" Ray asked. "I guarantee it won't be me. Before that boy left for El Paso, he looked me in the eye and made me promise to take care of her."

"Oops!" Michael said, covering his mouth with his hand. "I say we let Jordan tell him. And be forewarned, we'd better make damn sure nothing happens to our girl on the cruise."

It felt strange being alone in a car with Lucas Santana, but he'd insisted, even though Jordan was perfectly capable of driving herself. She'd been off crutches for two weeks but still had trouble putting all her weight on the ankle. When he'd called and told her what he was planning, she'd jumped at the chance to be there when he discussed it with Maria.

Shortly after he was discharged from the hospital, he'd contacted Jordan and asked if he could stop by the apartment. Initially, she'd dreaded seeing him again, thinking that with Bella now sitting in a Huntsville's cell awaiting her trial, she was through having to make nice with Lucas.

But the man who walked into her apartment that day

wasn't the same obnoxious jerk she'd met in the limousine. Clearly, his priorities had changed, and she'd seen a side of him she never would have believed existed until he broke down and cried when he'd talked about Maria and Diego Morales. She'd even found herself empathizing with him.

Finding out the woman he'd allowed to manipulate everything in his life was responsible for all that pain and misery must have been devastating. He knew he couldn't bring back Diego or Rusty for Maria, but he'd spent a lot of time trying to come up with a way to make it up to her.

After several conversations with the Dallas specialist who ran a rehab hospital catering to stroke victims, Jordan knew exactly how he could help. Although the private facility was world renowned, it was also pricey, and way beyond Maria's financial capability.

Lucas hadn't blinked or even asked how much it would cost him when Jordan suggested he foot the bill. And now they were on their way to visit Maria at the nursing home to tell her she would be transferred to the new facility in the morning.

"Jordan, before we go in, there's something I want to say." Lucas sniffed back a few tears. "The doctor tells me I would have been dead in a matter of hours if you hadn't sent help. I will always be grateful. If you ever need anything, all you have to do is ask."

She studied his face, trying to decide if this was just another attempt at seducing her into becoming his next conquest. She decided to give him the benefit of the doubt.

"We'd better get in there. I can't wait to see Maria's face when you tell her."

As they walked into the nursing home, Jordan couldn't stop thinking about how many times Maria had tried to tell her she was afraid. Unfortunately, they'd lost valuable time because Jordan had assumed Maria's fear was of her husband. But Maria had already figured out Bella was the one trying to kill her. It must have been so frustrating to be unable to get help, knowing Bella would try again.

When they got to her room, Lucas opened the door to let Jordan lead the way. Maria glanced up when she heard them and immediately noticed Jordan's limp. Her face showed her concern as she pointed to Jordan's foot.

"I sprained my ankle. It's good now, though." She plopped down in a chair opposite Maria's wheelchair, and Lucas stood behind her.

When Maria's eyes questioned why he was there, he took a deep breath and blew it out slowly. "Jordan and I are here to give you some good news. God knows you could use a little of that."

Her eyes darted from one to the other.

"Bella's in jail," Jordan started. "She's admitted to killing Diego because he was blackmailing her."

Maria's eyes grew wide.

"We also know she was the one who gave you the overdose of blood thinners," Lucas said, bending down on one knee to grab her hand. "She nearly killed me the same way."

"Do you know why Diego was blackmailing her, Maria?" Jordan asked. Although she had no intention of telling this woman that Bella had blamed Rusty's death on her, Jordan felt she deserved some answers, considering she'd almost gotten herself killed over it.

Maria shook her head.

"Oh well, it doesn't matter. They found the man who poisoned your son. He was dead in a field outside of town. Since Bella wouldn't say why she paid this man to kill Rusty, I thought it might clear up a few questions if we knew what Diego had on her."

Maria rubbed her forehead as if she were chasing away a migraine. Jordan decided the woman had heard enough depressing news for one day.

"I spoke to a specialist in Dallas who works with stroke patients. He's had a lot of success, especially with people like you who can't speak. He's agreed to admit you to his facility tomorrow morning to begin your therapy."

Maria turned to the window and stared for a few seconds before turning back to them. She used her thumb and forefinger to make the classic motion for cash.

"That's the good part, Maria. All you have to worry about is learning how to speak again. Lucas is taking care of the rest."

A lone tear slid down Maria's cheek. She reached under her blanket and pulled out the photo of her and Diego with her sister, Gia, and began thumping on it with her finger.

Jordan's first thought was, *Here we go again*. She took the photo from Maria's outstretched hand and showed it to Lucas.

He made a choking sound as he stared. "I loved Gia, you know. I was so sorry when she left me and went back to Mexico so suddenly. Then when I found out she'd died, I didn't think I would ever get over it."

Maria lifted herself out of the wheelchair far enough to snatch the photo from his hand. Maintaining eye contact with Lucas, she threw it against the far wall with so much force, it shattered into a million pieces.

Jordan's eyes widened and she cried out. She'd seen Maria angry before, but never enough to destroy a cherished photo. But when she studied Maria's face, there was no telltale sign of anger, no flaring nostrils or narrowed eyes. Instead, she was smiling as she pointed to the broken picture frame across the room.

"I'll get you a new one," Jordan said, thinking this must be Maria's way of saying, *I'm mad as hell and I ain't gonna take it anymore.* Since she couldn't express her anger verbally, maybe it was just the therapy she needed to heal.

Maria grabbed her arm and motioned for her to retrieve the picture. Jordan reached down and pulled out what was left of the frame, and the first thing she noticed was the piece of paper taped to the back of the photo. She turned to Maria and arched her eyebrows in question.

Seeing Maria bob her head up and down, Jordan pulled the yellowed piece of paper from the photo and unfolded it.

After several seconds, she glanced back up at Maria, who was now smiling like she'd just won the lottery.

"What is it?" Lucas asked.

Jordan pointed to Lucas, and again, Maria nodded. She handed it to him and waited silently while he read it.

The sound that came from him was full of pain, and he fell to his knees in front of Maria. "Rusty was Gia's child?"

When Maria verified it, he asked, "And I'm his father?" He didn't need an answer from her. Still clutching the paper that proved it, he hung his head and sobbed.

Jordan bent down and put her arms around him to comfort him. There was no way she could ever know how he must be feeling, finding out he'd had a son with the woman he'd loved. And realizing he'd never get to acknowledge that since the psychopath he'd allowed into his life had taken it all away from him.

Wearing the face of a broken man, he peered up at Maria. "I had no idea. Why did she go back to Mexico if she knew the baby was mine?"

Maria shrugged.

"Was it because she didn't feel the same way about me, or had she already known she was going to die?"

When Maria nodded in reply, her eyes showed the regret she obviously felt.

"And that's what Diego was using to blackmail Bella?"

Maria nodded before she lowered her head. As the woman's shoulders shook with silent sobs, Jordan could only hope she'd finally get some comfort knowing the burdensome secret she'd carried for so many years would no longer weigh her down.

After saying good-bye, Jordan and Lucas walked out to the nurses' station, where he made the arrangements to transfer Maria to Dallas in the morning. Then he and Jordan drove back to Ranchero. Lucas had taken the photo, assuring Maria he'd return it after it was reframed. He also promised that when she was able to leave the rehab facility, she'd come home to a wheelchair-accessible house with twenty-four-hour nursing care. She was still crying when they left, but Jordan knew there was a little joy mixed in with her grief.

"Why do you think Bella killed my son, Jordan?" Lucas asked when they were almost at Jordan's apartment.

"Greed. As your only living relative, she counted on inheriting your money after you died."

"I should have never signed that paper saying for all intents and purposes, we were in a common-law marriage." He spat out the words contemptuously.

"In retrospect, you probably shouldn't have. It guaranteed she would inherit your wealth when you died. Up to that point, she'd been prepared to wait as long as necessary. That's why she panicked when Maria told her that Rusty was your son. With the very real possibility of seeing all those years she'd spent with you wasted, she knew she had to act quickly to silence Maria. I guess she figured if she'd blurted it once, there was a real possibility she might do it again. Bella couldn't risk that. When her plan didn't go as she'd hoped and Maria didn't die, she probably assumed she could control Diego with money now that his wife was unable to talk."

"Then why kill Rusty?"

"I don't know, Lucas. Maybe she decided if she eliminated the real threat to her not getting your money, the rest of it would fall into place. My guess is she presuaded Diego and Maria to keep Gia's secret all those years mainly so you wouldn't try to get custody of your son. Maybe that was what she meant when she said Diego had been blackmailing her all these years."

"You think Rusty knew?" His voice choked on the last few words.

"No. From the short time I knew your son, I could tell he thought of you as a father, but I don't believe he knew the truth. Bella was beginning to see her plan unravel when Diego demanded more and more money. I think she did what she felt she had to in order to get what she believed was her hard-earned money."

She left out the part about Rusty's being involved with Bella in the cattle-rustling ring, as well as his affair with her. Some things were better left unsaid. His choked cry was proof she'd made the right decision. The man was in enough pain already.

When Lucas pulled up in front of the Empire Apartments and dropped her off, he reached over and grabbed her hand. "I forgot to tell you. I'm having a brand new Suburban delivered to your friend tomorrow morning. Tell him if he doesn't like the color, he can go to the dealership and pick whichever one he wants." When she nodded, he added, "It's the least I can do."

Jordan sighed and got out of the car, promising to keep

in touch. Totally exhausted from the emotional day and from hobbling up the stairs, she was looking forward to a hot shower and a bowl full of German chocolate ice cream from Braum's.

When she opened the door to her apartment and walked in, she was surprised to see her friends huddled in the living room, concern written all over their faces.

Pasting a smile on, she nodded.

"We have a surprise for you," Rosie said, grinning like the proverbial Cheshire cat.

Jordan sighed. "I hope it's a quick one. I'm done in, both mentally and physically."

"Not exactly what I wanted to hear."

She gasped, immediately recognizing the voice behind her. Twirling around, she came face-to-face with Alex— and he had a sinfully rich chocolate cake in his hands.

"Alex, how . . ."

"Don't even ask." He put the cake on the counter and took her into her arms. "Thought you might need this today. It's Myrtle's famous Better Than Sex Cake, one of your favorites."

"Jordan has never met a chocolate cake—or any other cake for that matter—that isn't one of her favorites," Victor said, rushing over for a closer look. "Yum."

Jordan stared up at Alex, seeing his concern despite the smile on his face.

"I'm okay," she said, standing up on tiptoes to kiss his cheek. "But I'll be even better when I find out how long you get to stay in Ranchero this time."

"As long as it takes to wipe the sadness from your face." Alex grabbed her and kissed her. When he released her, he held her away slightly and drilled her with his eyes. "Did that help?"

"Maybe a little. At least twenty more just like that and one or two slices of that cake might do the trick." She swallowed back the tears. "What are we waiting on? I'm starving."

"Hold that thought," he said. "Let's get some carbs into you. It's gonna be a long night."

RECITES

BELLA'S STEAK AND GRAVY

Boeuf Cuis au Jus de Viande

Yields 3–4 servings

1 pound (3–4 pieces) top round steak
⅓ cup plus 2 tablespoons flour, divided
1 tablespoon cooking oil
4 beef bouillon cubes
2 teaspoons pepper

Preheat the oven to 325°F.

Cut the meat into 3–4 single-serving-size pieces if it has not already been done. Trim *all* the fat. Sprinkle a little flour (approximately 1 tablespoon) on one side of the steak pieces and pound it in with a tenderizing hammer, flattening the steak. Turn and repeat for the other side. (If you use a butcher, you can ask him to tenderize the steak for you. Then, you can simply rub a little flour on each side of the meat.)

In a Dutch oven or skillet that has a lid, heat the oil over medium heat. Brown the steak pieces on both sides (2–3 minutes per side), working in batches if necessary so as not to crowd the pan. When all the pieces are browned, place them back in the Dutch oven, laycring them. In a bowl, whisk together ⅓ cup of flour and 2½ cups of water, blending well. Whisk out any clumps of flour, then add the bouillon cubes and pepper. Pour the mixture into the Dutch oven. The liquid should cover the steak and will become the gravy. Continue cooking on the top of the stove until bubbling.

Cover and transfer the Dutch oven to the preheated oven and cook for 1½ hours. After about 45 minutes, check the gravy for thickness: if it is too thick, add more water; if it is too thin, add 1 tablespoon of flour to 4 ounces of water and whisk until smooth before adding to the gravy. If the flour clumps, simply remove it with a louvered spoon. Taste it and see if it needs more pepper or bouillon cubes.

If you are doubling the recipe, add one bouillon cube at a time after the initial four cubes and taste after each one.

Serve with mashed potatoes.

BRENDA SUE'S WATERGATE SALAD

Yields 8–10 servings

1 can (20 ounces) crushed pineapple with juice
½–1 cup miniature marshmallows
1 can (14.5 ounces) red tart cherries, pitted and drained
1 package (1.4 ounces) instant pistachio pudding mix
¾ cup chopped walnuts
1 container (12 ounces) nondairy whipped topping such
*   as Cool Whip (low-fat version may be used, if desired)*

In a large bowl, mix together the first five ingredients. Fold in the whipped topping. Cover and refrigerate several hours before serving.

• • •

MYRTLE'S BETTER THAN SEX CAKE

1 package German chocolate cake mix, prepared
¾ cup hot fudge sauce
¾ cup caramel sauce
¾ cup sweetened condensed milk
1 container (12 ounces) extra-creamy nondairy whipped
*   topping such as Cool Whip*
4 Heath Bars (1.4 ounces each), chopped

Prepare the cake mix according to package directions and bake in a 13-by-9-by-2-inch pan 32–37 minutes or until a toothpick inserted in the center comes out clean. Cool for 20 minutes on a rack, then punch 20–25 holes in the top of the cake with the handle of a wooden spoon. Microwave the hot fudge sauce for 20 seconds and then pour it into the holes. Microwave the caramel sauce and the condensed milk separately and add one at a time just like the hot fudge sauce. Frost with the whipped topping. Sprinkle the Heath Bars over the whipped topping. Refrigerate.

• • •

ALEX'S LASAGNA

Yields 8–10 servings

FOR THE MEAT SAUCE:
  ½ pound ground beef, crumbled
  ½ pound bulk Italian sausage, crumbled
  1 large onion, chopped
  1 teaspoon salt
  2 teaspoons pepper
  3 cloves garlic, minced
  1 can (6 ounces) tomato paste
  1 can (28 ounces) crushed tomatoes, undrained
  1½ cups water
  1 cup medium spicy salsa
  2 teaspoons sugar
  1½ teaspoons chili powder

1 teaspoon fennel seeds
1 teaspoon dried basil
1 teaspoon oregano

FOR THE LASAGNA:
9 lasagna noodles (oven-ready lasagna noodles may be
used)
1 container (15 ounces) ricotta cheese
¾ cup grated Parmesan cheese
4 cups mozzarella cheese

Preheat oven to 350°F.

In a Dutch oven over medium heat, cook beef, sausage, and chopped onions until brown. Drain. Add the next twelve ingredients and simmer uncovered for 3 hours.

Bring a large pot of lightly salted water to a boil. Add pasta and cook for 8–10 minutes or according to directions. Drain. (If you prefer, you can use oven-ready lasagna noodles that need no cooking.)

Spread 1 cup of the sauce in the bottom of a 9-by-13-inch baking dish. Cover the sauce with 3 noodles. Cover the noodles with one third of the remaining sauce. Top with half the ricotta cheese, dropping by tablespoonfuls evenly on the noodles (3–4 dollops per noodle). Sprinkle with salt and pepper, then Parmesan cheese. Top with a third of the mozzarella. Repeat this entire sequence. For the last layer, use the remaining 3 noodles and cover with remaining sauce. Sprinkle the remaining mozzarella over the sauce and cover tightly with heavy-duty aluminum foil.

Bake in the preheated oven 45 minutes. Uncover and bake for another 20 minutes or until the cheese on top is bubbly. Let stand 20 minutes before serving.

BEEF DADDY'S BANANA PUDDING

Yields 12 servings

3 tablespoons cornstarch
1½ cups sugar
½ teaspoon salt
8 large egg yolks
2 cups heavy cream, chilled (divided use)
1½ cups whole milk, scalded
2 tablespoons butter
4 teaspoons vanilla (divided use)
4 large ripe but firm bananas
1 tablespoon lemon juice
1 box (12 ounces) vanilla wafers
1 tablespoon powdered sugar

In a saucepan, whisk together the cornstarch, sugar, and salt. Add the egg yolks and 1 cup of the cream and beat until smooth. Gradually whisk in the hot milk and cook over medium-low heat, stirring until the mixture is thick and begins to bubble in the middle, about 5 minutes.

Remove the saucepan from the heat and stir in the butter and 3 teaspoons of the vanilla. Allow to cool before spooning the mixture into a glass container and sealing with plastic wrap pressed on the surface of the pudding. Refrigerate.

When the pudding is cold, slice the bananas about a quarter-inch thick and toss with the lemon juice. In a large bowl or trifle dish, arrange a layer of wafers, then banana slices, then pudding, repeating three more times. Spread the final layer of pudding to the edges of the dish to seal the bananas. Cover again with plastic wrap pressed to the surface.

Refrigerate at least 3 hours and up to 2 days so flavors meld and the wafers soften. Just before serving, whip the remaining 1 cup of heavy cream until soft, then add the powdered sugar and the remaining teaspoon of vanilla and continue whipping until stiff. Serve the whipped cream on top of the pudding.

• • •

MARIA'S SANGRIA

Yields approximately 4 cups

2 lemons
2 limes
1 orange
½ bottle (750 milliliters) sweet red wine (I use Gallo
    Family Vineyards Hearty Burgundy.)
⅛ cup Cointreau
⅛ cup brandy
⅛ cup sugar
1 can (12 ounces) orange soda (diet may be used, if
    desired)
2 cans (12 ounces) ginger ale (diet may be used, if
    desired)

Cut each of the fruits in half. Chop half of the fruit halves into small pieces and place in a medium container with a lid. Squeeze the juice of the remaining fruit halves into the container. Add the wine, Cointreau, brandy, and sugar. Gently stir the mixture, then cover the container with the lid and refrigerate overnight. Refrigerate the sodas. When ready to serve, pour the wine mixture into a punch bowl and add the orange soda and the ginger ale. Add more wine or ginger ale to your taste. I usually double this recipe for a crowd and freeze a liter of ginger ale in a Bundt cake pan or a similar round pan to be used as an ice ring in the punch bowl.

• • •

BELLA'S BEEF STROGANOFF

Yields 4 servings

1½ pounds beef tenderloin
Salt
Pepper
Garlic powder
3 tablespoons flour, divided
3 tablespoons olive oil
1½ sticks butter, divided
1 medium onion, cut into thin strips
8 ounces fresh mushrooms, sliced
1 can (10¾ ounces) cream of mushroom soup
1 can (10¾ ounces) beef broth
1 cup sour cream
1 package (8 ounces) egg noodles

Trim all the fat from the steak, then sprinkle it with salt, pepper, and garlic powder. Slice the steak into ½-inch-thick strips and toss the strips with 2 tablespoons of the flour. Heat the oil and 2 tablespoons of the butter in a large skillet and quickly brown the beef, 2–3 minutes on each side. Remove the meat from the pan and set aside.

Heat another 4 tablespoons of butter in the pan. Add in the onions and mushrooms and sauté for 2–3 minutes until the onions are tender. Add the remaining tablespoon of flour to the vegetables as this will be the thickener for the gravy.

Return the cooked meat to the pan, then add the soup and the broth and bring to a boil. Reduce the heat, cover, and cook on low for 28 minutes, stirring frequently. Add the sour cream and cook for 2 minutes more.

Cook the egg noodles according to package directions. Drain. Toss the noodles with the remaining butter. Season with salt and pepper to taste.

Serve the meat mixture over the buttered noodles.

• • •

LILY'S LAYERED SALAD

Yields 12 servings

1 large head lettuce, rinsed, dried, and chopped, divided
¾ small head red cabbage, chopped
2 cups grated carrots
1 box (10 ounces) frozen peas, thawed
2 cups chopped cauliflower
2 cups sliced cucumber
2 large tomatoes, diced

1 cup mayonnaise (low-fat may be used, if desired)
½ cup dry ranch dressing mix
½ package dry Good Seasons Italian dressing mix
1 pound bacon, cooked and crumbled
2 hard-boiled eggs, chopped

In a large glass bowl, layer the ingredients starting with approximately 3 inches of chopped lettuce, then the cabbage, carrots, peas, cauliflower, cucumber, tomatoes, and remaining lettuce. Whisk together the mayonnaise and the ranch dressing mix and spread on top.

Sprinkle on the dry Good Seasons mix, then the crumbled bacon pieces, and end with the chopped eggs. Cover with plastic wrap and refrigerate overnight. When ready to serve, mix with salad forks.

• • •

BRENDA SUE'S CHICKEN SALAD

Yields 6 servings

4 large boneless, skinless chicken breasts
1½ stalks celery, chopped
¼ cup onion, chopped
1½ cups chopped walnuts
1½ cups seedless grapes, halved
⅓ cup sour cream (low-fat may be used, if desired)
1 cup mayonnaise (low-fat may be used, if desired)
1 teaspoon salt

1 teaspoon freshly ground pepper
½ teaspoon poultry seasoning
1 teaspoon garlic salt

In large pan, cover the chicken breasts with water and cook over medium heat until breasts are thoroughly cooked (about 30 minutes). Remove chicken from the water and cool. In a large bowl, combine celery, onion, walnuts, and grapes. Cut up cooled chicken into bite-size pieces. Add the chicken to the celery mixture. In a medium bowl, mix the sour cream and mayonnaise. Pour over the celery mixture and combine. Mix in the salt, pepper, poultry seasoning, and garlic salt.

Chill. Serve on croissants and store leftovers in the refrigerator.

· · ·

MYRTLE'S DIRT CAKE

La Suciedad Pastel

1 package (1 pound) Oreo cookies
4 tablespoons (½ stick) margarine, softened
1 package (8 ounces) cream cheese, softened
1 cup powdered sugar
½ teaspoon vanilla extract
3½ cups cold whole or 2 percent milk
2 small boxes (1.4 ounces each) instant vanilla pudding mix
*1 container (12 ounces) nondairy whipped topping such
     as Cool Whip*
4–6 gummy bears (optional)

Put the cookies in a food processor or blender and crush until the mixture looks like dirt. (It helps if the cookies have been frozen first.) Place one third of the cookie "dirt" into a trifle bowl or a brand-new, clean flower pot with foil covering the hole in the bottom. Set aside. Cream together the margarine, cream cheese, powdered sugar, and vanilla. Set aside. In another bowl, combine the milk and pudding mix and stir until pudding is dissolved. Add the pudding to the cream cheese mixture and hand-stir to combine. Fold in the whipped topping. Layer half the cream cheese mixture over the cookies in the bowl or flower pot, then add another third of the crushed cookies. Next, add the remaining cream cheese mixture, followed by the remaining crushed cookies.

Cover with plastic wrap and chill for several hours.

To serve, plunge the gummy bears (if using) into the top layer, allowing them to stick out above the "dirt." You can even decorate the dessert with a new plastic flower if you want. Serve with a brand-new plastic gardening shovel.

• • •

SANDY'S ALMOND BALLS

Yields 4 cups

⅓ cup water
⅓ cup unsweetened cocoa powder
¾ cup sugar (sweetener may be used, if desired)
Pinch of salt
3½ cups cold 2 percent milk
1 teaspoon vanilla extract

1 teaspoon almond extract
4 tablespoons Baileys Irish Cream liqueur
½ cup half-and-half
1 can whipped topping

In a medium saucepan, bring the water to a boil and add the cocoa, sugar, and salt. Stirring constantly, return this mixture to an easy boil, then simmer for another 2 minutes, making sure it doesn't scorch. Stir in the milk and heat to almost boiling. Do not boil. Remove from heat and add the vanilla, almond extract, Baileys, and half-and-half. Pour into four cups and top with whipped topping.

JENN MCKINLAY

Death by the Dozen

A Cupcake Bakery Mystery

Melanie Cooper and Angie DeLaura are determined to win the challenge to the chefs to promote their Fairy Tale Cupcakes bakery. Mel's mentor from culinary school, Vic Mazzotta, is one of the judges, but Mel and Angie will have to win fair and square. When Vic's dead body is found inside a freezer truck, Mel and Angie will need to use their best judgment to find the cold-blooded killer who iced Vic, or they may lose more than the contest—they may lose their lives . . .

INCLUDES SCRUMPTIOUS RECIPES!

PRAISE FOR THE CUPCAKE BAKERY MYSTERIES

"A tender cozy full of warm and likable characters . . . Readers will look forward to more of McKinlay's tasty concoctions." —*Publishers Weekly* (starred review)

"Delivers all the ingredients for a winning read."
      —Cleo Coyle, author of the Coffeehouse Mysteries

facebook.com/TheCrimeSceneBooks
penguin.com
jennmckinlay.com